MW01244418

ISBN-13: 978-1507685020
ISBN-10: 1507685025

Printed in the United States of America

BLACK MARIA

A
NOVEL
By

Michael Lucas

CHAPTER 1

Maria was born on a small farm in the blue-grass state of old Kentucky in 1986. She has a light brown complexion, hazel brown eyes, dark black arched eyebrows, and she wore her curly black hair in a natural bush that framed her head like a halo.

Maria was considered tall for a girl standing at 5'11". She possessed a shapely body that featured hips with and the right curves. Her nice, firm breasts sat straight up without the support of a bra. Maria was well put together. Her beauty was unbelievingly breathtaking and she knew it.

Over the years, many people told Maria that she looked liked a young Angela Davis (A strong black sister from The Black Panther Era), only more gorgeous. Angela was beautiful in the scholarly sense. Maria had the total package and then some.

Maria also had a brother who was two years younger than her. He was called Billy Boy. He had the same skin tone as Maria and he wore his hair in a short fade style that showed off his whirlpool of waves circling his crown. Billy Boy was a slender kid with an elevated height of 6'2", which made him a favorite among the young females who idolized him. He was treated as though he was a black god on Earth.

Their mother moved the family from Kentucky in 1989 after their father was killed. He died in a bar room fight with a two-bit drunk. Neither Maria nor Billy Boy could remember too much about their old man; nor could they recall having met him in the flesh or otherwise.

They moved to the nation's capital where they lived with their mother whose name was Marsha. They lived in the poverty stricken section of S.E. Washington, D.C. Marsha turned to alcohol after the move to Washington. She was constantly mourning her husband's death and trying to keep food in her kid's mouths. She ultimately became a cold-blooded alcoholic that drank everything her lips touched.

Marsha had been a beautiful woman at one time, but the years of alcohol abuse took a dreadful toll on her. It robbed her of her natural good looks and shapely body. Her pretty skin was once her pride and joy and also the object of plenty attraction. It had become faded and pale; bordering on grotesque.

Marsha worked as a janitor in a government office building. She cleaned floors and performed other odd jobs on request. Even though it wasn't something she enjoyed doing, Marsha figured she was lucky to get a job period. She had no education. In fact, the only experience she had when it came to working was farming, which she had learned in her home town of Inez, Kentucky.

When Maria turned eighteen years old on June 16, 2004, she decided that she was a grown woman. She couldn't wait to finish high school. She was a senior at Ballou High School. Maria knew this would be her last year before graduating and venturing out into the cruel world. Maria enjoyed going to school and being around her best friend, Sunny. The girls had plenty of fun going to parties and parks together. They snuggled close to various mannish teenage boys who were eager as they were to experience the adolescent joys of sex. Maria and Sunny were so close that they decided to give away their virginity at the same time with different boys. That was a couple of years ago when Maria turned sweet sixteen.

Maria and Sunny lived in the same building in the projects.

Almost in complete contrast to Maria, Sunny had a chocolate Hershey bar complexion with dark brown, doe shaped eyes with long black shoulder length hair. Her teeth were pretty and white and she had smooth lips that men dreamed of kissing.

Sunny stood almost 5'7", and like Maria, her body was equally outlined in every aspect. Sunny looked like she had been sculptured by Michelangelo. She was a sexpot and a main attraction for men of all races.

One day, as they were walking home from school, Maria turned to Sunny and said, "Sunny, girl I'm tired of hustling this weed shit. It ain't bringin' in no real cake (Money) and my mom ain't no help at all. All the cash she gets her hands on is devoted to the whiskey bottle."

Maria vented her frustrations.

"I don't know how she do it, but she still manages to get up in the morning to catch the bus all the way downtown for work. It doesn't seem to make any difference how drunk she was the night before. I hate to see my mom struggling that way in this repulsive ghetto life. I hate this shit!"

Maria raised her voice and that startled Sunny.

Sunny had never seen this side to her before. They were actually close. Sunny thought she knew everything there was to know about Maria until today.

"Girl, I might have to stop going to school. I need to get me a job to help my family out," Maria said.

She had sadness in her tone.

Sunny looked at her best friend with a serious expression etched across her beautiful, dark brown face.

It said, "I feel you girl. Things are hard on the boulevard for real. If that's your choice girl, then you know I'm with you till the bitter end Maria. We don't have to go straight home. We can jump on the Metro bus and go downtown to see if we can find a job right now," Sunny said.

That caused Maria to smile.

Maria knew all along that Sunny would support and stand by her no matter what she did. They were like real sisters, only more closer. That's a rarity among young women in D.C. area.

"Okay, Sunny. That'll work."

A few minutes later, the bus arrived and they climbed on to pay the fare. A few guys tried to talk to the girls, but they politely declined their offers. Guess they figured that they couldn't do nothing for them if they were riding public transportation. They had mansion on hill with boats by lake type dreams and a Metro bus transfer couldn't get them nowhere near those dreams.

Arriving downtown, they went everywhere possible from Chinatown to Pennsylvania Avenue trying to find work. As the day passed, they weren't too successful. Still, they were determined to accomplish their mission.

As they walked down this one particular street, they came across a robbery in progress. A jewelry store was being held up. Three young black guys with guns and black bandannas covering their faces came running out with bags of jewelry. The guys made it safely to the dark green Ford that was double parked and jumped inside. The car shot away from the curb amidst screeching tires and a cloud of dust and exhaust fumes.

Maria and Sunny glanced at each other in shock and disbelief.

"Girl, did you see that shit?"

Maria gasped.

"Hell yeah! Let's get the hell away from here before the police come and blame us for this shit," Sunny replied.

With that said, both girls took off running. Their long, lovely legs stretched double time as they beat a hasty retreat away from the scene of the crime. Once they were safely away, Maria spoke. Her eyes were wide with excitement.

"See Sunny! Girl, now that's the shit I'm talkin' about! Did you see that?" She repeated for emphasis.

"Yeah, I seen it," said Sunny.

She then added, "And it don't look like nothing good. We might as well head on back across town because ain't nothin' going to come through for us today. We'll try again tomorrow."

"Yeah Sunny, you right," Maria agreed.

"Besides, I've done enough walking today to hold me for another six months. My damn feet are killing me!"

On the long bus ride home, Maria couldn't stop thinking about the robbery. For some odd reason, it fascinated her. The thought of being daring enough to go out and take what you wanted instead of working or asking for it had never occurred to her before now.

"Sunny."

Maria spoke to her friend who was sitting right beside her.

"I've been thinking about that stick up. You know what?"

"What?" Asked Sunny with a raised eyebrow.

The suspicion was dripping in her tone.

"Fuck that job shit. We ain't going to get one any damn way. Not unless it's one of them Red Light District strip tease joints and that shit ain't for no bitches like us. Only them trick bitches do that kinda' freak shit."

"So what you sayin' Maria?"

"I'm sayin' that jewelry stick-up looked kinda' easy."

Now that it was out in the open, Maria sat back and held her breath. She was waiting on Sunny's response. She didn't have to wait long.

"Girl, what are you tryin' to do? That's a big step from selling weed. Then again, what the fuck we know about robbin' jewelry stores?"

"I'm not talkin' about jewelry stores," Maria said.

She was now sitting up straight in her seat.

"Well, what in the hell are you talkin' about then?"

Maria never batted an eyelash.

She calmly said, "I think our chances will be much better if we hustle banks."

Sunny's eyes grew to the size of baseballs.

"I know you tripping. You've been watching too much Set It Off or something. Tell me you're joking Maria."

Maria didn't miss a beat.

She replied, "Sunny this ain't no movie. I'm dead serious like Eve was when she tricked Adam into eating from the Knowledge Tree of Original Sin."

"Well, I'll be damned," Sunny sighed.

"I guess you really are serious because I have never known you to play around with religious issues."

Sunny looked at Maria with a serious expression. She loved Maria and would do almost anything in the world for her. Sometimes her friend intrigued her by some of the things she said or did or wanted to do; like now.

"You know Maria, sometimes I can't figure you out. You act like a damn boy at times."

They both laughed.

Turning to glance out the side window, Sunny caught a quick glimpse of an old dirty wino in threadbare clothes. He was pissing on the ground in full view of the public. Obviously, he had no shame or remorse. He didn't care who saw him. He saw Sunny's face staring out the bus window in disgust at him. He just smiled and gave her the finger.

She turned back to Maria. Sunny spoke with the wino on her mind and the thought of staying in the ghetto for the rest of her life.

"Sis, you know I'm with you. If we don't start doing something, we will never have anything. We will forever be poor and living in the ghetto."

Behind Sunny's comment, both girls fell silent and were content to just stare out the bus window at the downtown streets crowded with black people hurrying to and fro. Each person was wrapped up in their own individual thoughts.

A half an hour later, they reached their destination. They both stepped off the bus.

Maria said, "I'm going to take me a bath and soak my feet. I won't be back out tonight, so if you want me just come down stairs."

"I'm going to do the same thing because I'm exhausted," Sunny said.

"All that damn walking we done jive did a job on me too. If I don't come down stairs, I'll see you in the mornin'."

As they entered the apartment building, they went their separate ways. They had some serious thinking to do.

CHAPTER 2

***B*oth girls were up bright and early** the next morning. They were ready to do their thing. Sunny lived right upstairs from Maria in the same building. They always met up in the hallway before going anywhere together. They hated having to do that. The hallways always smelled bad and were filthy like a city dump. Most of the tenants around Congress Park Projects treated the buildings they lived in like shit. Most of them were either too lazy to take the trash outside to the trash dumpsters, or they simply didn't care. I guess they figured since they were living in a dump they might as well treat it like one.

Some of the people who lived in Congress Park, especially the neighborhood thugs and hustlers, had no problem with pissing right inside the hallways when they staggered home drunk or high on drugs. Their lack of good hygiene caused most of the buildings around Congress Park to reek with a foul odor, but Maria and Sunny's building was the worst.

"DAMN!" Maria said.

She was frowning and wrinkling up her nose.

"It stinks like shit in here. Smells like Blue Plains in this motherfucker."

Sunny agreed, "It does smell like the city's waste depot. You sho' can say that again, girl."

Maria changed the subject.

She said, "Sunny, you'll never believe what happened."

Sunny looked puzzled.

"So tell me."

"I have some bad news."

"Whaddaya' talkin' 'bout Maria?" Asked Sunny.

"Last night when I left you and went into my apartment, my brother, Billy Boy, told me he had just came from the hospital seeing our mom. He told me that she went to work drunk and messed around and slipped down a flight of stairs."

Sunny eyes grew wide with genuine concern.

"Is that right?"

"Uh huh. Girl, I was up all night. I started to come upstairs and let you know, but I decided to wait until this morning."

"I wish you would've told me last night. You can't keep things like that to yourself girl, because that's important. That's family Maria. Don't do that to me no more."

Maria looked at her friend and smiled. Maria loved Sunny just like she was her own blood sister.

"You right girl, that's my bad. It's just that my mind was so messed up last night when Billy Boy told me what happened that I didn't really wanna' see or talk to nobody."

"I understand," said Sunny.

"By the way, how is she doing now?"

"She's on the critical list."

"Damn, that's messed up for real."

"You know Sunny, I been thinkin' 'bout that conversation we had yesterday. I need to make a move real soon. Girl, my moms ain't got no insurance. She needs me now more than ever. I'm the only one she can depend on. You know Billy Boy don't know what to do. What I'm sayin' is that I'm gonna have to depend on you. Can I count on you?"

Sunny turned dead serious. When she replied, her voice was full of emotion.

"Maria, how many times do I have to tell you, I'm with you girl.

You know you can count on me. I told you that I'm with you until the end of time and nothing or nobody can change that. Ever. So how do we go about doing this stick up thang?"

"Well Sunny, I been thinkin' 'bout this for awhile. I just didn't know how to come at you with it until we seen that jewelry store get robbed yesterday. I didn't wanna come off on you 'bout something like that and have you think I was losin' my mind or something."

Sunny smiled, "I wouldn't have thought nothing like that girl. You know you can ask me anything."

Maria cocked her head sideways as though she was in deep contemplation.

She then said, "I know I could have asked you a long time ago, but I guess I was a little bit intimidated myself. That jewelry store caper made me bring it to your attention before I really wanted to. It was like it was meant to happen like that."

"I feel you Maria."

Sunny nodded. They exited the building and started walking to the bus stop.

"Ay'? You know Ruby? The girl in our third period Spanish class?"

"Yeah, I know exactly who you talkin' 'bout. Come to think about it, I've been seeing the two of ya'll doin' a lotta' talking lately. I was wondering what ya'll was kickin' it about. What's up with her?"

"Well," Maria answered calmly.

"You know she don't live over here on the Southeast side, right? She lives on the Northeast side of town over by Minnesota Avenue in Greenway. We been talking for the last four months about that stick up shit. She has a brother that be going up in them banks and coming off. She was telling me about all the cash he be comin' off within a few seconds time by jumping over them bank counters. Girl, she told me him and his boys be gettin' so much lucianno. She said she ain't never seen that much cash in her whole life. She said he be hittin' her off with some of that long cash too. I'm talking 'bout that Prada and

Chanel type cash. That's why she stay coming to school dressing so fly."

"Oh yeah?"

Sunny commented as her interest was aroused.

She could just see herself and Maria dressing fly in the latest and most expensive fashions. They would be throwing cash around like they had it to burn. Maria continued talking because she was now excited.

"Ruby says she's tired of her brother takin' care of her when she can do the same damn thing he's doing. She says she's been around him long enough and soaked up the game. When she ran down the method to going up in them joints, I knew she knew her shit. She probably knows how to rob banks just like him. She said whenever I'm ready to roll, me and her can lay our lick down and get paid. Sunny, I guess this is it. I'm ready and I think you are too. Am I right?"

Sunny laughed.

"Girl, from what you just said about Ruby, ain't nothin' to do but do the damn thang! Lets roll with it."

$ $ $ $ $

THAT FOLLOWING MORNING, they met up with Ruby at school. They found her by her locker talking to some guy.

"Hey Ruby!" Maria called from her locker.

"Let me holla' at you for a minute!"

"Okay girl," she said.

She closed her locker and stepped off on the guy without saying another word.

The 5'7", golden buttermilk, brick house with thick thighs pranced with hip-popping and sashaying grace. She blew past a group of overly attentive thug wannabes. Maria and Sunny could hear the whistles and catcalls that Ruby drew from them. Ruby's wild halo of short, corkscrew burnt, cinnamon curls made her stand out in any crowd. She had thin lips and a pretty smile that made you melt when she turned it on. The curve-showing D&G Nautical mini hugged her magnificent ass and hips like a surgical glove. Ruby was nineteen and still in the same grade with Maria and Sunny. She was far from dumb. In fact, Ruby was smarter than most of the girls she hung around with. She just started school late.

"Hey girl! What's up?" Ruby greeted.

"Them niggaz still goosin'?"

"Girl, you wild," Maria said.

She was looking over Ruby's shoulder with a smile. She spotted the guys still staring at Ruby' ass-sets.

"Yeah, they still goosin'. What's up though?"

"You got it girl," Ruby replied smiling.

"How you doing, Sunny?"

"I'm cool," she said.

They stood in the hallway talking for a while then decided to leave school. They walked down Martin Luther King Avenue, heading for the Anacostia Subway Station. They decided to go out to Pentagon City Mall where they could talk more seriously about the plan they devised to rob the bank.

Thirty minutes later, they exited Pentagon City subway station in Virginia, and walked right into the mall. They found a vacant spot near a wishing pond and sat down. They were looking at all the people walking around with shopping bags.

Ruby was the first to speak.

"We can be doing the same thing real soon if we do everything according to plan. This shit is serious. I've been looking at this one joint that looks real sweet. I told Maria about it a few months ago."

Ruby said as she directed her comments to Sunny.

Maria nodded.

"Yeah, I remember you talkin' 'bout it. So what's the deal on it now?"

Ruby laughed, "Sweetheart, that's what I'm tryna' tell you! Check this out."

Sunny and Maria drew closer, holding onto Ruby's every word.

She saw that she had their undivided attention.

Ruby continued, "Now, ya'll know I do a lot of ear hustlin' (Eavesdropping) when my brother has his boys over talking. They don't know I'm listening though, so they be real reckless with they shit. Well, anyway, the joint I'm referring to don't have any security guards inside the premises. They have four tellers. This is what we're going to do. When we go inside the joint to take it off, Sunny, you hold down the floor. Me and Maria will get the tellers and the safe. We'll leave out first. Sunny, you'll have to watch our backs. You will have the gun on all the people in the bank. You shouldn't have to shoot nobody. Believe me, they'll be terrified. Once we are outta' the bank I'll do the driving."

Ruby looked around to see if anybody was watching them.

"How does that sound? Logical, I hope."

"Are you sure about the security?" Maria asked first.

"Yeah, I'm sure. I've been watching this joint for a while now."

"Well, since you put it that way, it sounds good to me. Whaddaya' think Sunny?"

Sunny thought for a moment before replying.

"I agree with Ruby. When do we get paid?"

"The sooner the better," Ruby said.

She was resuming the leadership role.

"We been waiting long enough as it is. Today is Tuesday, so by Friday, we should be ready. We will meet at nine o'clock Friday morning at school. I'll have the car for us."

"Where you gonna' get a car from?" Maria asked.

"Let me worry about that," Ruby responded.

She was actually trying to sound more confident than she really felt. There was no turning back at this point.

Maria looked at Ruby, then nodded her head agreement.

"Okay Ruby. No problem."

Instead of returning to school, they hung out at the mall for the rest of the day. They were window shopping and browsing around. When they departed from one another, Maria and Sunny decided to visit Maria's mother.

Arriving at Greater Southeast Hospital around five that evening, Maria glanced at Sunny.

She said quietly," Mama don't look too good. Look at all them tubes runnin' in her arms, nose, and mouth."

Sunny comforted her, "She'll be alright Maria. You have to be strong, because you have a strong moms."

"I hope you're right Sunny."

While they stood there in the room, an Armenian doctor clad in a white coat entered the room to check on his patient. He noticed the girls and paused, secretly lusting over their thick, curvaceous bodies.

"Hello, young ladies. And whom might you be? Mrs. Valentine shouldn't be having any visitors at this time."

Maria spoke up while choking back tears, "She's my mother."

"Okay, so you are the daughter?"

"Yes I am."

"You and your brother are the only ones listed to contact in case of an emergency?"

"Yes, we are the only family she has."

"Your mother had a serious fall and the alcohol didn't make it any better. We had to do emergency surgery to remove a blood clot in her brain. She's now lying in a coma. It'll be up to her now to make it out of the coma. I know I shouldn't be telling you this."

The doctor said quickly after noticing the frightened look that came over Maria's face.

"I see that Mrs. Valentine doesn't have any insurance. The bills may get pretty high."

"That's all you worried about? Some fucking bills!" Maria snapped.

His words about money set her off like a time bomb.

"If you thought you shouldn't be telling me any of this, then why in the fuck are you speaking on the shit now? HUH!"

She raised her voice. That startled the doctor and Sunny.

The doctor stood there embarrassed, red faced, and with his mouth wide open. He was definitely unsure on what he should say next.

"You don't have to worry about the fuckin' bills," Maria said harshly.

"You can rest assure that they will be paid! You creep motherfucker! C'mon Sunny, let's get the hell outta here!"

Turning on the balls of her heels, Maria stepped away from the doctor who stood there in amazement. He was watching her long, beautiful legs glide across the shiny marble floor.

"Damn, if I wouldn't have put my foot in my mouth, I probably could've got her to have sex with me for part of the payments. I know she's not going to come up with all the money it takes to care for her mother," he thought before looking away to check on Maria's mother.

CHAPTER 3

AROUND 7:30 P.M. THAT EVENING, Maria and Sunny arrived back at their apartment building. They were in a cold, somber mood. Both girls knew their fate had been chiseled in stone. Upon entering Maria's apartment, they found Billy Boy chowing down on some Captain Crunch cereal mixed with ice cream. Helooked up from the kitchen table. Billy Boy put on his boyish smile and turned on the charm.

"What's up Maria?"

He greeted as he turned his gaze on Sunny. He gave her a sexy wink.

"Hey Sunny."

"Hey Billy Boy."

Sunny replied with seduction heavy in her tone.

 "With your fine self."

She added with a smile.

He pretended to ignore the compliment. Billy Boy turned his attention back to his sister.

 "Maria, did you go see mom today? If you did, how's she doing?"

"Yeah, I went to see her Billy Boy. She don't look good at all. The punk ass doctor had the nerve to say it's up to her to pull through. His bitch ass was quick to ask for some money though. I don't know, maybe they have done everything they can do," Maria said in a somber tone.

"So, what are we going to do? You know mom ain't got no insurance. It's up to us to make sure the hospital bill gets paid. Plus, make sure she gets the proper care while she's laid down."

"Don't worry," Maria said.

She was trying to sound more confident than she really felt.

"I'm going to take care of everything. You can count on that shit."

"I can help Maria," Billy Boy said quickly.

He felt like he had to do something. He was the only man in the house.

"How?" Maria asked.

"I can get a job or something."

"Nah, you don't have to do that. We'll do things the way we been doin' them. Ain't nothing changed. The only thing different is moms being in the hospital. She'll be okay."

"But Maria, where are you going to get the money to pay for the hospital bills? You know them bills can be jive high as a motherfucker. If you can do everything to help the situation, why can't I?" Billy Boy said.

"Like I told you young brother."

Maria smiled.

"I will handle this predicament that our family is in. I don't wanna' talk about it anymore."

Billy Boy grew silent. He acknowledged his older sister's authority. He knew that when she got in her present mood, it was best to just leave her alone. Maria was a stubborn woman with an iron will. Most of the time she acted like more of a mother around the household. Not only to her brother, but to her mother as well.

Sunny could sense the budding tension between the siblings.

She said, "Maria, if you don't need my assistance right at this moment, then I'm going to leave and see what's going on up stairs.

I wanna' make sure that everything is okay with my mom. If anything comes up with your moms, please come and get me. Don't hesitate to call if something comes up. I'll come right down, okay?"

Maria said softly, "Okay Sunny. I'll let you know without a doubt. I just don't wanna worry you with our problems."

Stepping closer to her friend, Sunny reached out and touched Maria on the arm.

"Girl, you know damn well you ain't worrying me. We been through too much for that kinda' shit," Maria laughed.

"You right, I'm trippin'. Next time I won't delay letting you know if something comes up."

"Bitch."

Sunny playfully said.

"You better not!"

Maria was pretending to be outraged.

Maria said, "Who you calling a bitch? BITCH!"

Both girls smiled at the double entendre. Billy Boy sat off to the side observing the play by play while shaking his head slowly.

"Ya'll crazy as shit. Ya'll calling each other bitches like it's the natural thing to do."

With her hands on her wide, ample hips, Sunny threw back her head.

She said real sassy like, "Well, Billy Boy, all women are bitches when they wanna' be. Don't start trippin' bout' no shit like that. I forgot. You still have a lot to learn about women!"

His pride was now on the line.

Billy Boy responded quickly, "Let me explain something to you Sunny. I'm not never trippin' bout no girls being called a bitch if that's what some BITCHES like to be called, that's your preference. What the fuck? That shit ain't no sweat off my back. And that lil' slick comment you just made about me learning about women, I bet you won't bet your money on how much I know about women. I'm toting real heavy and long down here Shorty."

He smirked and grabbed his penis through his Polo sweats.

"I guarantee you, if I put this dick in that tight pussy of yours, I'll have your fine ass hysterical! You'll be crying and moaning and tryna' climb the walls to get away from this dick. Don't let me hit you in the doggy style! Your little pretty ass would sho-nuff be in deep trouble."

Sunny looked over at Maria who looked away.

She moaned, "Mmm-Mmm. I guess he told you."

She instigated playfully.

"Girl, that little mannish-ass boy ain't tell me shit. Talking like he's a helluva' pussy handler!"

Sunny rolled her eyes.

" Billy Boy, I'll put this pussy on your lil' young ass and drive your young ass insane! I'll have your ass tryna' kill up the whole town, wondering who I'm fucking! It's a good thing that I look at you like you're my brother."

Dejectedly, Billy Boy looked at Sunny, knowing his chances at hitting her fuck box were real slim now. He always wanted to fuck her. He never knew how to go at her until she opened the door. Now that he turned on the aggression, she ran and hid behind that little looking at you like a brother phrase.

"See Sunny, you got it all twisted, looking at me like I'm your lil' brother, cause I damn sure don't look at you like my sister. I'm tryna' beat your lil' box up. What's up?"

"Look," Maria interrupted.

"Ya'll leave that shit alone. We got more important things to do than talk about some dick and pussy shit."

"Damn Maria, you know me and Sunny always go through our lil' thang. We always play around this way."

"Yeah Maria," Sunny agreed.

"You know I like talking and joking with Billy Boy like that. He keeps me on my toes about them young niggaz."

Maria laughed, "Shit, bitch you want some of that dick for real!

22

You just don't know how to ask for it! So cut the bullshit. Don't be scared, just ask for what you want, because fa'-real, fa'-real, I got Billy Boy making you scream and climb the walls just like he said."

Maria instigated some more.

"Yeah whatever. Fuck all that bullshit you talking 'bout girl," Sunny replied jokingly.

"You can go straight to hell."

Both Billy Boy and Maria started laughing at Sunny, who had to join in on the laughter herself.

"I'll see ya'll later, because I'm not tryna' hear that off da' wall shit. And Billy Boy, you over there smiling like it's some truth to what Maria said. If you really think it's any truth whatsoever to what Maria just said, I bet you won't hold your breath on it."

$ $ $ $ $

THE FOLLOWING DAY, the three girls met at school to go over their plans again and again until they got them right. There was no room for any errors.

Ruby repeated throughout the whole conversation, "Now that we're clear on that issue, check this out. I have this guy I know named Fast Black. He's a young dude around our age. He's down with the team. I talked to him about the heist we're trying to pull off. He's tryna' roll. I trust him because I've been knowing him since we were little kids. He's a thoroughbred soldier from my way. We don't have to worry 'bout him being weak or a snitch-nigga. Ya'll have my word on that. My word is bond. Oh! Another thing we need to do is go look at the joint we're hitting. We need to have our escape route already mapped out when we come up outta' there."

"When do you wanna check out the escape routes?" Maria asked.

"Well, Maria, we gotta do it today, because we only have a coupla' days before we tear that joint off," Ruby said.

"I don't know anything about robbing a bank," Sunny spoke up.

" My inner gut tells me that the best time for us to look at things is in the morning. That way, we'll know what's what and what routes to take. I hope I'm not moving too fast here. The way I picture it, we'll be robbing this joint in the morning time, right?"

"Absolutely Sunny," Ruby said with a smile.

She glanced at Maria, who gave an approving nod.

"When we talked the other morning, we did agree to hit the joint in the morning. You don't miss a beat Sunny. I like that. The only difference with our plan is that we'll have Fast Black driving for us when we come outta the bank. Now check this out. When we finish the job, Fast Black will take care of the guns and the car. We'll take the luciano with us back to school. We ain't trusting nobody with our cash."

"But you're going to trust them with our lives?" Maria said.

She had to voice her opinion.

"Ruby, this some serious shit we about to do. I know you trust Fast Black, but niggaz switch up quick when that pressure hits, you feel me?"

"Listen ya'll, you ain't' hear this from me. I keeps peoples business close to my chest, but the dude Fast Black don't be going for nothing. He killed two dudes that he found out were telling on a murder case. Slim is all the way official."

"He better be," Maria thought.

They left school to go hang out.

Early the next morning, the three girls drove around the immediate area of the bank they were planning to rip off. After deciding on an escape route, they climbed on the Metro and headed back across town.

"Ya'll really think we can pull this caper off?" Maria asked.

For the first time since she had decided to actually rob a bank, the faint stirrings of doubt began to creep through her mind. Ruby had been expecting it.

"Listen ya'll, all we have to do is stay focused on our mission and everything else will fall into place," Ruby assured them.

"Once we get inside the bank, we can't lose. I know without a doubt in my mind that nigga Fast Black will be outside waiting on us when we come outta there. Listen, this is my stop coming up. It don't make no sense for me to ride all the way back to the Southeast side. Shit, school is probably out by now anyway. So we have a day and a wake up before we do our thang ladies. All we have to do is lay back and chill until then. Then we'll rise to our destiny."

At the next stop, Ruby pulled the rip cord, signaling the bus driver to stop on Minnesota Avenue right across from Greenway Projects. Saying her good-byes to Maria and Sunny, Ruby exited the bus and jogged across the street.

$ $ $ $ $

THE DAY CAME SOONER THAN any of the girls had expected. They met up with Fast Black, a short, stocky built young black man with dark chocolate skin. Maria could see why they called him Fast Black. He was so dark. He was almost purple with a set of perfect white teeth. As a teen slangin' and bangin' in D.C.'s hardest hoods, Fast Black could never justify his evil deeds. He was bred to run the streets. Once he leveraged his street reputation, he would become one of the city's best drivers. He finally found a way to reconcile his demons.

Maria, Sunny, and Ruby all wore green army fatigues over their normal school clothes. That way, they could change quickly once they robbed the bank. They also carried glossy plastic hand bags in which to put the money they planned to take.

Fast Black was driving a dark colored 2004 Cadillac STS that was high style, high performance, and high tech. He sat parked around the corner from the bank near a church.

"Are ya'll ready?" He asked.

"This is the big one ladies."

"Enough with all that ladies shit."

Maria put her game face on.

"I'm ready to do the motherfucker. How about you Sunny? You ready?"

Glancing at Maria and Ruby, Sunny took a deep breath.

She said, "I got butterflies in my belly. My hands are sweaty as hell, but I'm ready as I'm ever going to be. So let's stop the bullshittin' and go get that luciano."

They hugged in the back seat after Sunny's statement. Fast Black gave an approving nod at the girls, as each one of them said a silent prayer, hoping for good luck in what they were about to do.

"Fast Black, give us about thirty seconds to complete the mission, and another thirty seconds to get back to the car," Ruby instructed.

"Start the timing in three minutes. If we ain't back by then, something must've gone wrong and it's your choice to leave or stay."

"You got me fucked up, Ruby," he snorted.

"The day I leave you, my mother is a hot bitch and I killed her myself. Ruby, I ain't going nowhere until I know for sure something went wrong. You know how I get down. They call me Fast Black, cause I balls the fuck out when I get behind the wheel. I know how to roll out. My name don't come from me leaving my partners behind in a hold-up. It comes from getting them home safely after the hold-up."

After Fast Black's little speech, the tension that had invaded the girls bodies eased up a little. They all relaxed and felt better about what they were getting ready to do.

It was now or never. Shit or get off the pot. Neither girl was about to back out now. Poverty and hunger pains had been with them all of their lives and now they were determined to do something about it.

CHAPTER 4

ENTERING THE BANK, all three girls went straight to work. By it being so early in the morning, not many people were there, which made it all the more sweet. The XD-Sub Compact 800 Series Special-Ops sub machine gun that Sunny clutched was strapped to her shoulder. The way she handled it left little doubt that she would use it if she had to.

"Okay people, you know what this is!" Sunny yelled.

That got everyone's attention right away.

"If you don't, it's a motherfuckin' robbery! I want all you motherfuckers on the floor right now!"

The few early morning patrons scrambled to the floor in a hurry. They didn't have to be told twice. The only thing on their minds was getting out of the bank safely.

Like professionals, Maria and Ruby leaped over the counter before the tellers had a chance to step on the silent alarm system located in the floor. They didn't waste any time cleaning out all the teller's drawers. Then they moved to the safe which had a timer on it.

"Shit! Fuck me!"

Ruby cursed under her breath after discovering that the safe was locked tight.

Out of the corner of her eye, Maria could see that Sunny was keeping a close watch on the people on the floor.

Seconds later, she heard Sunny scream, "FIVE SECONDS!"

As if they were reading each other's minds, Ruby and Maria leaped back across the counter with two bags of money. Without hesitating, they bolted straight out of the door.

"It's been fun. Now keep your fucking heads down and count to a thousand," Sunny ordered.

She was brandishing the sub-machine gun menacingly. She kept it aimed at the hostages as she backed out of the door.

Once on the street, Sunny quickly concealed the weapon. She lowered it to her side as she walked calmly to the car.

They held their breath as they tried to act normal while walking down the street towards the getaway car. They reached the corner without incident. As they started to breathe a sigh of relief, they spotted a rookie cop talking to Fast Black who was sitting in the stolen Cadillac STS.

It seemed like the cop was inspecting the car and asking a hundred questions at the same time.

"Yes, officer, my mother lets me use the car. I have to pick her up every day when I leave school," Fast Black stated.

He did not appear to be panicking at all.

In fact, he was acting in a calm and rational manner, considering the extreme circumstances.

"Let me see your driver's license and reges---."

The cop's attention was diverted by a call coming over his radio.

It announced that a bank robbery was in progress.

Being inexperienced, the rookie cop glanced at Fast Black, then down at his walkie-talkie. Then glanced at Fast Black again before making up his mind.

"Get outta' here and don't let me catch you out here no more," the cop warned.

He then took off running at top speed, deciding that the bank robbery call was way more important than harassing a teen taking a joy ride.

He bolted around the corner thinking that this could be his big break. He could catch the bad guys and look good in his superior's eyes. He ran right past Maria, Ruby, and Sunny. He never paid them the slightest attention. Lady luck was definitely with them on this sunny morning.

As soon as they climbed in the car, Fast Black pulled off. He was pumping the sounds of Bone Thugs 'n' Harmony classic **For The Love Of Money.** The Cadillac's tires screeched loudly against the pavement as Fast Black made two dangerous left turns. He hit the nearest highway. They were headed back to D.C. Sunny, Maria, and Ruby were in the back seat quickly pulling off their army fatigues. Soon as they finished, Maria told Sunny to climb in the front seat with Fast Black.

"Hurry up girl," Maria pressed.

"Me and Ruby going to lie down back here. They'll be looking for three females. Not a man and a woman."

Climbing over the seat, Fast Black couldn't help but notice her shapely behind as she lifted herself over the seat.

"Damn girl," he mumbled over the loud music.

"Your ass is wide as a motherfucker. We gotsta to holla at each other after we break bread at the crib."

"You can save all that shit," Ruby shouted from the back seat.

"We ain't even got away yet and all your freak ass can think about is some pussy. Just drive, horny ass nigga!"

Everyone in the car cracked up with laughter.

"Chill out Ruby. Damn. I'm just having a lil' fun to take the edge offa' thangs. Don't worry, you know I'm always 'bout black folks bid'ness."

Saying that, Fast Black swerved in another lane. He quickly took the Kenilworth Avenue exit.

The further they got away from the scene of the crime, the more they relaxed.

"LOOKS LIKE WE DONE PULLED IT OFF!" Maria shouted.

She began hugging Ruby.

"Not so fast girl," Ruby cautioned.

"We ain't in the clear just yet."

"Fa-real, fa-real, I thought that cop had me back there," Fast Black commented.

As he wheeled through traffic, he made a sharp turn on Sheriff Road. He kept his eyes out for the police.

"That bitch nigga was about to run the tags and shit on the car when the call came over the radio about ya'll putting in that work. Damn, that was a blessing fa-real. I thought I was gonna' have to crush his ass."

"It must be meant for us to get away,"Sunny said cheerfully.

"It must be if Black don't fuck shit up."

Ruby sucked her teeth irritably.

"Black, slow this damn car down before you get all of us late for speeding,"she groused.

"Okay Ruby. Don't panic on a nigga. Just remember, this is what I do. I steal cars and drive the hell outta' them. You gotta' keep that in mind Shorty. As soon as that rookie cop gets hip to the fact that we ran game on him, it won't take long for him to come to the conclusion that he let me get away. He knows what kind of ride I'm pushing. That's why after I drop ya'll off, I'ma get rid of this joint (Car.)"

"He's right Ruby!" Sunny said.

She was looking out the back window as they turned on Nannie Helen Burrough Avenue.

Ruby tried to calm everyone down.

She stated,"It's no need for everyone to be looking around and drawing any unwanted attention to the car since we're so far from the bank."

Fast Black kept driving fast. He nearly ran a red light. He slowed the car down, looked both ways, and pulled off again.

"Black, you lunchin' like shit!"Ruby yelled.

"You gonna get us caught up Boy!"

"No I'm not, we almost there anyway. About ten more minutes and you girls will be in Ballou before the bell rings for second period."

Ruby felt more relaxed as she thought about the money bags they had.

"From the looks of things, there's gotta be a lot of paper in these bags. Mostly big faces."

Sunny gave Ruby a knowing smile.

"Whaddaya' going to do with your half Ruby?" Sunny asked.

Maria spoke up, "She don't mean no harm Ruby. Sunny, you can't be doing that. I mean we cool and all, but some people don't be telling out all they bid'ness."

"Thanks Maria for putting me up on game. I was jive out there. I'm sorry Ruby."

"Forget about it. Shit ain't nothing," Ruby said.

Fast Black reached Naylor Road in Southeast.

He kept speeding until he reached Alabama Avenue. They were soon pulling up in front of Ballou High School.

"Well, as promised, here we are ladies. It didn't take long to pull this caper off did it? If I didn't know any better, I'd say ya'll did this shit before. Check it though, I'ma bout' to go burn all the clothes and shit to make sure nothing comes back to us. So ya'll leave all that shit in the car. I'll hold on to the machine gun. We need to put it back before your brother misses it. Hurry and roll on out so I can take care of my bizness and ditch this hot ass car. I know this motherfucker is burnin' up by now. I'll meet up with ya'll later at Maria's crib so we can break bread."

As Fast Black pulled away from the curb, all three girls were laughing over what he'd just said. For the rest of the day in school, the hours seemed to drag by like molasses. They couldn't wait until school was out so they could find out exactly how much money they had from the heist they did. Finally, when it seemed like they couldn't take the suspense any longer, the 3 p.m. bell rang. It alerted the girls that school was officially over for the day. Sunny, Ruby, and Maria left school in a hurry. They were more than anxious to get to Maria's place.

After destroying all the evidence and everything else that could've linked him and the girls to the crime, Fast Black headed to Maria's house around 7 p.m. This time he was driving a stolen, silver bullet hued convertible, 2003 Aston Martin Vanquish.

Inside the apartment, Sunny, Ruby, and Maria sat around the living room counting the stacks of fifty and one-hundred dollar bills. They'd been counting it over and over to make sure they had the right amount.

"I think we got close to a hundred and twenty thousand dollars here," Ruby said excitedly.

"That's not bad for a few seconds of work," Maria said.

She already was spending the money in her head. She knew most of it would go to her mother's medical bills and the rest would be for the groceries and the rent.

"You ain't never lied girl. Shiiid', I think that's good for some project bitches that's never seen this kinda' money before," Sunny added; still counting the money.

Ruby laughed, "Speak for yourself, girl. I've had this kinda' money in my hands before. Remember, my brother does this shit for a living."

"Well, I'll say this," Sunny insisted.

"This was our first time going up in a bank. We ain't exactly experts in this robbery shit. I think a hundred and twenty thousand is pretty damn good."

"Ain't no doubt about that," Maria agreed.

"By the way, how much do ya'll think we should give Fast Black?"

Ruby shrugged, "He did do a good damn job. That's not to say he was a big help to us. Plus, he didn't leave us when the cop was sweating him. I say that he deserves about fifteen thousand. That'll leave us with a hundred and five thousand to split, which is about thirty-five thousand a piece, give or take a little."

"Sounds good to me," Sunny smiled.

"Damn Sunny," Maria said.

"That's more money than we ever seen in our lives or had in our pockets at one time."

"So I guess that means it's no problem with breaking off fifteen thousand for Fast Black?" Ruby questioned.

She knew they wouldn't deny him for all that he did that day.

"Hell no!" Maria and Sunny said in unison.

"It's all free money anyway," Maria added.

Ruby started counting Fast Black's share of the loot and put it to the side.

"Good. It's a done deal then. Now come on and lets break this bread down before Fast Black gets here. I hope he's alright."

"If something went wrong, we would've heard about it by now," Maria reasoned.

"I guess you're right Maria. Yeah, we probably would've heard from him by now or seen something on the news."

After they finished counting, dividing, and stashing their shares of the money, they sat around the living room talking and waiting for Fast Black's arrival. About fifteen minutes later, they heard a knock on the door. All three girls grew deathly silent.

"WHO IS IT?" Maria called out.

"It's me, Fast Black."

"Hold on a minute, before you open up the door," Ruby told Maria with caution.

"I wanna make sure everything is in order. I'ma make sure Fast Black's money is right on the table just in case he tries some funny shit."

After Ruby went to get his money, she sat it down on the coffee table. She then nodded at Maria. That was the signal for her to open the door.

"Go ahead and open the door."

"Hey Maria," Fast Black said.

"Boy, we thought something had happened to you when we didn't hear from you right away."

Stepping into the apartment, Fast Black's eyes immediately went to a pile of money sitting on the coffee table.

"Yeah boy, you had us worried to death," Ruby said.

 She entered the living room from the bedroom.

"No bullshit," Sunny added.

"Why you ain't call nobody? We were all worried about you. What took you so long to get back with us?"

He took a seat on the couch without waiting to be told.

Fast Black said, "Well, I didn't have no problems getting rid of the car. I had to put the machine gun in a safe place until Ruby can put it back where her brother had it. Dig Ruby, you know I know your brother and the way he be carrying shit with hitting them licks. It won't be long before he hits another one. So we best be about putting that joint back soon as possible. Anyway, the reason I took so long to get back across town was because I had a little trouble stealing another ride. It took me a while to find the joint I wanted. Ruby you already know if it's not fly and fast, I'm not fuckin' with it," he said with a smile.

Smiling, Ruby said, "You sho' right about that with your thieving ass. Ain't that a bitch? This nigga got the nerve to be choicy with his stealing behind."

Everybody cracked up with laughter.

"Fuck all that," Fast Black said jokingly.

"What's my break down on the loot ya'll snatched today?"

"Damn! You geeking like shit Slim! We got you," Ruby said.

She was faking like she was mad.

"When it comes to money Ruby, I needs all mines. You know how I be on one with them bitches. My mother always tell me I got a talent from God. If I go back to school and get my education I could be a genius with the kinda' brain I got. The streets is all the education I need. So I just don't listen to her. Ruby, you know me better than Sunny and Maria. You know I do what I wanna do to get that cake. Anyway, that's enough about me explaining about wanting mines. Where's that bread at?"

Ruby took the three $5,000 wrapped stacks of money off the table and passed them to him.

"Here you go. That's fifteen thousand."

Without hesitation, Fast Black said, "Good looking Shorty. This

34

is gon' let me do the motherfucker for about a week and some change."

"Damn!" Ruby said.

"You weren't bullshitting when you told me that you be splurging all that money huh?"

Sunny and Maria looked on in amazement. They were trying to hold back their questions. Fast Black had been blowing more money on a constant basis than they'd ever seen. They both wondered how long he's been doing it.

"All I know for sure is that I'm gonna take ten and put it down on a nice ride. I will probably get that new Caddie STS joint. That way I won't have to keep worrying about stealing anymore cars and shit to get around the city.

"That's sounds like a good idea Black," Ruby said.

"I don't know. We might just put some of our loot together and buy us a ride, probably that Chrysler 300 C joint."

Always the cautious one out of the bunch, Maria said quickly, "Hold up Ruby. We can't be moving that fast; buying all types of cars and shit. We should at least wait a while before we start spending this money. Fast Black you should wait too. I watch all these cop shows. I know that the FBI always waits to see who starts spending money right after a robbery. They wait to see what area the money is being spent in so they can concentrate on that particular neck of the woods."

"Maria is right," Sunny said.

"Yeah," Ruby agreed.

"Maria's right Black. I don't know what the fuck I was thinking about in the first place."

Suddenly, Sunny had a bright idea.

"Ya'll know what? I remember reading or I seen it somewhere that some folks robbed a bank and took the money to another location and exchanged it. You know, swapped it out with another business that wasn't in the same city where the bank was robbed."

"How the hell we gonna' do that without arousing any suspicion?" Maria asked.

"Hold up Maria," Ruby said.

"I just might have an idea. I don't know why I didn't think of this before. Now that I think about it, every time my brother hits a bank, he spends the money around town in gambling spots. So listen, this is what we're gonna' do. We're gonna exchange it in the casinos in Alantic City. All we have to do is drive to New Jersey and shoot a little dice at the crap tables. We lose a little at the black jack tables and shit. Then we take the chips back to the windows to swap it out for some fresh legal money."

Nodding her head, Maria said, "I like it, but there's just one problem."

"And what's that?" Ruby asked.

"How the hell are we going to get to Alantic City?"

"No problem," Ruby answered.

"The way I see it, we'll let Fast Black buy the car he wants. Then we'll have him drive us to New Jersey so we can take care of bizness."

Fast Black gave Ruby a sharp glance. After Maria's warning about the FEDS watching out for anyone spending large sums of money following a bank robbery, he was a little leery about doing anything with his cash.

"Not so fast Ruby. I may wanna exchange some of my loot for some fresh cash before I go buying any new cars. Shiiid', Maria's right. Whatever I do, I must put protection on myself as well."

"Yeah, you're right Black," Ruby said.

"But since you'll only be exchanging fifteen thou', you can do that right here in the city before you go down to the car dealerships. I doubt very seriously that the FBI will get hip to you spending that money."

Fast Black smiled, "A'ight Ruby, I'll tell you what. I have a spot where I can clean up my money. Once I do that, I'll cop my Caddie. If that don't work, don't worry. I got a backup plan to get you girls to Atlantic City. Whatever happens, I got it all covered. A'ight?"

The three girls looked from one to the other then nodded in Fast

Black's direction.

"We comprende," said Ruby.

She had a devilish smile while throwing a Spanish word at him that she'd learn in school.

As an afterthought she added, "So is everybody satisfied with their cut?"

When nobody said a word, Ruby stood up.

"Good," she announced.

"That means this meeting is over for now. We'll get back together tomorrow. In the mean time, Maria, don't you think you should be checking on your moms?"

Catching the hint, Maria quickly stood up.

"Yeah girl, you're right. I better get ready to go check on my mother. Black, we'll holla' at you later."

As Fast Black got up to leave, he found that he had developed a new found sense of respect for Ruby and her girlfriends. He could do nothing but good things by hanging with them.

"Yeah, we definitely can have a good future together," he thought.

He headed out the door to go take care of his business.

CHAPTER 5

CLOSING THE DOOR, Ruby asked Fast Black to drop her off across town in a joking manner. Fast Black knew she didn't like riding in his stolen car, but he played along with her anyway.

"Shiid', c'mon if you rolling, cause I gotsta' go get this money cleaned up," he said.

He stood at the door and listened to Maria and Sunny laugh.

"I don't want to get robbed of this money. That's all Black."

"Ruby, you trippin' like shit Moe! You robbed a bank for money. Now you're worrying about getting robbed? Ain't that a bitch?"

Maria and Sunny walked over by the door.

Maria decided to put her two cents in.

"Ruby, quit faking girl. You know damn well your ass ain't about to get back into no hot ass car with Fast Black. Especially not now."

She was pretending to be insulted.

Ruby said sharply, "It's not that I don't wanna ride with my homie. It's just that we done came too far to go out like suckers. It ain't 'bout taking unnecessary chances."

Fast Black started back pedaling, signaling an end to the conversation. It was getting late and he still had business to take care of before sunrise.

"That's my cue ladies. I can take a hint. Look Ruby, you call the shots. I'll see you back across town in a little bit. How are you getting home anyway?"

"Don't worry Black. I'ma call a cab."

Without another word, Fast Black turned and started to head downstairs and out the building. The girls closed the door. Ruby was about to pull out her cell phone when Billy Boy walked through the door and caught her by surprise. Ruby looked like she had been hit by a thunder bolt. Without making her call, she expertly slid her cell phone back in her pocket.

"Who the fuck is that?" Ruby asked as she turned to Maria.

"Aw, that ain't nobody but my lil' brother, Billy Boy," Maria smiled.

She glanced at her brother.

"I told you about him remember?"

"Oh yeah," Ruby confirmed.

She relaxed a little.

"But you never told me that he was tall and fine as a motherfucker!"

Sunny gave Ruby a nasty look while turning up her nose.

"Don't start that shit girl. Billy Boy is way too young for you."

Secretly, Sunny had a crush on Billy Boy. She was just too ashamed to let it be known. She wasn't about to stand there and let Ruby flirt openly with him without her saying anything.

"What chu' talking about Sunny?" Ruby asked.

She was licking her long, red tongue over her full luscious lips while staring at Billy Boy. She was openly lusting.

"Shiid', he looks mature enough to speak for himself. Ain't that right, Boo?"

Seeing the way Sunny had spoken up just confirmed in Maria's mind what she'd suspected all along.

"*I knew that slut had a crush on my brother*," Maria thought with a knowing smile.

"Ladies look, we are not about to have no cat fights or confusion up in here about my brother," Maria said.

She then introduced Billy Boy to Ruby, "Ruby, that's Billy Boy, my younger brother. Billy Boy, this Ruby a real good friend of mines."

After acknowledging Ruby, Billy Boy looked around the apartment and said, "Whassup wit' cha'll'? You girls up in here having some type of party and didn't invite a brotha'?"

"Nah boy," Maria said.

"We ain't having no party. We just had to catch up on some homework. Mainly our Spanish. Comprende'?"

Running his hands through his wavy hair, Billy Boy smiled and said, "Si', I comprende."

"Anyway, smart ass," Maria said.

She assumed the role of big sister once again.

"Where have you been?"

Billy Boy shrugged, "I went over my man's house."

"Well," she pressed.

"You should've called and let me know where you were so I wouldn't have been worried about ya."

Glancing over at Ruby, Billy Boy felt slightly embarrassed and felt he had to say something.

"Hold up Maria, I'ma grown-ass man dog. When you start talking to me like you're my mother? You might be older than me, but don't forget that I'm the big brotha' round' here. Besides, Sunny and Ruby are here, so don't try to play big in front of them! You trying to make me look like a child!"

Amused, Ruby smiled and poured coals on the fire.

"You got a point Billy Boy. You sho' is a man and ain't no man 'sposed to let no bitch talk to him any kind of way like he's a child."

Ignoring Ruby, Maria looked at Billy Boy and realized just how much he'd grown up and how much she really loved him. She would do anything to protect him from the dangers she knew lay smoldering out there in the mean streets of Washington, D.C., better known as **CHOCOLATE CITY.**

"Billy Boy, I would never try to belittle you and you know it. The reason why I asked is because you didn't call me and let me know what's up. Plus, you didn't answer your phone. You are my only brother and I don't want anything to happen to you. That's all. You already know that with moms laid up in the hospital and everything, I just feel we should be aware of where one another is at all times. You never know when they may need us at the hospital."

Before Billy Boy could respond, Sunny spoke up.

"Billy Boy, you know we worry about you all the time. Boy, don't start acting all cute just because Ruby is here. You know her fast ass got a crush on you."

"Why don't you mind your own biz-ness and leave mines alone," Billy Boy said indignantly.

Paying him no attention, Sunny focused on Ruby. She was the main force who was threatening to take Billy Boy away from her. Even though she didn't let it be known, Sunny still was going to defend her territory. Her territory was Billy Boy. That's it and that's all.

"I thought you was calling a cab Ruby?" Sunny asked.

Taking the hint, and peeping the nasty look, Ruby decided to ease up off of flirting with Billy Boy. At least for tonight anyway. For the rest of the night, the girls along with Billy Boy, stayed up talking until the sun rose up in a bright blue sky. By then, Billy Boy had gotten to know a lot more about Ruby. Not once did any of the girls slip up and mention a word about the bank robbery they'd done.

Maria didn't want her brother knowing anything about that side of her. Plus, she didn't want him involved in any kind of way. Maria knew that if he ever found out, he'd want to be a part of it. That's just the way he was. Maria figured the less he knew, the fewer problems would arise with trying to keep him away from robbing banks.

Ruby and Sunny left the apartment early that morning. Ruby caught a cab and Sunny walked upstairs to her apartment. Neither of the girls went to school that day. Billy Boy didn't go either. He was just too tired after staying up talking all night.

*T*HE NEXT THREE WEEKS PASSED without incident or any

mention of the bank robbery. That made the trio relax. Fast Black had switched the money from the bank robbery with fresh, unmarked bills he had picked up in a few after-hour gambling spots. Finally, he felt safe enough to go to Chevy Chase Cadillac car dealership and put a $8,500 down payment on a 2001 midnight blue Cadillac STS with all black leather interior.

He had to get used to riding around in his own car. For once it wasn't stolen. Fast Black picked up the girls one bright afternoon and drove them up to Atlantic City. There they could exchange the bank money with casino money. Maria decided to exchange some of her money for a cashier's check so she could pay some of her mother's hospital bills. All of this took place during the month of April. That left only a few months before Maria and her girlfriends were scheduled to graduate from Ballou High School.

One night while they were all sitting around in Maria's living room, Maria paced back and forth.

Her pacing prompted Ruby to ask, "Maria, what the hell you keep pacing for?"

"I wonder what's taking Black so long to get here? I have to be at the hospital to check on my moms before visiting hours are over."

"Girl, you know that he's got that new ride and don't know how to act. Black's probably somewhere right now with a bitch. Anyway, don't sweat the small shit. He said he would come and scoop us up and he will. He knows how important it is to get you over there to that damn hospital to see your mother. He's got a mother he loves, so he knows what's up, trust me."

Before Ruby's words could sink in, there was a knock at the door.

"Who is it?" Maria called out.

"It's me, Fast Black. Open the door."

Maria opened the door with a no nonsense look on her pretty face.

"It's about time your ass showed up," she snapped.

"I thought I was gonna have to call a cab. Where have you been anyway?"

Fast Black chuckled, "Shorty, I   been turning corners with the STS all over this ma'fuckin' city. I'm sorry I'm a lil' late, but don't worry. It won't take long for me to get you to the hospital. They don't call me Fast Black for nothing. Didn't I tell you that before?"

His smirk caused all three girls to laugh.

"Well, let's see if you can live up to that name smart-ass. We need to get to the hospital before visiting hours are over," Ruby said.

He was faking a surprised expression.

Fast Black said, "Damn Ruby. You should know better than anyone that I can get ya'll across town better than anyone in ten minutes flat."

"Then what are we waiting for?" Maria asked.

She was already heading for the front door.

"We've been waiting on your ass for two hours."

"Well lets rock and roll," Fast Black said.

He was itching to get back behind the wheel of his pride and joy.

As they headed out the apartment building, Fast Black held the door open for the girls to exit. Maria greeted a few of the hustlers and other girls she knew as they walked towards Fast Black's car.

"Oh, he wit' chu?"

A big, dark skin thug named Fat Ace yelled out. He was holding his hand inside his waist.

"I thought I was gonna' have to air his ass out," he said.

Fat Ace was a guy that was known to shoot first and ask questions later. He liked Maria, but never had the balls to ask her out. He feared rejection. Fat Ace wasn't the most handsome guy in the hood. His heart and drive to get that money by any means made his chubby frame sexy to most gold-digging women in the hood. No, it made him more of an easy target for the conniving women who chased after men with money.

"Go head with that shit Ace."

Maria called out as they reached Fast Black's Cadillac STS.

"This my peoples, so let that be."

Fast Black just stared at the big guy. He made a mental note to stay strapped from now on.

"Even though Maria said something, niggaz still cruddy 'round here and he won't catch me slippin'," he thought.

He got in and opened the doors for the girls.

Once inside the Cadillac, Fast Black drove like a professional stock car racer. He hit Suitland Parkway within seconds. He jumped on Martin Luther King Avenue which was a straight shot to Greater Southeast Community Hospital.

After a few minutes of speeding, Maria looked over at Fast Black and smiled.

"You're really trying to get us there with the quickness huh? Cause your foot ain't let up off the gas pedal yet. Just make sure you're careful nigga. Shit won't make no sense if all of us end up in a hospital somewhere. We'll be laying next to my mother for trying to get there quick," Maria quipped.

"You sure right about that shit," Sunny added.

She was laughing her ass off. That in turn caused Ruby and Maria to laugh.

Fast Black grunted. He watched the sights fly by as he raced the Cadillac STS towards the hospital.

"Just relax Maria. I got this ma'fucka. Believe dat'! Ya'll safe with me. No matter how fast I drive, I ain't gonna' do nothin' to put ya'll in harm's way. Long as I'm behind the wheel, ain't shit going to happen to ya'll. You can bet on that!"

"Black," Ruby blurted.

"Why you get the same kind of Caddie' that you had when we robbed the bank?"

He never took his eyes off the road.

Fast Black replied, "I thought I told ya'll about that when we was up in Atlantic City?"

"Nah nigga, you ain't tell us shit," Ruby said.

"Well, it's like this. I wanted something faster, but the car dealers wanted too much loot for what I wanted. I got this one on a good bargain. I'm jive glad it jumped off this way."

"Me too," Sunny agreed.

"This Caddie' floats like shit. I fucks wit' this joint."

"Thanks Shorty. Listen, I seen this nice Chrysler 300 C that'll fit ya'll to a tee. I can get ya'll a nice-ass deal from the dealer on that joint. He lets me cop them joints without all the hassles. It's been a minute now since the caper, so ya'll should be able to cop a ride without any suspicions, you dig!"

"Awww, Black is getting tired of us ya'll," Ruby said playfully.

She meant every word.

"It ain't that. It's just that I be having shit to do sometimes. I know if ya'll get a ride, you won't have to depend on me or anybody else to take ya'll wherever ya'll need to go. Feel me?"

"You do have a point Black," Maria said.

"That's what's happening fa-real, fa-real," Sunny said, snapping her fingers.

"Yeah, I guess, since our money is cleaned up. Ain't no way anything can be traced back to us or the bank," Ruby said.

"On top of that, we'll be graduating in a few months. We might as well do it up in official style. Hell, we only have one life to live. We should live it to the fullest."

As Ruby was finishing her statement, Fast Black was making a sharp left turn directly into the hospital's parking lot. The smooth, graceful moving car came to a stop. It sounded like a small G-4 jet landing.

"I told ya'll it wouldn't take me long to get here. So ya'll want me to put the ball in motion concerning ya'll getting a car?"

They exited the car and headed towards the hospital's entrance.

Ruby casually said, "It's cool with me, but I have to see what Sunny and Maria say. All I know is it don't make any sense to have money and not enjoy the fabulous things in life."

Maria had been seriously considering Fast Black's proposal to get a car every since he'd brought the idea up, but she didn't want to seem too anxious.

"I don't know. First, I have to see how high my mother's medical bills are going to be. If it ain't too much, I can throw something in to get us a ride."

*I*NSIDE THE ANTISEPTIC SMELLING BUILDING, the

foursome stopped at the nurse's station on the floor Maria's mother was housed on. Maria spoke to a short, heavy-set white nurse with bleached blond hair.

"Can you tell me anything on my mother's condition?" Maria asked.

"Ms. Valentine, your mother is still in a coma from the accident. She does come out of it from time to time. However, it's only for a few seconds at the most. You all must keep your faith in God and believe that he'll take care of the sick and disabled."

Maria tried to smile, but it hurt too much inside.

"Thank you very much for your kind words, but I need to ask you what are her expenses for her care?"

"I beg your pardon?" The nurse asked politely.

"I'm referring to the cost of my mother's medical bills. How much is it going to cost to keep her getting care here?"

"Well, I have to punch a few numbers into the computer to get an exact figure. Do you mind holding on for a moment?"

"No, not at all," Maria said.

The nurse went straight for the flat screen computer terminal.

It didn't take long for the nurse to find what she was looking for.

"Okay Ms. Valentine. I have it for you right here. Up until today, her bills total $12,500."

"Good Lord! That's a lotta' money! If this is going to be like this, I'ma have to hit me a few more banks," Maria thought.

She pulled out two cashier's check totaling $15,000. The nurse accepted the checks and glanced down at the amounts. She looked puzzled.

"Is there something wrong?" Maria asked.

"Well," the nurse said.

"Everything is fine except for two things."

"And what's that?"

"First of all, you gave the hospital an extra twenty-five hundred dollars. Secondly, you didn't write out the hospital's name on the checks."

Maria managed a thin smile.

"That's my bad. I meant to put the name of the hospital on them. Do you have an ink pen I can use?"

The nurse handed Maria a pen so she could fill out the checks properly.

Maria filled in the essentials. She commented matter of factly on the extra money.

"As for that extra twenty-five hundred, can you please put that towards my mother's next bill? I know another one is coming real soon."

She pretended to ignore the obvious sarcasm dripping from Maria's tone. The nurse nodded her head in a way that let Maria know that she understood and sympathized with her plight.

"Sure thing Ms. Valentine. If that's what you want me to do. I'll be more than happy to do so. In fact, how about I give your mother an account number and credit the money to that account under her name so the hospital won't try any funny stuff?"

"That's cool with me," Maria said.

She was softening up. She now understood that the nurse was a genuine woman.

"Do they still have my mother in the same room she was in the last time that I came to visit her?"

"Yes ma'am. I hope you all have a pleasant visit considering the circumstances," the nurse said.

The three girls along with Fast Black started walking down the long, spotless corridor. They were all wrapped up in their own thoughts.

Once they entered her mother's room, Maria tried to hide her emotions. The flowing tears soon betrayed her. Automatically, tears flowed down her pretty face. That made Fast Black swallow. He was choking back tears of his own. Reaching over, Sunny put her arm around Maria and hugged her.

"Don't cry Maria," Sunny whispered.

"It's going to be a'ight."

Fast Black stood off to the side trying to shake the smell of death that invaded his nostrils. He hated hospitals. They reminded him of cemeteries. He glanced down at Maria's mother. She was lying in bed still as a rock.

He shuddered when he thought about himself in the same predicament.

"*I'd rather be dead than be a vegetable,*" he thought.

He watched Maria walk over to her mother's bed and take a seat in the chair beside it.

Glancing at all the tubes in her mother's arms and nose made Maria sad beyond words.

"Hey mom. This is me. Maria. I hope you can hear me. I'm doing fine. So is Billy Boy. He didn't come today because he was still asleep when we left. I didn't want to wake him up. You know how grouchy he gets. I know that's not a good excuse for him not coming to see you, but I promise to bring him along the next time I come visit you."

She looked over at her three friends.

Maria said, "These are three of my best friends in the whole wide world. You already know Sunny. The other girl is Ruby and this here is Fast Black. He thinks he's a helluva' driver and I guess he is."

Ruby, Sunny, and Fast Black all smiled.

Even though it was Maria's understanding that her mother couldn't hear nor comprehend what she was saying, it still made Maria feel better just talking to her and being in her presence. It was more mental than physical.

"Moms we love you. Me and Billy Boy need you. You have to get better and come up outta' that coma and come home to us. You have to embrace life with a firm grip and be strong. You are all we have. Please don't let us down and give up. I know you can pull through this. You have always been such a strong and wonderful mom."

When Maria turned around, she spotted Sunny standing to the side of the room dabbing at her eyes with a handkerchief. When Sunny looked up, she stared at Maria through eyes filled with sympathy and understanding.

"Maria, your mother is going to make it. I know she is. I can feel it in my soul."

"She sure will Maria," Fast Black and Ruby added in unison.

Sunny continued, "We've known each other since we were little girls. You were like a sister to me Maria. So you know how I feel about your moms."

"I know Sunny."

Maria nodded. Maria had been holding on to her mother's hand when suddenly she felt a jolting squeeze. Maria jumped up quickly like she had been hit with a bolt of electricity.

"Did ya'll see that?" Maria asked.

She was looking around the room in a state of heightened excitement.

"My mom's just squeezed my hand! Mom I know you can hear me!" Maria said.

She was gazing down into the wax-like face of the woman who had given her birth.

As tears continued streaming down Maria's face, she poured her heart out.

"Moms, I know you're a fighter. Please don't stop fighting. You hear me? We are here waiting to take you home. Sunny, come here. Sit down and talk to her for a minute while I go get the nurse."

As Maria rushed from the room, Sunny took her place in the chair. She sat beside the bed and stared at Mrs. Valentine.

"Mom, you'll be okay. We have faith in you and we have faith in God. We are all praying for you to get well soon. We know that God is watching over you. Maria and Billy are always telling me how much they love and miss you and how badly they want you to come home. I always tell them that you will be up and out of this place sooner than they think. So please hurry and get well. We all need you back home."

Just then, Maria and the nurse entered the room. Ruby, Fast Black, and Sunny all watched curiously as the nurse went over and checked Mrs. Valentine's vital signs. She then adjusted the tubes administering the intravenous fluids into her pale, drained body.

"All right, now children," the nurse whispered gently.

"Visitation hours are over Mrs. Valentine. She needs her rest. You all can come back tomorrow if you'd like. Our patient has had enough excitement for one day."

Obeying the nurse's orders, Sunny got up from the chair and backed away from the bed. She was still looking down at Maria's mother. Maria walked over by the bed then bent over and kissed her mother on the lips.

"Mom, I'm leaving now. You will be with me every second of the day and night until you come home. I want you to remain confident in yourself and be determined to pull through this. Not only for yourself, but for me and Billy Boy. We can't wait till' you come home."

"Don't worry," the nurse assured Maria.

" I will look after your mother while you are not here. It is always good for one of you to come visit and talk to her. I wasn't sure before, but now I am. Your mother can hear every word you say to her. You are perhaps the biggest reason for her rapid recovery. Just try to make sure you come visit tomorrow."

"You can count on it," Maria said.

She turned to the others.

"Ya'll ready to roll?"

Her friends nodded yes. They all walked out of the hospital room. The nurse stared at the kids with a huge smile. In her heart, she truly believed that Maria was a good girl who really cared about her mother. Most people forget about their loved ones when they need them the most.

"But that's just how life is," she grimly thought.

She then resumed tucking Mrs. Valentine in under the hospital sheets.

"You're lucky," she whispered.

"You've got a daughter who really loves you. You get better now and go home to her. You hear me?"

CHAPTER 6

*T*HE HOSPITAL VISIT WAS painful for Maria. She didn't regain her composure for almost four hours after she got home. She stayed in her bedroom for most of that time crying. The memories of her mother lying helpless in that hospital room depending on machines to keep her alive were clear and heart wrenching. Sunny and Ruby stayed in the living room. They were showing Maria their support.

They were all over Maria as soon as she came out of her bedroom to get something to drink. They hounded her about being strong for the family during this time and how was she going to pay the future medical bills. They even offered to give Maria some of the money they had stashed away from the bank robbery. Maria refused, feeling too proud to accept their help.

After making sure that Maria was okay, Ruby called a cab to take her home. After Ruby left, Sunny gave Maria a sisterly hug and went home to count her money. All Sunny did was count her money and think about different ways to spend it. Because of Maria, she decided to wait on spending it. The whole situation with Maria's mother had shaken Sunny up pretty bad. She knew Maria would need some more money.

As the days quickly turned into weeks, the girls, Fast Black, and

Billy Boy stayed at the hospital by her mother's bedside. When they weren't at the hospital, Maria was pressing Fast Black to take her back to Atlantic City. Maria wanted to flip the little money she had left. Maria was damn near broke and didn't like it one bit.

"I'ma think about it Maria," Fast Black told her one day while sitting in her house.

"What's there to think about Black?" Maria pressed.

She didn't want to reveal the fact that her pockets were hurting for certain again. Although Maria had a little over $6,700, she felt that was nothing compared to all the money she just had. Stepping up to the plate and paying all the bills really took away from her small fortune.

"Listen Black, life is short and serious. You see what happened to my mother. She didn't get to go nowhere outside of D.C. I had plenty of time to think about things while she's been away. I have to get some money some kind of way so I can help my mother and do all the things I want to do before I die," Maria's voice cracked.

She stared at Fast Black with her eyes brimming with tears.

Fast Black put out the marijuana laced cigar he was smoking. He looked at Maria's shapely body. She stared back at him, looking sad.

Fast Black frowned in disgust.

"*These broads think I'm they personal cab driver or something,*" he thought.

"Black, don't do that boy," Ruby spoke up.

"You 'spose to fuck with us, but yet every time we ask your ass for a ride somewhere, you start acting all funny and shit."

"No I don't," he pouted.

He was trying to deny the fact that Ruby just picked his cards.

"Yes you do Black. Look, just do this for Maria. When we come back, we won't bug you about shit no more," Sunny said.

She batted her bedroom eyes at him.

"I heard that one before," he mumbled.

"When you tryna' go Maria?"

Maria gave Fast Black a mischievous smile.

She said, "Ain't no time better than right now. I just told you that life is short and serious boy."

Throwing his head backwards, Fast Black released a burly sigh.

"Get ya'll loot together. I'ma go get some gas and shit. I'll be right back."

"Thank you Black," Maria said.

She gave him a hug.

"Yeah whatever," Fast Black groused.

He left. While he was driving towards the weed spot, Fast Black called a female to postpone their dinner date. It was his turn to take out Big Booty Angie. She was one of the sexiest females who was very well known Uptown for fucking and sucking guys into comatose-like sleeps. Fast Black made arrangements to see Angie on another day. She agreed and Fast Black thanked God for blessing him with another chance to get at the sexy red-bone.

Fast Black drove around Galveston Place and bought a few bags of Strawberry Hydro weed. He headed to 51 Liquor store to get some cigars and drinks for the trip. He drove back to the gas station on Alabama Avenue to fill his gas tank. Fast Black returned to Maria's hood thirty-five minutes later. He scooped her, Sunny, and Ruby up and they were on their way.

"Here you go Ruby. Twist that up for me," Fast Black told her.

He jumped on the Baltimore/Washington Parkway.

Looking in the brown bag he gave her, Ruby scrunched her face when the strong aroma of Hydroponic weed invaded her nostrils.

"Oooohh. Dis' dat' dro' ya'll," Ruby beamed.

"We gone be high as shit by the time we get up there to get our gambling on."

"And you know it," Fast Black said.

He popped in The Rare Essence Live P.A. CD. They drove for a few hours smoking weed, and drinking Remy and Moet Rose' cocktails. They were laughing, joking, enjoying the ride, and the

54

comradeship. They made it to Atlantic City a little after 8:30 p.m. They grabbed a quick bite to eat and went straight to the casinos at the Trump Plaza Hotel.

Maria was blown away, but played it cool while watching all the people from various nationalities on the crowded casino floor. They were betting small, big, and playing the slot machines. Ruby and Maria headed for the crap tables while Sunny and Fast Black took a chance at the card table. Maria had $6,000 worth of chips. She planned to risk everything she had left to make more money.

In less than one hour, Maria had lost $5,000 worth of chips. She only had two $500 chips in her hand. Seeing the frustrated look on Maria's face, Ruby gave her $3,500 worth of chips.

"Go head' and get cho' man girl. I know how it is. Just get me back when you can," Ruby said.

Maria grabbed the dice and went to work.

She was trying to re-create the sure-fire shot that Billy-Boy showed her one time a few months back.

Maria started shaking the dice.

She and Ruby, along with everybody, crowded around the crap table.

They heard a female yelling, "AAAAAAHHH! OMIGOD! OMIGOD! I'M RIICCCCCCHHH!"

Maria looked up and saw that the voice was coming from none other than Sunny. Sunny was jumping up and down after winning a huge pot at the poker table.

"Ease up Sunny with all that geeking-ass shit!" Fast Black smirked.

He was happy for Sunny, even though she just won a few thousand from him. Fast Black loved seeing black people get money, no matter how they did it.

"Oohh, okay Black. I'm just so happy boy. AAAAAHHH!" Sunny laughed.

She started raking up the pile of chips.

Back at the crap tables, Maria concentrated on the roll she learned from Billy Boy. She lost another $1,500 before things turned around for her. A f t e r getting a hot hand, Maria turned her last $3,000 into $24,800. Ruby won a quick $12,000 betting on Maria's hot hand.

"Damn Shorty! You jive punishing these peoples!"

Maria heard a man whispering in her ear as she rolled and won another pile of chips.

"BET IT ALL!" Maria yelled.

She was feeling cocky. She looked over her shoulder and spotted Fast Black and Sunny crossing their fingers.

"Don't cross your fingers! This ain't luck! You better get with me! Ruby just won big fucking with me! I'm on fire, I'm telling you!"

Maria smiled.

People around the table started placing their bets on Maria. Fast Black bet his last $2,300 on Maria. Sunny bet the $18,000 she walked away with from the poker table.

Maria shook the dice.

She told Ruby, " You better blow on these girl! They are burning my hand!"

Maria said as she tossed the dice high in the air.

Everybody watched in awe. They were hoping and praying for a win as the dice seemed to glide through the air in slow motion.

"SEVEN! ANOTHER WINNER!" The crap table attendant yelled over the roar of the cheering crowd.

Maria rode her hot hand until every one of her friends raked in a pile of chips. When they'd got enough of the gambling, they left and splurged a few thousand on a plush suite inside Trump Plaza to crash in for the night.

The suite looked like it was laid out for the Queen of England. Sunny ran and dove on the gigantic king size bed. Ruby headed to the bathroom to take a nice-hot bubble bath. Fast Black went to the fully stocked bar and grabbed a gold bottle of that **Ace of Spades** champagne. Maria got on the phone to share her good news with Billy Boy. Fast Black, along with Maria and Sunny, chilled on the sofa and drank for a while.

"Maria, you crushed them peoples tonight. You better hope they let us leave this ma'fucka after the way you twirked' them peoples," Fast Black said.

His tone was full of excitement. He had won close to $43,000 betting on Maria tonight. He couldn't fathom how much money the casino lost tonight on the crap table.

"I had to Black. My mother needs mo---"

"AY BLACK! Can You Come Here For A Minute?" Ruby called from the bathroom.

She cut Maria off.

"Mmm-Hmmph!" Sunny and Maria hissed in unison.

Fast Black stood up and went to see what Ruby wanted.

Entering the bathroom with the champagne bottle, Fast Black nearly choked on the swig of champagne he'd just took. He was staring at Ruby's naked frame sitting on the edge of the Jacuzzi- style tub.

"Come on and get in here with me Black," Ruby smiled while looking directly at him.

"You ain't neva' gosta' tell me twice," he laughed.

He quickly locked the bathroom door and rushed on over to the Jacuzzi.

"All that money and weed got me horny as shit, Black," Ruby said.

She was unbuckling his navy blue True Religion jeans to pull out his hulking man-meat. She started licking and kissing his boner. Fast Black took another swig of the champagne. He put his other hand on the back of Ruby's head. He was urging her on to handle her business.

Going to work, Ruby glanced up into his eyes and started sucking the life out of him. She deep-throated his fuck pole.

"Mmmm.You ready Black? I need to feel this big dick deep inside my pussy," she moaned.

She rubbed his dick all over her face.

After stripping out of his clothes with the quickness, Fast Black jumped in the Jacuzzi and bent her over.

"Spread them legs girl. You said you wanted it," he demanded.

He grinded his hard pole on her glistening pussy lips. He pulled her back and penetrated her tight fuck box with a painful thrust.

Intoxicated, their sexual hunger went into over drive. Fast Black slammed his thick wanger in and out of Ruby's warm wet tunnel. He then pulled out quickly.

"Ahhh! Ssss boy! Put it back in Black!" She gasped.

He plunged back inside, then snatched his meat out again as Ruby tried to make her pussy muscles lock him inside her.

"Ssss Black. C'mon boy. Stop teasing me," Ruby begged.

She wiggled her soft ass at him. She felt his thumbs brushing against her hard nipples.

He slid his thickness back inside, fucking her up to the edge of the Jacuzzi. Ruby cocked one knee onto the edge of the Jacuzzi. She felt his dick rocking her insides all the way to her aching clitoris.

"Aaahh Black! Sssssss! I'm Ca-Cummmin' Black! I'm CUUUUUMMMMMMMIIIINNNGGG!" She shrieked.

She bucked her ass wildly into his pounding piston. She bit her bottom lip. Tiny splatters of love juice exploded out of her filled up pussy and slid all over his sawing love muscle.

"AAAAAHHH BOY! SSSssssssss! OMIGOD! OMI! Black!" She gasped.

She was loving the way his dick filled her tight wetness.

"Got Dayyum' Ruby. You got that good ole' ha-box," he groaned.

He made the ugliest fuck face he could muster as she clenched onto his stabbing manhood. She fucked him back like she knew all the secrets to pleasing him.

They started that loud slapping noise type of rapid fucking.

They both were yelling out loud and cursing. Fast Black from the orgasm erupting from his glistening boner and Ruby from her oozing pussy quaking like a tender gigantic nerve. They collapsed in the Jacuzzi with no more energy. They fell asleep in the water hugged up like newlyweds.

CHAPTER 7

*T*HE MONTHS HAD PASSED since the festive night in Atlantic City. Maria's mother took a turn for the worse instead of getting better as everyone had expected. The medical bills piled up. That left Maria with only $17,000 remaining from all the cash she won in Atlantic City. Part of her winnings had been used for the down payment on a 2001 platinum Toyota Camry luxury sedan. Maria also used some of the money to buy some new clothes for herself and Billy Boy.

Sunny decided to buy a dark blue 2000 Ford Mustang and Ruby settled on a 1999 dark burgundy and black Cadillac Seville. When each of the girls climbed behind the wheel of their new cars, they felt like they owned the world.

It was early June. All three girls graduated early from Ballou high school. They were proud of their accomplishments. Most girls they knew had either dropped out of school willingly or were forced out to due to getting pregnant.

Ruby had missed her period two months in a row after the one night stand she had with Fast Black. She went to the doctor and learned that she was six weeks pregnant. Ruby told no one about the pregnancy. She quickly paid to get an abortion. Ruby felt that she was too young for kids, especially by Fast Black. He was someone who loved to run the streets more than she did.

Sunny and Ruby met Maria at her apartment to discuss the upcoming prom. They were all excited about the event. They changed their minds a hundred times when it came to what they were going to wear. Billy Boy sat there listening, observing, and marveling over the complexity of women and what they went through just to go out to a party.

"Billy Boy, you know I went to see mom today," Maria said out of the blue.

"Oh yeah? How's she coming along? Is there any change in her condition?"

"Well," Maria started.

"When I entered her room and sat in the same chair I always sit in, she seemed to be aware of my presence."

"You say that every time you go see her," Billy Boy thought.

"Whaddaya' mean?" He asked.

"Was she conscious, or what?"

"It's kind of hard to explain," Maria said.

"I mean, when I held her hand and started talking to her, she squeezed my hand. It was as if she was letting me know that she knew it was me in her room. I was looking at her face. I don't know if it was my imagination. It seemed like she was smiling at me. I can't be sure, but it sure did seem that way."

Sunny and Ruby glanced at each other while sitting on the couch. They both knew how bad Maria wanted her mother to get well. They figured that she was maybe seeing more in the light gestures than there really was.

Maria continued,

"The doctor told me that she is coming along swell. He said she is a strong person. If she keeps up the work, she should come out of that cataleptic condition she's in. Do you understand what I'm saying?"

Billy Boy didn't know what the hell Maria was talking about.

He could only nod his head.

He replied, "Look, Maria. I can dig where you coming from. Well, I think I can. I love mom just as much as you do. I also feel as concerned over her condition as you do, but what I'm trying to say is this. I don't wanna' get in your bid'ness or anything like that, but girl, you're the only sister I got in this whole wide world. Only God knows what's gonna' happen to moms. So right now, I gotta pay more attention to you and your well being."

"What are you talking about Billy Boy?" Maria asked in a serious tone.

She leaned in closer to him.

"I'm talking about you and all this money you've been coming up with. You done bought a rack of new clothes for me and yourself, a new car, plus you still paying mom's hospital bills. C'mon Maria, you been spending way more than what you told me you won up in Atlantic City. Even Ray Charles can see that you spending more than you say you won. Now just come clean with me so I won't be in the dark if shit comes down on you or me. You owe me that much Sis."

Sunny and Ruby started squirming like they had ants in their panties over on the couch. All of a sudden, it got very hot in the room. Nervously they glanced at Maria, wondering what her excuse was going to be.

Clearing her throat, Maria took a deep breath.

She started explaining, "Billy, you have a point about what you're saying, but I don't wanna talk about it right now."

Staring at his sister, Billy Boy knew whatever was going on had to be serious. The only time Maria called him Billy, instead of his nick name, was when she was in a serious, no nonsense mood. Billy Boy decided not to press the matter any further. Instead he keyed in on what she was saying about the prom tonight.

"Tonight is a big night for me and my girlfriends. We are trying to get ourselves together for the prom tonight. Besides, you are the lucky one who will be driving us three attractive women to the big event. Right now, you have your hands full. So just be happy for your sister and her friends tonight, okay?"

Billy Boy looked at his sister and smiled. He loved Maria and would do anything she asked.

"Okay, Maria. As soon as all of this is over, I want your promise that you'll fill me in on what's going on, deal?"

"Okay," Maria promised.

"You got my word. After the prom you and I will sit down and talk about whatever you wanna' talk about. Is that cool wit' chu'?"

"Yeah, that's cool. I'm going to hold you to your word. Don't think for one moment I'm going to forget, eva'!"

Maria laughed and turned to Sunny and Ruby.

"Are ya'll ready to change into our prom clothes?"

"Ain't no doubt about it," Ruby said.

She sighed in relief and was glad that Maria changed the subject.

"Girl, I have everything I'm going to wear right here. How about chu' Sunny?"

Sunny clicked her tongue against the roof of her mouth.

She said, "Are you trippin' or something girl? You know I brought all my things over here earlier today."

Ruby laughed, "I keep forgetting you live right upstairs. Let's go get dressed then."

Sunny and Ruby followed her into her bedroom. Billy Boy watched all three of them with a curious expression. He knew whatever was going on with Maria, the other two had to be involved in some kind of way.

"Billy Boy," Maria called over her shoulder.

"Yeah, whassup'?"

"Make sure you dress to kill. You have to represent for your sister boy. I know you got enough fly shit in there to choose from. In other words, don't dress up like a thug like you usually do."

"There you go again with that bullshit Maria," Billy Boy playfully said.

"I done told your ass about tryna' act like you my moms. Why don't you chill the fuck out with all that shit?"

"Aw, boy," Maria said.

She stopped in the doorway to her bedroom. She threw her hands on her hips.

"Just put something nice and classy on please. Because me and the girls are truly going to be some classy, diplomatic bitches tonight Baby Bro'."

"Maria," Billy Boy said.

He had a look of disdain.

"Why you wanna talk like that? You know how much I hate hearing ya'll calling yourselves that word. Hell, you the one acting like some kind of thug."

"Billy Boy, don't sweat the small stuff, child. You know we always talk this way. It's cool as long as no other dudes or bitches jump out there and call us bitches. It may be a serious misunderstanding. Ain't that right ladies?"

Waiting impatiently for Maria to move out of their way so they could get inside her bedroom and change into their clothes, Ruby and Sunny quickly nodded their heads in agreement.

"See there Billy Boy, what did I tell ya'? Look, do you think you can be ready in an hour or two?"

Billy Boy shook his head as if he was hearing something he simply couldn't understand.

He stated, "You got me twisted Sis. Women are the ones always taking all day to get dressed. It'll never take me no damn hour to get dressed," he said.

He stepped off and headed towards his bedroom.

As the girls disappeared inside Maria's bedroom, someone knocked softly on the door. That stopped Billy Boy in his tracks. For no apparent reason an image of the police flashed through his mind. That shook Billy Boy with fear. Creeping over to the door, he looked out the peephole and couldn't see nothing but black.

"Who is it?" Billy Boy said in a low voice.

"It's me, Billy Boy. Fast Black! Open up baby."

Relieved, Billy Boy snatched the door wide open. Fast Black

stepped inside the apartment with another guy following him. Both were dressed in some fly-ass Versace Chinese collar suits with matching black Versace slip-ons. The expensive outfits could feed a few hundred people in a small third world country.

"What's up Billy Boy?" Fast Black greeted.

"Ay', this here is a good friend of mines. His name's Shooter."

Shooter was known for exactly that: **Shooting anybody that rubbed him the wrong way and for the right price also.** Shooter was a light skin kid who was about 18 years old with a very bad temper. He started robbing banks at the age of 13. He didn't talk much. He let his guns do all the talking. Shooter didn't have any problem with keeping anybody in **check** if he felt disrespected. He kept them **checking** into the city's morgue. Robbing banks and killing people was a way of life for him.

Billy Boy looked the two young men up and down.

"Damn," he exclaimed softly.

He quickly adding a whistle of approval.

"You two niggaz look Oh-So Fly."

They walked towards the living room.

Fast Black said, "I wanted to surprise Maria and nem' by taking them to the prom tonight. That's why I brought my mans and nem, Shooter with me."

Truth be told, Fast Black couldn't get Ruby off his mind after the mind blowing sex they shared in Atlantic City. Every time he went out with another girl or had sex with one, he always thought about Ruby. Even though he was fighting it, Fast Black knew he was booty whipped by Ruby.

"Oh Yeah," Billy Boy said.

"That might be a problem Slim."

"Oh yeah, why you say that?" Fast Black looked at him.

"I know they don't have no dates. Maria already told me they didn't."

"You're right," Billy Boy affirmed.

"I mean you're half way right. The plans changed Black. You see, they didn't have any dates, not at first. Then Maria asked me to escort them."

Fast Black looked at Billy Boy and smiled.

"C'mon Slim. You're going to escort all three of them?"

Billy Boy nodded.

"Damn, Billy Boy. I know you ain't gon' block a nigga like that? I'm saying me and my partner got all sweet to have fun with Ruby and her partners. That ain't cool lil homie. That ain't cool at all," Fast Black complained.

Billy Boy shrugged.

He didn't want to ever rain on anyone's parade.

Billy Boy simply said, "Listen Slim, I'ma go ask them and see what's up. If they say they cool with it, then it's cool with me. I'm just going off what they told me Slim, that's all."

Billy Boy cleared the air. He was staring at Shooter who looked sneakier than the disciple who betrayed Jesus Christ.

"I doubt if they heard ya'll come in. They just went into Maria's bedroom to get dressed. Just chill out and grab a seat. I'll be right back."

"Okay lil' man," Fast Black said.

He was rubbing his hands together.

"We'll be right here when you get back, cause we sure as hell ain't got nowhere else to go tonight," he said.

He then winked at Shooter.

"Ain't no question, Bob," Shooter said.

He took a seat on the couch.

As a bank robber, within the last 18 months, Shooter had taken nearly $350,000 out of six banks. Shooter and Fast Black were close friends who met at the Oak Hill Juvenile detention facility. They hooked up together once they got back on the streets and became crime partners. Shooter did all the robbing and killing. Fast Black did all the driving.

As far as planning the actual robberies, Shooter always acted alone. He vowed to never take anyone on the inside with him. Shooter figured it was a good policy. It increased his share of the money because he didn't have to split the money evenly with a partner. It also narrowed down the prospects of having someone rat him out. Shooter knew he'd never rat on himself and he wanted to keep it that way. He threw Fast Black a few thousand dollars here and there. Fast Black was cool with that because he wasn't doing anything more than driving the getaway car. Shooter figured that was more than fair since Fast Black wasn't taking any real risks by going up in the bank with him.

Shooter didn't trust too many people. Fast Black won his trust while they were housed in Oak Hill. When Fast Black told Shooter about the three girls who also robbed banks, quite naturally Shooter's interest went up. Especially when Fast Black mentioned that the three girls were stand-up thoroughbreds. Fast Black figured that since the girls wanted to be in the business of robbing banks, then meeting Shooter was in their best interest.

Even though Shooter had agreed to meet Maria and her girlfriends, it had never crossed his mind to go out on any jobs with them. After Fast Black told him how sexy and fine the three girls were, Shooter had to meet them. Besides, Shooter didn't see how taking three fine, young, beautiful girls to a prom could hurt anything. On top of all that, he had a pocket full of big face hundreds and nowhere to go. Not to mention he had just bought a brand new outfit.

Shooter's jewelry consisted of a solid-rose gold watch with diamonds around the face and a sparkling bezel. His rose-gold diamond ring cost more than Maria's mother's first medical bill. In ghetto parlance, Shooter was sharper than a switch blade knife and shined brighter than the full moon.

Billy Boy returned to the living room.

He said, "Listen up ya'll, Maria told me to tell ya'll as soon as they finish dressing, they'll holla' at cha'll. She told me to tell ya'll to make yourselves comfortable, you dig?"

Fast Black smiled, "Yeah Billy Boy, we understand."

"Do ya'll want something to drink or anything before I go get ready for the prom? Shit I gotta' hurry up if I wanna look all fly like you and your man."

Shooter said, "Nah Slim, we don't need nothing. We ain't gon' hold you up from getting fresh."

The three young men laughed. Billy Boy walked off towards the back of the apartment where his bedroom was located so he could get dressed. They all could feel the magic in the air. It let them know that the night ahead was going to be special indeed.

CHAPTER 8

*T*WO HOURS HAD PASSED and Billy Boy was dressed.

He waited along with Fast Black and Shooter for the appearance of Maria and her girlfriends. Billy Boy sported a light blue, Armani pin-stripe two-button suit with a navy blue knit shirt and a pair of dark blue Stacy Adams. Although Maria paid for them, Billy Boy always made it his business to choose his own clothes. For a boy his age, Billy Boy was very fashion conscious and knew how to dress very well.

Shooter started the conversation, "Say Young? That outfit looks jive sweet on you Slim. Where did you cop it from?"

Pleased by Shooter's compliment, Billy Boy puffed out his chest with pride.

He said, "Me and Maria went shopping in Georgetown. I don't remember the name of the store, but it sure had some pretty slick shit up in there. As a matter of fact, I copped most of my outfits there. I don't know how in the world I forgot the name of the joint. I guess I wasn't paying that much attention."

"Yeah, they do have some pretty Alias spots up there in Georgetown Mall," Shooter acknowledged.

"That's it. That's the joint right there Slim!" Billy Boy said excitedly.

"I don't know how I forgot the name of that place."

Shooter shrugged as if it was nothing.

"It's not like you forgot. You probably just got caught up scoping out all that fly-ass shit up in there. I can see that happening. Like I said, they got some real Alias spots out that way. Hell, I have forgotten the names of most of the stores inside the joint myself."

For some reason or another, Shooter found himself liking Billy Boy more and more. At that moment, the girls came walking out of the bedroom. They looked absolutely gorgeous.

Maria wore a curve-showing, two-piece Valentino ensemble that consisted of a hot pink suit with short skirt and a white sheer D&G lace blouse. Maria's tiny feet were nicely adorned by a pair of white and pink $780 Giuseppe Zanotti slip-on, high heel pumps. Her light brown complexion and sandy hazel brown eyes set her long, black, curly hair off to perfection. She was the portrait of beauty.

Sunny had on a black, curve-hugging Georges Chakra sleeveless mini-dress that gave her enviable figure an adorable and sexy flare. Her chocolate colored body strained against the dress that revealed the black satin bra and matching bikini panties she wore underneath. Sunny's long, jet black hair was down to her shoulders and kept neatly in place by a black and white bandana that was tied around her forehead. She left it dangling loosely over her left shoulder. A pair of Christian Louboutin, black and white, open-toe, high heel, ankle sandals allowed her pretty toes to peek out suggestively. Even though it was highly unconventional to wear a bandana to a prom, there was nothing about Sunny that could be said to be conventional. She was a ghetto girl to the core.

Ruby's ruffled, white frock dress was a sight to behold. It hit her just around mid-thigh. It showed off her big legs and thick thighs. Her black and white, $629 Alberto Fermani Co-Op, alligator booties had her walking the line between serious and sexy. Ruby's hair was still cut short and colored cinnamon. Instead of wearing it in a curl, she had it done up in a stylish, short pixy cut and tapered in the back. It brought out her buttermilk skin complexion. Fast Black caught a natural hard-on while staring at Ruby. He wanted to make love to her right then and there, but kept his cool.

"In due time. In due time. I'ma tap that ass again. And when I do, I'ma make her ass fall in love with me for real," Fast Black thought.

Maria said, "Hey Black. What's all this about? You talking about taking us to the prom?"

All three boys stood there speechless with their mouths hanging wide open. They were absolutely astounded by the girl's appearance.

Fast Black recovered quickly.

"First of all, let me clear my throat! You ladies look very lovely tonight and that's no bullshit. And damn, Sunny," he said.

"I never seen a girl rock a bandana to the prom like that. You jive working that ma'fucka! I mean, you straight killing the game. You look really good."

"Ease up with all the compliments, big boy," Billy Boy smirked.

"You know Sunny's my date for the prom."

Billy Boy looked at Sunny who lowered her head to keep him from seeing her blush.

Ruby interrupted the conversation.

"You three young men look jive slick yourselves. So, who's your friend Black?" She asked; referring to Shooter.

He was standing there like the cat had his tongue, because his mind was locked in on Maria.

Any fool could see Shooter had been hit by the thunder bolt of love. He could not believe this young girl was so damn attractive. For him to be mesmerized by her beauty was something new and strange to him.

Fast Black called out, "Shooter! Shooter!"

He was obviously awe struck.

Shooter finally answered, "I'm sorry, Fast Black. It's just that, it's just that I was spell bound by all this beauty around me."

He noticed that all three girls were laughing at him.

"Yeah Slim."

Fast Black chuckled.

"I jive can see that, but let me introduce you to these sexy honeys.

First, I'ma hip you to the one who really seems to have caught your full, undivided attention. Her name is Maria. The other one is Sunny and that's my girl Ruby. You know her brother Ike."

"Oh yeah, I seen shorty around before," Shooter confirmed.

He was keeping his eyes glued to Maria.

"But I never was familiar with her the way I am with her brother. Anyway ladies, all of ya'll look captivatingly beautiful on this lovely evening."

All three girls thanked him for his compliment, knowing he was sincere.

"So, Fast Black?" Maria asked.

"Are you going to answer my question about the prom?"

"No doubt, I'm going to answer it. It's like this. Since ya'll didn't have anybody taking ya'll except Billy Boy, I was wondering if it would be cool for me and Shooter to come along too? Shit, I didn't even know Billy Boy was taking ya'll til' a few minutes ago. All three of us can show you ladies a real wonderful time, you dig me?"

Maria looked over at Sunny and Ruby.

She then said, "I don't have any problem with it. Then again, ya'll look too clean not to be our dates for tonight. Billy Boy, you don't have no problems with this do you? I mean, you are our official chaperone tonight, so whatever you say goes."

Billy Boy looked at Shooter and Fast Black who were pleading with their eyes for him to say yes.

He let them sweat for a minute or two before saying, "Nah, I ain't got no problem with it. Ain't no hassles with me. I know I just met Shooter, but he seems like a pretty good dude."

Sunny and Ruby spoke at the same time, "It's cool with us then."

Walking away from Ruby, Sunny said, "I see ya'll even brought us some carnations."

Fast Black smiled, "Damn, I almost forgot. Me and Shooter picked them up at the flower shop. We didn't know what color to get, so we purchased three white ones. That way, they'll go with whatever outfit ya'll have on."

"I heard someone say before, that flowers were one of the most sweetest things God ever made but forgot to put a soul into," Sunny said.

"However, we already know that God is the greatest of planners so therefore he didn't forget anything. I just had to say that about the flowers because it sounded good. Know what I mean?"

Ruby laughed.

"C'mon Sunny, stop preaching and give me some of that good weed you been smoking on."

Everybody cracked up with laughter.

"No bullshit, you know if you start preaching, we'll never get to the prom," Billy Boy added.

"Anyway," Maria said.

"We really appreciate this ya'll. God may not forget about things, but we sure as hell had forgotten about copping some flowers for the prom. You know damn well a girl can't go to a prom without wearing a carnation."

"It's getting late," Billy Boy sang.

He was imitating the classic Floetry song.

"C'mon ya'll, if we don't get up outta' here we may not have a prom to go to," he said.

He was growing a bit impatient.

"You right Billy Boy," Maria agreed.

"C'mon, all of us can take my car. That way we'll all be together. Black, you don't mind driving do you?"

"Nah, that's cool with me."

Fast Black grinned.

"If everybody's ready, let's get outta this joint."

It was around 7:30 p.m. when all of the young people jammed inside Maria's car. The summer breeze was nice and pleasant. It accentuated the fading sun which had turned a blazing red as it slowly disappeared into the early twilight.

BY THE TIME THEY ARRIVED at the prom, the party was in full swing. The dance floor was crowded with young bodies dancing to the fast paced sounds of Young Jeezy and Akon's hit "I'M A RIDER!"

When Maria and her companions entered the auditorium, they were immediately noticed by the mob of teens who were standing around drinking the alcohol spiked punch. They were patting their feet to the latest hip-hop tunes. A couple of their female classmates approached them.

"Hey! What's up wit' cha'll ladies?" Asked Cindy.

She happened to be the class clown.

"Damn, ya'll jive crushing shit with them outfits. Sunny, the way you rocking that scarf around your head, you know you got shit on lock. I ain't never seen nobody rock a scarf like that. Especially not at a prom. Now, that's original."

"Yeah, no bullshit," agreed Chunky Vicky.

Vicky was one more doughnut away from being a straight up fat girl, but she stayed so fly and dressed so sexy. She had a lot of boys chasing behind her, trying to get her goodies.

"Sunny, you doing the ma'fucka and your chaperones ain't doing so bad eva'. Maria ain't that your brother, Billy Boy?" Vicky asked.

She pointed over to where he stood looking shy.

"Yeah Vicky, that's him," Maria said.

She was feeling proud of her younger brother.

"My one and only flesh and blood brother."

Billy Boy tried to stop blushing. He felt like a silly school boy on his first date standing next to Sunny who had an iron grip around his arm.

"Damn! He's cute," Vicky pressed.

"Sunny, the way you're holding onto his arm, you act like he's your man or something."

"Don't even try it Vicky," Sunny said defensively.

"Billy Boy is like a brother to me. He's just escorting me to the prom tonight out of the goodness of his heart."

Sensing that she hit a nerve, Vicky decided to leave well enough alone. She turned her attention to Fast Black and Shooter.

"So, who are these other two fine gentlemen?"

"This is Fast Black. He's my date for tonight. You can step the fuck back Vicky," Ruby playfully said.

The way Fast Black was looking tonight she didn't have a problem with giving him some more of her goodies.

"The other cutie-pie that's standing by Maria is Shooter," Ruby said.

Shooter and Fast Black both nodded at Cindy and Vicky.

"Well," Maria said to the two intruders.

"Where are ya'll dates at?"

Cindy rolled her eyes.

"They over there standing by the punch bowl. You just reminded me and Vicky that we gotta get back over there with them. We just wanted to come over and holla'. You know, pay our respects. Who knows when we might see each other again? You know how strange life can be."

Sunny looked up, "Ya'll going somewhere in the near future?"

Cindy shrugged her slender shoulders.

"Well, I been thinking about joining the Navy. Vicky is on her way to USC out in Cali', but I guess she can speak for herself."

They all turned their attention on Vicky.

She said, "Thanks for telling the whole world Cindy, but any way."

She continued, "Yeah ya'll, I got accepted to USC about a week and a half ago. My father has been planning this for me probably before I was born. You see, he's a Trojan and wants me to follow in his footsteps. He's already paid my tuition and everything. He feels like I'm his only chance to live again and do the things that he never got to do. I want to let him know that his dreams weren't a waste of time. I don't want him to die without knowing or seeing that he made good on his solid investment."

Maria stood there listening. She was thinking about her own father and what kind of relationship she might have had with him had things turned out differently.

"Besides, I want to make him proud of me. I'm the youngest out of six kids. I have two sisters and three brothers. My oldest brother got killed in some dumb ass street beef. My other brother is in the feds doing 25 years. Look ya'll, I don't wanna be here telling my life story. It will only have me standing here in tears."

Vicky smiled weakly. Everyone near her heard her voice crack.

"This is our prom ya'll. It's a joyful time and everybody is 'sposed to be happy. This is the night we should be happy and thankful to the Lord that we made it out of school. I will obtain my PhD and become a doctor so that I can help poor kids. That's my whole ambition and to get plenty of dick in the process," she said.

That caused everyone to laugh.

"Yeah, I'm going to join the Navy," Cindy added with a light chuckle.

"I'ma work Uncle Sam to get all the benefits he's offering. That way I can go to college and get a loan to do it quicker. I'm not leaving D.C. unless I have to. I plan on enrolling in Howard University to study Criminal Law so I can help some of these young black brothers who have been wrongly convicted. A lot of them white lawyers feel like the brothers are guilty so they don't do their jobs. They basically sell them out. If a person is innocent, it doesn't make a bit of difference what color they are. You have to fight and get them off. I'ma fight for them all the way to the White House lawn if I have to. The reason why I specified the black brothers is because most of them are railroaded into the prison system from what I've been reading."

"Look Cindy," Vicky said.

"I don't mean to interrupt you, but our dates are coming this way. I guess they got tired of waiting on us, girl. Let's head them off before they get over here."

All five girls hugged and kissed and said their goodbyes.

Vicky and Cindy made it half way across the dance floor. Maria and Sunny yelled behind them.

"We forgot to tell ya'll that ya'll looking real good in them outfits!"

Vicky and Cindy stopped dead in their tracks. They turned around and then all three girls busted out laughing. They caught up with their dates and linked arms. They proudly strutted across the dance floor. Their firm asses bounced beneath their skin tight dresses. Glancing back over their shoulders, they rolled their eyes exaggeratedly. That caused Maria and Sunny to laugh out loud.

Ruby didn't think it was all that funny.

She quipped, "Those bitches ain't gonna never stop flirting. They could become a doctor or a goddamn Admiral in the Navy and they still gonna' be hoes."

Fast Black and Shooter looked at each other amusedly.

Fast Black said, "I know one thing. They sure in the fuck know how to work them asses and hips!"

"No bullshit, Slim," Shooter agreed.

Billy Boy felt like he just had to put his two cents in.

"You can bet cash money on that and come out a guaranteed winner."

"What you know about somebody's ass and hips?" Sunny grilled him.

Billy Boy looked at her like she was crazy.

"Sunny, I done told your ass before 'bout sleeping on me with that brotha' shit. All you gotta' do is set that pussy out to me and I'ma knock sparks out cho' lil' ass shorty. I'm talking about electrifying your entire ma'fuckin' world."

"That's right Slim," Fast Black laughed.

"Don't go for nothing Billy Boy."

Sunny glanced at Maria and Ruby.

"Did ya'll hear that? Billy Boy must really think he can handle me."

"Damn right we heard it," Ruby laughed.

"You started it Sunny. The way he's talking, he might can handle your ass."

Sunny pivoted back around to face Billy Boy. She put her hands on her hips.

"Youngster, I keep telling you. If I lay this hot pussy on your ass, them people from the mental hospital will be coming to get you from climbing the walls hollering out my name at the top of your lungs. You'll be begging me to come back to you. They might fuck around and put you in a straight jacket for lunchin' out. You can't handle this pussy boy, I'm telling you."

"Ooooohh!" Maria laughed.

"Sunny went real deep on that one."

She instigated and all three girls laughed.

"You know me and Billy Boy always play like that," Sunny capped.

"C'mon Billy Boy, let's dance."

"That sounds like a good idea," Billy Boy said.

He then followed her out on the dance floor.

A live band was performing on stage. They were singing an old Earth, Wind, and Fire classic entitled "**KEEP YOUR HEAD TO THE SKY!**"

Embracing one another, Sunny and Billy Boy began moving slowly in each other's arms. They swayed and rocked back and forth to the enchanting sounds of the music.

Maria and Ruby looked at Fast Black and Shooter.

"Are ya'll just going to stand there looking stupid, or are ya'll gonna dance with two lovely and lonely girls? C'mon all you gotta' do is stay close to me and slide your feet. I promise I won't lose you."

"I doubt if you'll lose me Maria. I just don't be dancing like that," he said.

Maria frowned, "Don't start all that bashful shit boy. Even

gangsters slow dance sometimes. I know a big strong man like you ain't going to let a healthy sista like myself dance all alone?"

With his manhood being challenged, Shooter rose to the fight.

"C'mon baby girl. Let's do this."

As they headed for the dance floor, Ruby glanced over at Fast Black.

"I don't know what your ass is still standing there for. C'mon, let's tear this motherfucking floor up."

"Only if you tear up the bedroom with me later on."

Fast Black smirked and pulled Ruby into his embrace.

"I'll think about that while we dance Black. Is that fair enough?"

She smiled while looking into his dark brown eyes.

He kissed her passionately on the lips.

"All a nigga can ask for is that you to play fair," he said.

He pulled her on the dance floor where they started to dance the night away.

CHAPTER 9

"STEP IN THE NAME OF LOVE. Snap my fingers. Groove in the name of love."

The four of them sang along with the band's rendition of R-Kelly's hit song. They all joined Sunny and Billy Boy on the dance floor. They danced through two more songs before departing off the dance floor. They sat down at one of the cabaret style dinner tables.

Sunny was the first to speak.

"Billy Boy, you tired my ass out. Especially, when the band played that last fast song."

Billy Boy smiled.

"You were jive working me for a minute shorty. I'm talking about getting it in on the serious tip."

"You really think I was jamming to that joint, huh?"

"I'm serious," he insisted.

"You were doing your thing Sunny."

That's when it dawned on Sunny that Billy Boy was about to say something slick out of his mouth. He didn't disappoint her.

"Sunny, just imagine. If you feel like I wore that ass out on the dance floor, just visualize what I'll do to you in the bedroom! You will be the one climbing the walls, not me."

Sunny sighed.

"Are you still on that? I thought we had moved on to other issues. Oh, I forgot. Your mind don't transport that fast. I thought we were through with that subject days ago. You gotta come with something newer than that shit."

Billy Boy didn't get a chance to respond before Ruby started talking.

"Billy Boy, I'm not cutting you off or anything like that, but I wanted this to be somewhat of surprise for everyone. I guess telling ya'll now is as better time than any. We only have a couple more hours before the prom is over. Then we have somewhere else to go where we can enjoy ourselves."

Impatiently, Sunny said, "Ruby, just tell us what you're talking about. Shit! The prom will be over by the time you get around to saying what's on your mind!"

"Well, excuuuuusssseee me!" Ruby said playfully.

"Anyway, about two days ago before I came over to your place, Maria, I made reservations at the Hilton Hotel. We have a top floor suite for tonight."

"Shiiid'!" Maria blurted.

"Bring that shit on. That sounds real cool to me. Maybe we can invite Vicky and Cindy to the prom's after party. After all, we don't know when we might see 'em again."

"Yeah, I feel so much sympathy in my soul for them for wanting to do all them nice things. I hope they accomplish their visions. I have a lotta love for them. To tell the truth, maybe I do feel a little envious. Not that much. Just a little tiny bit."

Maria said, "I feel somewhat along them lines myself. But like you said, Sunny, we pray that God blesses them to achieve their dreams, because that's what they want. It will never stop us from being their friends."

"Being young females," said Ruby.

"We are going to feel a little green with envy, but look at it on the bright side. We made it all the way through school without getting pregnant. We are driving our own cars. We have nice fashionable wardrobes. We have some loot put away."

"You are right about everything," Maria interrupted.

"Except one thing and that's that most of my money is gone. After I pay this next bill when I go see my moms, I will be nearly broke. I'm not mad or disappointed about it, because I'm going to do whatever I can for my moms."

Billy Boy looked at Maria but never said anything. He was also heartbroken about their mother.

Ruby said, "Yeah Maria, we know about your situation with your mom. But like you and Billy Boy already know, whatever we can do to help, just give us the word. We're your friends boo. Me and Sunny will assist you in any way we can. If you need anything, just say the word."

Shooter sat there silently taking in everything that was being said.

He asked, "Maria, what's going on with your mother?"

Before Maria could answer him, Billy Boy spoke up.

"Shooter, our mom is in the hospital. She's in a coma from an injury she suffered from falling down a flight of stairs at work."

"Damn," Shooter replied.

He was shaking his head. He wondered if they were trying to sue the company about the accident.

"That's really sad for something like that to happen to ya'll mother. Since I met ya'll today and feel like a part of the family, consider me a new friend. A true friend. Me and Fast Black been friends for a long time, so I'm mainly talking about my new friends. Anyway, I want ya'll to know that whatever I can do to help out with ya'll moms, you can definitely count on me. Money ain't a thang eva'."

Everyone at the table smiled at Shooter for stepping up and showing his support. Maria stared at him admiringly. She now had new found respect for Shooter.

Suddenly, Maria said, "Look, we ain't gonna' turn this into one of those sad prom nights. Let's sit back and have an enjoyable time tonight."

Vicky approached the table carrying a cell phone with a camera on it. Vicky took a few pictures of all of them sitting around the table.

"They have a nice image on the wall over there. Let's take a few pictures together. Everyone is taking their prom pictures over there by the photographer," Vicky said.

"We need to take some pictures by ourselves and with our dates."

"That's cool with us Vicky," Maria said.

"But before we go over there, I'd like to say something. Well, I'm the one who's asking, but it's coming from all of us. You can ask me whatever. Ruby made some reservations at the Hilton Hotel. The suites are big enough for all of us to hang out in there and chill for the rest of the night. We want you, Cindy, and ya'll dates to hang out with us."

"That sounds great to me! We don't have anything else lined up to do after the prom. I doubt if they mind. Most likely they'll be with it. You can count us in," Vicky said.

She went over to tell Cindy and their dates about the invitation to the after party.

They partied at the prom until after 11:30 p.m. then left. Vicky, Cindy, and their dates came to the prom in an all-white, rented stretch Hummer-H2 limousine. Fast Black was still driving Maria's Camry. Figuring they'll have more room in the limo, Cindy invited them to ride out to the hotel with them. Everyone climbed in the limo except Ruby. She stayed with Fast Black as he drove towards the hotel.

Soon as they pulled off, Fast Black broke out two joints of Hydro.

He said, "Fire these joints up."

"You ain't slick boy!" Ruby said.

They sped across town getting high.

"I don't know what chu' talking about Ruby. I'm just funnin'. That's it. That's all. Don't trip, I'ma hook you up real nice so you can get a few nuts off, a'ight?"

High, horny, and excited, Ruby felt her pussy pulsating in anticipation. She gave Fast Black a dirty look as they drove through the streets around Uptown with three-story row houses on them. Stopping at a traffic light, Fast Black rubbed his dick through his slacks and smiled mischievously at Ruby.

"Ruby, I don't think I can wait til' we get to the hotel," he said.

He pulled over on a side street. Feeling good and high off the Hydro, Ruby didn't object when he pulled over. He parked across the street from an old abandoned elementary school.

"Go 'head and lean your seat back," he told her.

"I need to hit that real quick before we hit the hotel," he smiled.

He reached for Ruby's breasts and cupped them. He flicked his fingers over her nipples. He then leaned over until his lips were sucking on her breasts through her dress.

"Ssss. Mmmm Black."

"Open them legs for me Ruby," he huffed.

He hiked her dress up until Ruby's naked, soft-butt cheeks touched the leather seats. Fast Black quickly inserted two fingers inside her moist pussy before she had a chance to move her thong to the side.

"Wait. Sssss. Wait boy!" She giggled.

She lifted her ass up and pulled her thong off until it hit the car floor.

"You rushing to get up in this pussy ain't chu'?"

"You know I ain't had you in over a month and some change girl," he said.

He kissed her and started working his middle finger around her slick hole. She started humping back on his finger. That let him know she was hot and ready.

"Yeah Black. Right there baby. Mmmm-Shit," she moaned through kisses.

He inserted another finger.

"Ssss. Ra-right there Black," she gasped.

She was releasing her pussy juices all over his jabbing fingers.

Fast Black's fingers felt like they were probing a wet sponge. He got hard instantly. He was ready to dig up in her tightness.

"Damn Ruby," he said.

He pulled his fingers out of her clenching pussy and started licking them loudly.

"You know what your pussy tastes like?"

"What boy?" She giggled.

He pushed his fingers into her mouth. Ruby sucked on his invading fingers like she was sucking on a lollipop. She got off on tasting her own sweet juices.

"Mmmm. It tastes sweet and delicious," she moaned.

She was sucking all of her juices off his fingers. That made his dick jump inside his trousers.

"No bullshit," he said.

He quickly climbed on top of her in the passenger seat. Ruby helped him lower his trousers as she stretched out in the seat. Fast Black pushed the seat back as far as it would go. He grabbed her right ankle to lift her leg up. He let it rest on the dashboard. Ruby braced her other foot on the steering wheel. He went to work kissing on her glistening pussy lips. He made hot swirls on her aching clitoris until she grabbed his ears roughly.

"OMIGOD BOY. SSSSStop. Black. SSssss. What are you? Doing to me?" She moaned.

His nose pressed against her pussy. He started shaking his face back and forth. He pushed his nose deep enough inside her wet slit to drive her crazy from the pleasurable friction.

"Aaaahhh. Sssss. Black . Oooohh Black!" She howled.

He ran his long tongue all through her pussy lips. He slightly nibbled on them while pressing her mound real hard against his snaking tongue. Ruby's breathing got deeper and deeper as he bit down on her budding clitoris. She could do nothing but grip the back of his head and try to pull his face away from her pussy.

"Get the fuck offa' my head," he growled.

He shook his head to knock her hands down.

"I got dat' ass now and I ain't letting go. Grrr," he growled.

He went back to sucking her pussy greedily. By now, Ruby's pussy was so wet she could've slid a whole baseball bat inside it. Fast Black got off on making her twist and turn in the seat. She was trying to get away from his tongue love. He ate and licked her pussy for a few more minutes before her whole body began to shiver.

"OOOOOHHHH! BLACK BOY! I'M CA-CUUUUMMMMMMMMIIINNGGG!" She screamed.

She exploded all over his tongue and face. He tried to push his head deeper into her gushing fountain.

"Ssss. Mmm-Mmm-Mmmph. Yesss Black," she moaned.

She hooked her right leg around his head. She tried her best to fuck the shit out of his face. His long tongue slurped most of her gooey love gunk out of her steaming fuck box.

"C'mon Black. I want that dick. C'mon boy, hurry up," she begged.

She was now aching hard for his dick.

Fast Black came up off her pussy and grabbed hold of her ankles. She slid roughly down the seat. Her back and head were flat on the bottom of the passenger seat. When he got her in the position he wanted, Fast Black guided his stiff rod inside her quivering wetness.

"Mmmm-Shit. Damn, dis' dick feeels soooo good. Fuck me hard Black," she grunted while looking up at him.

"Boy, I miss dis' big ole' dick! You better fuck me good too nigga! You hear me? Fuck me Black!"

Fast Black pumped hard and fast. He shuddered with every stroke because of the way she was talking dirty to him. He loved that shit.

"I said Fuck Meeee! Sssss! Mmmm Yess!" she huffed.

She gripped his plunging love muscle with her pussy muscles and rode out his brutal dicking. He pounded her pussy, then pulled out, and quickly slammed it back in, pounding harder and harder. He pulled out again. He jammed himself back in deeper and deeper, until he lost control in her gripping tightness.

"Fa-Fuck Me Black! Fuck Me Boy! Fuck Meee!" She screamed out.

She was feeling his warm dick spasm as he exploded deep inside her pussy. Soon as she felt his hot semen gushing up in her fuck box, Ruby climaxed again.

"Oooohhh Black! You La-Like that Boy?" she moaned and rotated her hips real hard.

That made her pussy suck his dick inside as deeply as it would go.

As he extracted his limpness a few minutes later, Fast Black turned on the air conditioner to get rid of the strong smell of sex. They found some wet wipes in Maria's glove compartment and used nearly all of them to clean up.

"Black, you gotta start wearing a rubber," Ruby said.

She was wiping out the last of his warm semen.

"This shit is too messy."

She wiped her pussy again. She then balled up the wet wipes and tossed them out the window.

"Yeah, a'ight," he laughed as he pulled off.

"Next time I got chu'," he lied.

He pulled into traffic and sped towards the hotel.

They met with the other four couples at the hotel about an hour later. Ruby arranged for them to have a big feast and prom cake at the hotel. Ruby also purchased a few bottles of Cristal', Ace of Spades gold bottles, and four bottles of Dom Perignon' 1985. All of the champagne bottles were chilled inside gold buckets filled with ice. There were also trays with weed, E-pills, and blunts.

As they entered the hotel suite, everyone was sitting down in the buttery living room area. They were looking at Fast Black and Ruby strangely. It was probably because Ruby's hair was a mess. Fast Black went about the living room like nothing never took place between them. He took a quick tour of the suite. He walked in and out of the two large bedrooms that had a Jacuzzi in the middle of the floor.

"Damn Ruby! It's a good thing you gave us the keys! We would've been mad as shit waiting on your ass!" Maria complained playfully.

She already knew the play that took place between Ruby and Fast

Black.

"Don't start that shit Maria."

Ruby gave her a funny look.

"Me and Black just stopped to get some gas. That's all."

"Mmm-Hmm!" Sunny teased while looking at Ruby's wrinkled dress.

"Damn Ruby! You must have paid a small fortune to get a spot like this. This some rich and famous shit for real," Vicky said.

She changed the subject. Ruby wanted to run over and hug her for it. Even though Ruby loved sex, she didn't like putting her business out there like that.

"Tell me about it Vicky, but the money was well spent. Money is made for spending. It ain't no thang'. I'm not tripping. The most important part is for us to have the best time of our life and that's what I wanted for us, you know?"

"I feel you girl. I'm definitely doing that," Cindy said.

She sat on her date's lap and smiled like she just won the lottery.

"Yeah, I couldn't let ya'll really know how this joint was laid out. It wouldn't have been a bombshell for ya'll. I just want us to have a helluva' time tonight."

"Ruby, this is really like dat'," Sunny said.

"And you really like dat' for doing this for us."

"Yeah girl. We'll never forget the wonderful time you showed us tonight," Cindy added.

"It's a good thing Vicky brought the camera with her."

They all agreed with Cindy's statement.

"I almost forgot! Me and Vicky never introduced ya'll to our dates. Maria, Sunny, and Ruby already jive know them," Cindy said.

"Yeah, we hip to Roland and Keith," Maria said.

"We all took the same classes with them at one time or another."

"Well, Roland and Keith, this is Maria's brother, Billy Boy. He's Sunny's date. This dude's name is Fast Black. He's Ruby's date," Cindy said.

She was smiling at Fast Black.

"And this other dude right here is Shooter. Those are not their real names, but that's what they go by. I do know one thing, they're three fine ma'fuckaz."

Everyone laughed.

The five young men shook hands and got to know each other.

After the introductions, they sat around on the comfortable chairs and couches. They were drinking champagne, eating, smoking, and popping E-pills.

Cindy and Vicky talked more about their plans for the future.

"Have ya'll thought about what ya'll going to do after school?" Vicky asked Ruby, Maria, and Sunny.

"Well Vicky, right now I haven't thought too much about the future," Maria said.

"My mom is still in critical condition. Me and Billy Boy have our hands full taking care of her situation. That's our full time job right now. She's the only blood family we have. We love her so much and want her to be around for a long time."

"I jive been thinking about opening up a business," Ruby said.

"What kind of business?" Cindy asked.

"I'm thinking a fly-ass clothing store that specializes in women's clothing. I'ma have some personal designers to design some exclusive shit too."

"That sounds a'ight Ruby," Sunny said.

She knew Ruby's addiction to high fashion would definitely help her in her business endeavor.

"I haven't decided what I wanted to do yet. I will get into something legal though. Maybe me and Maria can pitch in with Ruby and the three of us can be business partners and maybe expand into more types of business."

Everyone smiled.

"Yeah, I like the sound of that," Ruby said.

"We'll come up with something, but right now it's time to party!"

She said laughing.

Billy Boy turned on the CD system. The young people drank, ate, and got high until around 4:30 a.m. Billy Boy and Sunny were so drunk and high that they passed out on the couch in each other's arms. The other young people were sleeping too. The only ones still awake were Maria, Shooter, Ruby, and Fast Black.

"What time do we check outta' this suite Ruby?" Maria asked.

She stared at Shooter who returned the look with a wink.

"We got this joint until midnight tomorrow," Ruby said.

She exhaled the last of the chronic fumes from the blunt she was smoking with Fast Black.

"Well, Ruby, I'm jive sleepy. I'm going to lay down in the bedroom and get some sleep," Maria said.

"Why Maria?" Ruby blurted.

"We should make the best out of our stay here. You never know when we'll be able to get together again like this," she sighed.

"Never mind. Go ahead and get some rest. I'll be out here talking to Shooter and Black."

"I'm jive tired too," Shooter said.

He was looking at Maria.

"I need to get some rest myself. If it's okay with you Maria, I'd like to hang out with you a minute before I crash out."

"I don't care. I'll see ya'll in a little bit," Maria said.

She proceeded to step off.

"Besides," Ruby called.

"It won't be long before me and Black fall asleep out here."

"Yeah right," Maria thought.

She was walking towards the bedroom. Shooter followed close behind her.

Shooter had been mesmerized by Maria's beauty all evening. Maria was also attracted to Shooter. As soon as they entered the bedroom and closed the door, Shooter took Maria in his arms and kissed her tenderly. They kissed like old lovers.

Maria had never had sex with a man on the first night before she met Shooter. Shooter tested the waters with Maria from the first moment they touched the dance floor. He made it known that he wanted her. It only took a few songs, his smooth personality, and some Issey Miyake cologne. The way he treated her, he had a way of melting Maria down. It started out with a few soft touches on her waist. Next came a kiss on her neck and so on. Shooter palmed Maria's soft behind as he whispered sweet nothings in her ear. Before they even left the prom, Maria couldn't get enough of Shooter. She enjoyed the way they connected with each other.

They started to undress each other in the darkness. Maria wore a Victoria's Secret white bra and bikini set that revealed her magnificent light brown body. Her wonderful curves were bursting out of her bikini underwear. Shooter removed her panties. He gasped for air at the spectacular sight of her naked body. Her neatly shaved, dark brown silky hair decorated her pussy perfectly.

He grabbed Maria and pulled her closer to him. They fell down on the bed. Maria spread her pretty legs wide open for him. Shooter took her tits into his mouth and sucked on them tenderly. They were both filled with passion. While guiding his hard shaft into her hot, wet pussy, Maria cupped his hairy balls. She massaged them while she kissed him deeply on his full lips. Shooter responded with pleasure while snaking his wet tongue in and out of her mouth. It took them no time to step up the tempo. As he thrust his dick up and down her torrid pussy, she raised her pelvis bone upward to meet his jabbing thrusts. That made her cum instantly.

She put her legs halfway up in the air. That allowed his hard girth to slide deeper and deeper inside her honey love. He put his hands under her nice, soft, pear shaped ass. He slyly slid a finger inside her asshole.

"Ssss. Ooohhh Shooter!"

She moaned with satisfaction.

Shooter looked down at her.

He said, "Damn! You're one beautiful girl, I mean woman. I wanted you from the first time I laid eyes on you. I never came across a woman that was as beautiful as you."

He fucked her harder with each word.

"If I have, I never noticed."

"Oh. Ssss," Maria huffed.

"It fa-feels sooo good. Don't talk boo. Just fuck me."

She let out cries of pleasure as their tempo increased with pounding fury. They went at it on the bed like two convicted criminals who were just released from prison after doing several years locked away with no sex.

They exploded into a drenching orgasm of melting butter. They went right back at it a few moments later. They traded positions and kept fucking harder and harder as if they were racing to reach that golden, climatic plateau.

"Damn Maria," he panted.

He pulled out of her tightness. He looked at his dick glistening with her love cream.

"You wet as shit!"

Maria had gotten used to taking that massive boner. She had even grown attached to fucking the handsome stranger. Even she had to admit the sex was top-of-the-line. While he buried his dick deep inside her stretching snatch, Maria started really feeling Shooter's girth up in her stomach.

"Oooooooohhhhhh. Mmmmmmmmhhhhmmm. Don't stop Shooter. Don't stop!" She screamed.

He plowed in and out of her love oven with rough intensity.

"I'm Cuuummmmiiinnng Boo! Ooohhh Shit! I'm Cuuuummmmiiinnnggg!" She cried.

She was lying on her stomach and taking his plowing with euphoric joy. As she climaxed back to back on his hard penis, he continued fucking her hard and deep inside her hot expanding pussy.

"Aaarrrgggh Shit! Ma-Ma! MARIAAAAHHHHHH!" He

bellowed.

He pulled out his exploding dick and shot thick globs of hot semen all over her ass cheeks and lower back.

"Ooohhh. You Nasty Shooter," she giggled.

She twitched several times as the last of his warm load dripped on her. After their intimate love bliss, they laid in each other's arms and feel fast to sleep.

*I*T WAS THE MONTH OF JULY. Three weeks had passed since the memorable night at the Hilton Hotel. Maria started to tell Billy Boy a thousand times about where she'd gotten the money from, but she decided against it. She thought it would be better if he didn't know anything. Billy Boy never asked her anymore about where the money came from. Maria cruised in her Camry in route to the hospital to see her mother. She thought about how Shooter had been a big help to her financially and romantically. He'd paid the hospital bills for her the last couple times. He dicked her down real proper like whenever she wanted him to. Maria didn't want to keep accepting money from him.

He told her numerous times, "Maria, you my bun'. You know you're more than welcome to it. What's mines is yours."

"I just like doing shit for myself," Maria thought.

She knew that she still had to get some money to pay the upcoming hospital bills. Maria pulled the Camry into the hospital's parking lot and got out. She took the elevator up to the 4th floor where her mother was located. She spotted the doctor making his rounds as she came off the elevator. Maria decided to speak with him for a few minutes before going in to see how her mother was doing.

"Doc, how's she doing?"

"Well, Ms. Valentine, your mother doesn't seem to be improving any. You know a situation like this takes some time. It's pretty hard to tell right now about her recovery. She may go on this way for months before something happens. Don't worry, she'll be alright under my care."

After she finished talking to the doctor, Maria entered her mother's room and sat down in the chair beside the bed. Her mother still had the I.V. tubes feeding liquid into her body. Maria talked to her mother while fighting back the tears. It hurt her every time she came to visit to see her like this.

"I'm praying that you will hurry up and pull through this situation. I meant to tell you the last time I was here that I really missed you at my graduation. It was really nice. I wish you could've been there to see me, Sunny, and Ruby walk across the stage. Billy Boy is doing fine. He's going to complete high school. I'll make sure of that. We are greatly concerned about you. We pray every day that you make a full recovery from this condition and come home to us. Mom, I don't have a job or anything like that. I will get one soon. I will take good care of you, even if it takes more money to get you well. I'll do whatever it takes. I just need you to pull through for me and Billy Boy. We worry about you in here so much. We love you mom."

Maria talked to her mother for two hours before she left. She was trying to deal with this tragedy the best she could. Maria rushed out of the hospital to her car. She was filled with sadness. She knew she had to leave her mother all alone again. She missed her mother so much. Not a day passed that Maria didn't get down on her knees and pray for her mother's full recovery. However, Maria had to stay focused on the real world if she wanted to survive. She needed to make a way to support herself, Billy Boy, and also keep paying for the expensive medical treatment that her mother was receiving.

CHAPTER 10

DRIVING BACK TO THE HOUSING PROJECT where she lived, Maria thought about the last two weeks. She had been pressing Shooter about robbing a bank with her, Ruby, and Sunny. Shooter was like a Catholic Pope when it came to robbing banks.

"I know he's damn good. He has to do a job with me," Maria told herself.

She parked the Camry on the side street of the project building. Maria heard a few dudes calling out her name as she walked towards her building. She waved politely and kept it moving. Maria was faithful to Shooter. She didn't want to give anybody around the hood any wrong ideas that she was looking for another man.

When she entered the building, Shooter came from out of nowhere; startling her.

"Hey babe'," he said as he hugged her.

GOD DAMNIT SHOOTER!" She fussed.

She broke from his embrace.

"Boy, you scared the hell out of me. Where did you come from anyway? I didn't see your car out there."

"I parked around the corner. I been waiting on you for an hour now. I started to go up to Sunny's spot when I found out that you wasn't home. I decided to just wait on you."

"I went to see my mom," Maria replied.

She gave him a kiss on the lips.

"I kinda' figured that's where you went. How's she doing?"

"Not so good," Maria confessed sadly.

"Damn baby girl," Shooter sighed.

"I'm sorry to hear that. You know what you've been asking me about?"

"Yeah."

"Well, you know that's why I'm over here. We can kick it about what you been asking me about."

"C'mon then," she said.

She grabbed his hand and led him inside the apartment. Shooter sat down on the living room couch.

"Maria, where's Billy Boy?"

"I don't know. He went out somewhere. He didn't tell me where he was going. I think he went to play some basketball. You know he thinks he's Kobe Bryant. He can't stay away from them courts. That's a good thing today. I really don't want him knowing what's going on, you know?"

"Yeah, I feel you," Shooter said.

He turned on the TV.

"So what do you want to holla at me about Shooter?" Maria said.

She eased closer to him on the couch and laid her head on his shoulder.

"Well, I've been thinking about what you been stressing about. I changed my mind about not going on a bank job with ya'll. I usually don't go against my gut for shit, but I know you need some loot for your moms and shit. I jive ran into this sweet ass joint. I been looking at it for a minute. The way I see it, I'ma need ya'll assistance to pull this caper off. I'm telling you Maria, I'm only doing this just this one time and I mean that shit," he stated firmly while looking into her eyes.

"I'm glad you decided to take us with you boo," she smiled.

She kissed him passionately .

"Like I said Maria, only this one time!"

He repeated himself after disengaging from her soft lips.

"Okay," Maria said.

She then thought, *"That's cool with me. I know I can manipulate him with this pussy to do anything I want. I need some money for my mother and one bank job ain't going to do it. I'ma get him to go with the flow. Watch!"*

"When will you see Sunny and Ruby again?"

He invaded her thoughts with that question.

"They come through all the time. You know I can see them whenever. Sunny lives right upstairs and Ruby ass practically stays here whenever she's not chasing Fast Black around the city."

Fast Black turned the tables on Ruby with his oral skills. Now Ruby was looking for Fast Black in the daytime with a flashlight. She was steady trying to get some more of that bomb head from him. She was tongue and dick whipped. She would never let him know it. She feared that he may try to dog her out. Ruby did things on the sly like show up at Fast Black's house when she knew he was about to go hustle for the day. She would get him to hit her off real quick with some good dick and tongue love, then go on about her business.

"Well, you know we gonna' have to get together real soon. We need to go over a few things as to how we are going to go up in that joint and come off. It shouldn't be too hard to come up with a plan. I have an idea."

"What kind of an idea?" Maria asked.

She was rubbing her hand along his thigh.

"To take some caramel candy from a baby. The joint is that sweet," he smirked.

She fell over into his lap laughing.

"And you know how good that caramel candy is? I'm not going to get into all the details with you just yet. I want to wait and kick it with all ya'll together. You know I won't ever give ya'll no inaccurate information."

"I know that boo."

"Maria, I know we haven't known each other that long physically, but I always knew and loved you mentally. You were the woman I always saw in my dreams."

Maria started laughing again.

"I'm dead serious Maria. You knocked me down on my knees

when I first saw you in person. No woman has ever made me feel that way. This is why I know you were meant for me. I would never put you, Ruby, nor Sunny in a bad predicament. I love ya'll too much. That came from the little time we been hanging out together."

Maria called Sunny and Ruby. She told them to come over to her house. They arrived quicker than greased lightening. Fifteen minutes later, they were all together. They were chilling, smoking, and drinking in Maria's living room.

After the last blunt, Shooter got everyone's attention.

"Ay' check this out ladies. First I would like to say that I have never done a bank job with anyone before, especially no women. It never came up in my thinking. I normally work alone. For some reason, I have confidence in ya'll. I like the way ya'll carry shit. We are going to roll together on something I got in the works. It's a piece of cake like I told Maria. I wouldn't tell ya'll anything wrong. I received the inside scoop. At the end of this month, an armored truck will be bringing a rack of loot. They bringing in the big shipment so the bank will have enough loot to last throughout the month. Ya'll already know that's a nice piece of change."

"You motherfuckin' right that's a nice piece of change! So when we rollin'?"

"Hold fast Ruby," he grinned.

He admired her enthusiasm.

"I received the info' straight from the horse's mouth."

"What does the security look like?"

"I'm glad you asked that question Sunny. From the way I was told, the armored truck will slide through with the loot before the bank opens up. The bank opens at 9:00 and the armored truck is 'spose to slide through at 8:00 in the morning. Now I thought about taking the armored truck on some Dead Presidents shit, but that would be too risky. It would probably get us all caught up. They always have three-to-four guards riding with big loads like that. So this is what we gonna do. We gon' wait til' nine o'clock when the bank opens and go up in there. That'll be much better for us and a lot less complicated, you know? They only have one guard in the bank. The vault will still be open after the armored truck rolls out. The only weapon the guard will have is a Glock. I'll handle him. I'll have ya'll backs. I'ma have that heavy shit with me; that Mossberg pump. Niggaz be scared to death when they see that big ma'fucka. They be tryna' give you everything in the country to not get hit wit' dat' big ma'fucka. I'ma hold the floor down. Ya'll basically keep the same routine ya'll had with the first bank. Ya'll hit and grab as much money as you can. Don't be bullshitting."

"Never that Shooter," Maria said.

"What date do you have set for us to hit this joint?"

"Well, today is July Fourteenth. I think around the thirty-first will be a good day to roll and hit that joint. That gives us around sixteen days to make sure we have everything in order."

"Bring it on then boo," Sunny said.

"No bullshit. From what chu' spittin', I know it's going to be a big payday. I'm willing and ready to do the motherfucka!" Ruby added.

"I heard that!" Maria said.

She stamped the girls' approval of Shooter's idea about getting the money without being harmed.

"Oh, another important thing is getting away from me, or should I say the most important thing?" Shooter paused.

"Look, I got three .380 pistols that I think ya'll should carry just in case. They're very light, compact, and easy to conceal. They're just the right size for a woman. Other than that, it's a go. If ya'll have any more questions, just let me know."

"Shooter, I'm speaking for all three of us here," Ruby said.

"And I know they'll agree with me about what I'm getting ready to say. The way you talking sounds real good to us and we agree with your plan. You just lead the way and we'll follow."

"Well, if ya'll ain't doing shit tomorrow, we can slide through and check the joint out to see what we're up against. We can check out the surrounding areas so we can be all the way on point about what channels to take for our escape route," Shooter said.

"You know we ain't doing shit now," Sunny blurted.

"We can go check that shit out right now."

A few seconds of silence hung in the air before everyone started nodding and agreeing with Sunny's idea.

"Ya'll ain't too tipsy? I don't want no fuck ups," Shooter said.

"I've been doing this shit for a long time now. Any minor slip-up can determine your life or death."

"Boy, stop being all paranoid. We straight!" Ruby said.

That gave him the confidence to go along with them.

"A'ight, we taking my ride," Shooter said.

He got up and headed for the door. They were right on his heels.

They exited the building and followed Shooter over to an all black Cadillac Escalade with butterscotch leather, light tinted windows, and 20" chrome rims. Shooter bought the SUV some time ago after scoring big on a bank robbery.

They climbed inside the Escalade with Maria sitting up front with Shooter. Ruby and Sunny sat in the back. Shooter turned on the screens in his headrest for the girls watch while he drove.

"Show off!" Ruby playfully said as they pulled off.

"Don't take it personal Ruby. When you getting money, you can stunt how you wanna' stunt on them peoples every now and then. You dig me!" Shooter laughed.

The girls shared a laugh with him.

Twenty minutes later, they pulled off of Addison Road on the Maryland side of D.C., near Fairmont Heights High School, and exited the Escalade. They walked about four blocks to the bank. Once they arrived, they walked around and checked out the territory thoroughly. To the passers-by, they looked like four high school students deciding on whether or not to enter the bank.

"I told you this shit was the sweetest!" Shooter exclaimed.

"I know we can tear this motherfucka off."

They circled the bank a few more times. Ruby noticed the bank had a front and back entrance. At that moment, her mind started working on an escape plan.

"Damn ya'll! This joint is too sweet," Ruby blurted.

"We can slide through the front door, and get ghost right out the back door. We can have Fast Black waiting for us at the back entrance when we come out. You is using Black right?"

"Hell yeah! You know that's my man, Ruby. I been hipped Slim about this joint. But I ain't gave him no details on any escape plans yet," Shooter said.

"When you give him the scoop, make sure he gets a car with four doors on it," Maria spoke up.

"Because when we come out the bank, we ain't gon' have no time to be bullshitting tryna' get up in the car."

"I got all that," Shooter nodded.

"Ya'll just make sure to remind me when we meet up with Black. Hopefully, next time we come back from out this way, we'll be going back to the city some rich ma'fuckaz!"

The three young girls smiled after hearing Shooter's declaration. The four of them walked back to the Escalade and climbed inside. They arrived in Maria's hood about 15 minutes later. Shooter pulled the Escalade alongside the curb in front of Maria's building.

"I'ma holla at cha'll later on. I need to catch up with Fast Black so I can give him the scoop."

"Okay Shooter," Ruby and Sunny said in unison.

They exited the SUV and left Maria behind.

Once they were gone, Maria kissed Shooter passionately and undid his pants. She let out a deep moan as she freed his manhood. She stroked his dick a few times and then pulled back.

"I know you coming back through this way to see me right?"

She squeezed his thick boner while looking into his eyes.

"You know I need to feel this big ma'fucka deep inside my pussy."

"I got chu'. Don't even trip," Shooter said.

He looked at the young woman who held the key to his heart.

"Well, just in case you forget, here's a little reminder of what you'll be missing," she said.

She went to work and took him deep into her warm-wet mouth. She sucked up and down on his stiffness like a lollipop. She licked all over the head and then eased his thick fuck muscle back inside her steamy, slick mouth.

Maria made loud slurping sounds as she sucked his dick. She jerked him off from the base of his dick with both hands. Her pussy tingled with delight of having his wide, rock-hard boner deep in her mouth. It slid back and forth while radiating its own heat. He slid in, then out, then back inside her mouth like he was fucking her pussy.

"Aaahh Shit. Damn Maria!" He groaned.

She quickly removed her soft lips from his dick with a loud popping sound. She kissed the head of his dick and sat back up like nothing ever happened.

"Mmmmm," she licked her lips and giggled.

She was looking at the shocked expression on his face.

"Well, I'ma see you later."

"Maria, don't play."

He looked at her like she just took some money from him without his consent.

"Girl, look at my shit. I know you ain't gonna' leave me like this are you?"

"I just gave you a little reminder of what you'll be missing if you don't come back tonight. Bye boo," she giggled.

She exited the Escalade. She closed the door and blew him a kiss before sauntering off to her building. Shooter watched Maria moving up the walkway putting an extra switch in her strut.

He squeezed his dick.

"I'ma burn that pussy up tonight," he thought.

He pulled off sexually frustrated and mad as hell at Maria for doing him like that. He couldn't keep her off his mind while he drove towards his apartment. That was exactly the impression Maria wanted to leave on him. Shooter couldn't wait to handle his business in the streets. That way he could rush back to Maria's bed and let her finish what she started in the Escalade.

BY THE TIME MARIA ENTERED THE APARTMENT,

Ruby and Sunny were chilling in the living room. They were smoking on a plump spliff of Blueberry Hydro. Ruby offered Maria the spliff as she sat down. Maria declined. Her thoughts were on Shooter. She had never sucked a man's dick before. She knew he had the avenues to help her out with paying for her mother's medical expenses. Maria felt that sucking his dick was only a minor price to pay to get what she wanted. Plus, she genuinely liked Shooter.

"Where's Billy Boy at Maria?" Sunny asked.

"He left outta' here early this morning. He didn't say where he was going. He should be back soon though. Ain't no telling with him. He probably somewhere playing ball."

"Okay, anyway, I'm hungry as shit. I haven't ate nothing all day. I could eat a whole bull right now," Sunny said.

"No bullshit. I jive got the munchies myself," Ruby added.

"It's some fish in the ice box that's already been seasoned down real good," Maria told them.

 "I was going to fry some fish for me and Billy Boy. It's more than enough to fill your bellies. Ya'll go ahead."

"What else do you have to go along with the fish?"

"Ruby, do you hear this greedy-ass bitch?"

"Yeah, I heard her Maria. Sunny did ask a good-ass question. We do need more than just some fish to get full."

"Okay. Okay. I feel what you bitches is saying. Do ya'll really think I'd ask ya'll to eat with me and only have some fish?"

Ruby and Sunny gave Maria a funny look when she got up and headed for the kitchen.

"Ya'll fix the cream style corn and blue berry muffins that are in the cabinet. Grab a few cans of green peas out of there too. I'll hook up the fish, macaroni and cheese, and the grape Kool-Aid," Maria said.

"I'll cook the green peas, corn, and muffins. We don't need too many bitches in the kitchen at one time," Sunny said.

"Maria, lemme' make the Kool-Aid. You know that's my

specialty," Ruby said.

That caused the girls to laugh. Ruby headed towards the kitchen to join Maria. The three girls started on their task of preparing the meal.

$ $ $ $ $

*M*EANWHILE, BILLY BOY WAS soaring through the air.

He was taking his team to another victory by dunking the ball on a lanky defender. He was constantly drawing cheers from the crowd. Billy Boy had been hustling the courts all day. The 5-on-5 full court pick-up games around Barry Farms were $150 per man. Billy Boy's team had won several games before calling it quits. They earned a little over $2,800 apiece.

Billy Boy was hanging from the rim with a smile. A lanky guy pushed Billy Boy in the air as he let go of the rim.

Billy Boy turned aggressively on the lanky man.

"Slim, I know you ain't for real? You tryna' hurt me?"

The lanky man paid no attention to Billy Boy. He stepped straight towards his gym bag.

"You better get da' fuck on lil' nigga, before I get mad!"

Billy Boy felt disrespected and knew he had to do something, or be labeled as a bitch-ass nigga with a nice b-ball game.

"NIGGA, FUCK YOU!" Billy Boy raged.

He punched the lanky dude in the back of the head.

Soon as the dude turned and took a wild swing, he caught Billy Boy in the neck with the blow. Billy Boy rushed him and it was on from there. The two young men were locked up in battle. They were fighting hard straight gutter-style right in the center of the basketball court. Hustlers, sexy young women, and other people from the hood stopped what they were doing to watch the fight. The referees and a few respected men from The Farms jumped in the middle. They tried to pull the two combatants apart while they swung wildly and cursed each other out.

"Nigga, I'ma crush your bitch-ass if I ever see you again!" Billy Boy barked.

A group of young men drug the lanky man away.

"Nigga, I know you faking. I'ma make sure you see me though! Believe dat!"

The lanky man fired back while his homies held him at bay.

Billy Boy wasn't scared to stick around on the court after whipping the lanky guy's ass. A few dudes that knew Billy Boy told him about the guy he just beat down. They let Billy Boy know the guy was known all around the city for firing that pistol at whoever rubbed him the wrong way.

Before Billy Boy could say anything, rapid gunshots exploded all around him. The lanky guy rushed towards the crowd surrounding Billy Boy. He was firing aimlessly. Fearing for his life and shaking nervously, Billy Boy took off. He sprinted through **Barry Farms** basketball court. He scaled the ten foot fence quickly. Billy Boy bolted across Suitland Parkway with tears in his eyes. He was dodging the speeding cars. He was scared to death. He had never been shot at before in his life. Billy Boy made it safely across Suitland Parkway and kept running in a zigzag motion. His legs were burning so bad that he wanted to stop, but he knew he couldn't. His life depended on it.

$ $ $ $ $

BACK INSIDE MARIA'S HOUSE, the girls all sat around the kitchen table eating the delicious meal they made together. Ruby was smacking loudly, which irritated the hell out of Sunny. Her actions alerted Maria that she liked her cooking.

"Ay'! Do ya'll really think we can tear that bank off?" Sunny asked.

"Shooter already knows the layout about the loot. He knows how shit runs inside the bank. Just on that alone, it looks pretty damn good to me," Ruby said.

She spooned up some creamy style corn. Ruby talked and chewed at the same time.

"As long as we stick with our game plan, we should be straight."

"You have a point Ruby," Maria said.

"And I don't think we'll have any problems. We'll be a'ight, so don't worry Sunny. Like Shooter said, it's sweet. It ain't nothing but a piece of cake."

They all smiled and went back to eating and didn't confabulate about the bank robbery anymore. Ten minutes after they finished talking about the bank, Billy Boy came through the front door with a loud bang. He startled the girls. He rushed through the living room and ran straight towards his room without saying a word.

The girls had no time to react. They looked at Billy Boy like he was crazy. They then went back to eating their food. They were wondering what the hell was up with Billy Boy. After getting himself together, Billy Boy returned to the kitchen.

He said, "Damn, I smell that good got'damn aroma of fish and cornbread up in the air. It sure smells like dat! Where's my plate?" He inhaled while entering the kitchen.

"Not cornbread, but blueberry muffins, Carl Lewis."

"Well, I was close Sunny," he said.

He ignored her slick remark about him running through the house earlier.

After Billy Boy ran across the Suitland Parkway, he ducked inside a strip bar somewhere in Maryland. He called a cab from the pay phone. Billy Boy left his cell phone and all of the money he'd won from the games in his gym bag. All he had on him was the $150 he left the house with inside his shoe.

"You want me to fix you a plate, boy?"

"Naw, Maria. I'm cool. You go on and finish eating. I can fix my own plate," he said heading towards the stove.

"Ay', make some room for me at the table," he said fixing his plate.

He was happy to still be alive and able to see his sister, Sunny, and Ruby again.

"Boy, your ass ain't that damn big. It's enough room at this table for you," Sunny told him in a sassy tone.

"Yeah, you may be tall, but your legs can still fit under this table. Where have you been anyway?" Maria questioned in a motherly tone.

"I was out playing some basketball, but I think I'm through with all that shit."

"Why? You love basketball!" Maria said.

She was taken aback by his statement because she knew how he loved playing basketball.

"Them sucker-ass niggaz be hating on me way too much. I gotta' wreckin' one of dem bammaz today over that shit. I said that's it after that," Billy Boy said.

He conveniently left out the part about the shooting because he knew Maria would have a hissy fit.

"Damn, them niggaz hatin' like dat' on you? You must be really like dat?"

"I'm jive a'ight Ruby, but my passion is pool. I can shoot the colors off them balls. Just ask Maria and Sunny. I always beat them when we used to play High and Low and Nine Ball. I tried to get some money for my big sister to help out around here. That ain't work out cause I had to leave my shit when I got ta' fighting that nigga. I'm sorry Maria."

"Don't worry about it Billy Boy. I'm just happy that you're home. That's all. We'll worry about the bills later."

"Naw, I'm just fucked up that you been doing all the work 'round here. You are taking care of me and moms."

"Billy Boy, I do appreciate you wanting to help out, but you have to be careful out there. I can't have you and moms laying up in the hospital. I'd really go crazy then. I don't need you to give me any money. I don't need it. I have enough cash put up for us."

"Yeah Billy Boy, now that you mentioned it, I do remember you beating us in pool when we were younger," Sunny said.

She was trying to change the subject. Sunny didn't want them getting all emotional at the table because she knew she would start crying.

Billy Boy fixed his plate and sat down at the table between his sister, Sunny, and Ruby. Even though Maria told him that she didn't need his money, Billy Boy still wanted to help out.

"I'm the man of the house. I'm suppose to be the one making sure everything is everything around here," Billy Boy thought as he dug into his plate of food.

CHAPTER 11

*T*HE TIME WENT BY QUICK and now it was time for the

heist. Early that morning, everyone met up at Maria's apartment and went over their plan.

"Basically everyone knows what to do right? The same way ya'll hit the first bank ain't no different. The only difference this time is we'll be getting a whole lot more loot," Shooter smiled.

"But seriously, ya'll know we can take this joint. We have the vantage point because this is a thundering summer morning. For some reason, it's raining on our parade," he joked sarcastically.

"But a little rain ain't gon' stop our show. Even though it's pouring down raining like cats and dogs. Shiid', this is the best time to rob a bank. The police can't get to the scene all that fast because they be taking precautions and shit while speeding on rain slick roads," he said.

"So do you have the bags to put the money in?"

"Yep."

All the girls nodded together. They held up the bags for him to see.

"Good. Now we all know Fast Black is the driver. Also, I will be the last one to leave out the bank cause I'm watching ya'll back to make sure ya'll get away safely. That should cover everything."

"I hope so," Maria said.

"Because I want to get out of here before Billy Boy hears us and wakes up."

On that note, the five of them departed from Maria's apartment. They scrambled into an H-2 Hummer that Fast Black had stolen. They had about fifteen minutes before they reached their destination. They arrived at the bank a little after 9:15 . Fast Black let them out about 12 feet away from the bank.

Before swarming out of the car, Shooter asked, "Are ya'll ready?"

"Yeah," they said in unison.

They exited the Hummer sporting dark green sweat suits with hoods on them. As they walked towards the bank, Fast Black drove the Hummer around back and parked near the rear exit. Everyone knew their position when entering the bank. Yanking the door open quickly, Shooter went straight for the guard, took his gun, and made him lay down.

"THIS IS A ROBBERY!" "DON'T MAKE IT A HOMICIDE! NOW EVERYONE GET ON THE GOT DAMN FLOOR! NOW!" Shooter announced.

While Shooter controlled the floor, Maria, Sunny, and Ruby didn't waste any time jumping across the counter as though there was no tomorrow. They went straight to the vault. They kept their guns tucked in their waist-lines. They filled the bags quickly. They stuffed them until they had to mash down the money with their shoes.

"YA'LL HAVE FIVE SECONDS!" Shooter yelled.

They closed their over flowing bags. The girls harvested the rest of the money and flung the bags across their shoulders. Then they leaped back across the counter. The three of them left quickly. They made their way towards the back entrance for a fast escape. Shooter was right behind them watching their backs all the way out the door. He kept his eyes on the people in the bank.

Fast Black was right there waiting on them. It was still pouring down raining when they came out. The people that were on the street never noticed a robbery was taking place. They were too busy trying to get out of the torrid rain and loud sounds of thunder.

$ $ $ $ $

AT THE SAME TIME, the scene at the hospital was out of control. Several visitors had to move out of the way so they wouldn't get ran over by the medical staff who ran down the hallway with emergency reviving equipment.

One of the nurses entered Mrs. Valentine's room. She was making her daily rounds and got the shock of her life. Her life support machine had flat-lined! The nurse's panic button went off. She ran out into the hallway screaming for help and alerting all the staff in the area that a patient was dying.

"HELLLP MEEE! THIS WOMAN IS DYING! I NEED HELLLP STAT!"

The nurse yelled and ran back into Mrs. Valentine's room.

As the doctors and several nurses rushed inside the room, they saw the nurse giving Mrs. Valentine CPR. She was trying her best to revive the comatose patient. They all moved in trying to help the nurse overcome the daunting challenge of reviving a comatose patient. All of them were overcome with a surging fit to save Maria's mother. Even though most of them doubted that she could be revived.

In the midst of all the attempts to resuscitate her, Maria's mother never regained a heartbeat. With defeated looks, slumped shoulders, and tears in a few of their eyes, the medical staff stood there listening to the painful flat line sounds of DEATH blaring from Mrs. Valentine's life support machine.

After some of the medical staff had left the room, two nurses unplugged the wires of the life support machine. They covered Mrs. Valentine's face with a sheet. Maria's mother passed away at the same time Maria and her friends were robbing the bank.

$ $ $ $$

FAST BLACK PULLED AWAY FROM THE REAR OF THE BANK after making sure everyone was out of harm's way. He sped through several back streets. He cut through Fairmont Height High School's parking lot. He then jumped back on Addison Road speeding towards D.C.

"I think we done pulled it off. We are home free now Black. Home Free Boy!" Shooter laughed.

He smacked Fast Black in the back of the head.

"Ay', you know where to drop us off at right?"

"Yeah Shooter. I know Slim. You told me a million times," Fast Black said sarcastically.

He continued speeding towards the rendezvous spot. They arrived at Shooter's black Escalade in no time. It was parked out of eyesight in a small alley next to Deanwood's Metro Station. They quickly took off the green sweat suits and changed into different clothing inside Shooter's Escalade.

"Ay', throw all your clothes that you take off in here," Fast Black yelled from the Hummer.

After that was done, Shooter and the girls leaped into the Escalade. They left Fast Black sitting in the Hummer.

"Ya'll drive safe!" Fast Black said.

"I'll take care of the shit on my end. "

"And I got my end covered too. I'll see you later on at my spot," Shooter said.

"How far is your car from here?"

"Over there in Mayfair. But don't worry about me, just get the hell out of here," Fast Black said.

He watched as Shooter pulled off and turned on Sheriff Road.

Fast Black waited for ten minutes until they were out of sight. He began dousing the Hummer with gasoline. When he was done, he tossed a lit book of matches inside the SUV and took off running for Mayfair Mansion where his car was parked. By the time Fast Black made it up the hill near TNT Soul Food Restaurant, the Hummer was consumed in flames. Any potential evidence linking him, Shooter, or the girls to the bank heist was burned.

Shooter drove the Escalade down the rainy street towards the Southeast side of D.C. very carefully. He wasn't trying to break any traffic laws. He wanted to stay away from any unwanted difficulties.

"I can't believe it. I'm still in a little shock that we came off so quick with all this money," Maria smiled.

She looked around to see if any cop cars were following them.

"Yeah, I think we done came off real pretty," Ruby added.

"Yeah, it sure does look pretty," Sunny giggled.

Her comment caused everyone in the SUV to howl with laughter.

"Ya'll looked jive sweet the way ya'll took that joint off," Shooter complimented the girls.

"Yeah, it kind of felt like I was transformed into another person or something," Sunny said.

"It must've been the adrenaline pumping. I was on a mission to get all that loot and get the hell up outta' there."

"I almost tripped running my big ass out the back door," Ruby playfully said.

"I couldn't tell. For real, ya'll did a helluva job today ladies!" Shooter said again.

They all smiled at his statement.

THE TIME ELAPSED QUICKLY AND before they knew it, they were at Shooter's apartment building climbing the stairs. They came to a stop at the apartment door. Shooter put the key inside the lock to open it. The four of them made their way inside the apartment. They grabbed the closest seat they could find.

Shooter lived by himself in a studio-styled apartment near Simple City Housing Projects. It was somewhere on Hillside Road. The bedroom and the living room were hooked together. The kitchen and the bathroom were separate rooms. The hardwood floors were the color of a freshly chopped oak tree. Shooter had a king size bed that sat in the middle of the floor. It had a gold bed frame with beige and light brown couches and chairs to match. The huge LCD flat screen TV that hung from the wall showed a City of the Gods DVD. That was Shooter's favorite movie. The stereo system and Play-Station 3 sat inside a glass enclosed shelf directly under the TV. Taking in the apartment, Maria knew this was Shooter's playboy palace. She wondered how many women he brought here to have sex as they poured the money on the bed.

"You sure do have a nice place here Shooter," Maria said.

"Yeah, thanks. I try to make this a comfortable atmosphere where I can unwind and feel good."

"I heard that," Ruby said.

"But fuck all that for now, we have to count this bread."

"Yeah, let's go 'head and count it up. We need to know how much cake we're working with," Sunny added.

They all started to count the money. They counted for over an hour. They placed it in neat stacks of $10,000. They miscounted about five times before getting the count right. When they did get it right, they all looked at each other with dumb looks. They had counted out $1,342,000!

"Got Dayyum!" Maria blurted.

She broke the silence.

"This is a lot of fucking money! A million point three and some change! I can now say we came off like the MOB!"

"A Milli-A Milli-A Milli. A Million here, A Million there," Ruby giggled.

She imitated the rapper Lil Wayne.

Shooter stepped up and spoke, "Check this out, ya'll know I have to pay the people that put me down with this lick. I also have to square away Fast Black for his help."

Sunny asked, "How much do you think they should get Shooter?"

"Whatever we give them, they'll be happy with it, but we all have to agree on it first. We have a mill-ticket here and that's a lot of fucking money. I think we can spread a little love in the right places. You do right by others, that shit always comes back tenfold."

Shooter schooled them.

"First thing's first, I think we should break bread equally. Then we put together something for Fast Black. I'll handle the folks on my end with my share of the loot," he said.

That made the girls feel good and guilty at the same time. Good, because he was splitting the profits 50/50 and was willing to pay the people that gave him the tip out his share. Guilty, because they felt bad about not wanting to pay the people in the bank.

Shooter counted out the money and stopped when he reached $335,500. Shooter told each girl to count his money and asked them to tell him how much it was.

"This is $335,500 Shooter," Maria said after counting it up.

She simply repeated what Sunny and Ruby had just told him.

"That will be our shares to do as we wish with it. I'ma give Black $50,000 out of my share and handle the people at the bank," he said.

He counted out the money for Fast Black. The girls counted out their shares of the money.

While Shooter was putting the loot in the bag for Fast Black and his inside connect, Ruby, Sunny, and Maria each gave him $70,000.

"Fuck is all this for?" Shooter asked.

"It's for putting us down with the move," Ruby said.

"Yeah. It's a little appreciation money, that's all," Sunny added.

"Yeah. We threw Black's money in there too. Give him what you want to outta that," Maria said.

She gave him a kiss on the lips.

"Ya'll never cease to amaze me," Shooter grinned.

He already had his mind made up to give Fast Black $150,000. That way, he wouldn't have to touch any of his money. He would still be able to pay his inside connect at the bank.

"You know this is the most money I ever had in my possession at one time in my whole life!" Maria exclaimed.

She threw her share up in the air. Sunny and Ruby did the same thing. They started throwing money at each other. They were making it rain money inside Shooter's apartment.

"I'm glad everyone is happy," Shooter said after they were finished having a ball.

"Now can ya'll please clean up all this loot, so we can get moving?"

It took another hour to clean up all the money and divide it up equally again.

"What are ya'll going to do with all that bread?" Shooter asked.

"The first thing I'ma do is take care of my mother's bills before I think about doing anything else."

"Ruby, we can purchase that business you were talking about. Maria, you can contribute a little something after you take care of your mom's bills. If Ruby really wants to invest in a business, we can make up the slack on your end Maria."

"Right now, I don't know what I'm going to do Sunny. I will let you and Maria know something soon," Ruby said.

"Before ya'll start spending that money, I hope ya'll know how to clean that shit up first."

"Shooter, we will clean the loot up before we do anything else. Don't worry babe, we got this."

Shooter just looked at Maria and smiled. He knew he had him a gangsta woman on his team.

"Shooter, when do you think Fast Black will show up?"

"You know Ruby, Fast Black is never in a rush to get his paper. I might not see him for another two days. He knows his money is safe with me. "

"Like a vault safe. Yeah, we know how secure that can be," Sunny capped.

That caused everyone to laugh at her remarks.

Shooter responded, "It's a lot out of harm's way than it was at first."

They all laughed again. Shooter went and put his money away.

It was about 6:45 that evening when they departed from Shooter's apartment. It had now stopped raining and the sun was shining. That made the 85 degree weather feel like a 100 degrees with the humidity factor. It didn't take any length of time for Shooter's black Escalade to arrive around Maria's projects to drop them off.

"I'll catch up with ya'll later on. Make sure ya'll do the right thing. Keep them nosy people out of ya'll business. When people know things, they like running their mouths. That's one of the reasons why I been able to outlast most people in the bank game. I keep them nosy ma'fuckaz outta' my business."

While Shooter was telling them this, they stood on the sidewalk with the Escalade's doors open. The three of them absorbed Shooter's advice with all ears.

"You're absolutely right Shooter. We didn't come this far to get jammed up. We won't run our mouths. Like I told you back at your place, don't worry, we got this. We'll always put protection on ourselves babe."

"Okay then. I'll see ya'll later."

The three of them said alright as Maria shut the doors. She blew Shooter a kiss as he pulled off. A rack of dudes started calling, whistling, and trying to holler at the three girls as they walked towards Maria's building. They waved politely and kept it moving. As they entered the building, they could still smell the filthy pollution of piss and garbage in the hallway.

"Sunny, we need to move away from here and get us a better place to live. If Shooter can live in a nice place, we can too."

"Yeah, I feel you Maria. We can move into another spot. We sure have the money to do it. Shiid', for real-for real, all three of us can get a place together."

The conversation stopped right there once Maria saw her brother's face. Instantly, Maria knew something dreadful had happened. Billy Boy looked at her with blood-red eyes. That was a clear sign that he'd been crying. Before he could get the words out, Maria had a bad feeling about what was going on. Maria dropped to her knees and started crying. You could hear Maria's painful cries and wailing all over the housing projects.

No one knew the aching pain that Maria carried in the pit of her heart. Billy Boy grabbed her and picked her up off the floor with the help of Ruby and Sunny. When they finally pulled her up off the floor, Maria was distraught and didn't know if she was coming or going.

"Moms passed away at 9:10 this morning," Billy Boy said softly.

When Maria heard the revelation of her mother's death come out of his mouth, the pain struck more ferociously. In her heart, it felt like thunderbolts of lighting were striking. Maria couldn't believe what she heard Billy Boy say.

Ruby went into the kitchen to get Maria a glass of water in an effort to calm her emotions down. Maria was hysterical. She sat on the couch rocking back and forth.

All Maria kept saying was, "I can't believe my mom is gone. She can't be gone. She just can't be."

$ $ $ $ $

MARIA AND BILLY BOY BURIED THEIR MOTHER a week and half later in a small private service. There were no blood relatives at the funeral. They didn't have any. The only people that showed up were Sunny and her mother, Juanita. Ruby, Fast Black, Vicky, Cindy, and Shooter all came out to give Maria and Billy Boy support and comfort behind their loss.

MONTHS FLEW PASSED QUICKLY AFTER THAT

DREARY AND SAD DAY. Two weeks after the funeral, the three girls along with Billy Boy, took the Greyhound Bus out to Las Vegas to clean up the bank money. The reason they went that far was because they didn't want to take another chance with the casinos in Atlantic City. They had a ball while they were there. They stayed in the best hotels Vegas had to offer. They even obtained some extra money from gambling in the casinos. That was an added plus to their bank rolls.

The girls thought Billy Boy didn't have a clue as to what was going on. Truth be told, Billy Boy knew the little schemes they were pulling. He didn't want to utter any words to them about it and buss' their bubble. He was content with living lavishly in the three-story brick house that Maria moved them into after their mother died. The house had five bedrooms and four and a half bathrooms. The first floor had a spacious kitchen and living room that Maria had laid out with expensive furniture, exotic plants, and oil paintings. The house cost Maria, Sunny, and Ruby close to $285,000 to buy and decorate it.

The girls put down most of the payment for the house with Shooter's help. He knew somebody that knew somebody in the real estate game that hooked the girls up. Every day they decorated the house, Maria kept bringing up the subject of robbing another bank. Unbeknownst to her, Maria had become addicted to robbing banks and touching that fast money. Now that her mother was gone, she had no reason to rob a bank. It was as if she was under a spell.

Billy Boy was aware of all this. He used to hear the girls talking around the house when they first moved in. Maria had the master suite on the third floor. All three girls would lay around in their nightgowns, lingerie, and tight undergarments talking about everything under the moon; especially the bank robberies.

Maria also had put on a few extra pounds over the last few months. It only enhanced the stunning, lovely, light brown complexion she had. Sunny and Ruby thought Maria was just going through some deep depression and dealing with it by eating food. There were no other faults to be found in her body. She was a young girl that would be 19 years old in a couple more months. Maria already had the body of a woman.

Sunny's body had filled out a little bit too. Her chocolate Hershey body started looking very good to Billy Boy. I'm talking good enough to eat. Billy Boy even had a few wet dreams about making love to her. They still flirted and talked nasty to each other, but it never went any further than that. Billy Boy wanted to fuck the shit out of Sunny, but he just didn't know how to go about doing it.

Ruby and Fast Black were still creeping on the low-low, but Fast Black had let the money change him. He started tricking his money off on other women. He started spending less time with Ruby. She saw the signs and just backed up from Fast Black. Ruby decided it would be better to be friends with him than enemies. She knew all men were dogs and accepted the fact that Fast Black wasn't any different.

Creeping quietly like a ninja through the house, Billy Boy put his ear to Maria's door and listened as Sunny spoke.

"I'm glad we put our money into buying this house. It makes me feel good to have a home like this and not have to work for years to get it."

"Yeah, but it costs to maintain a house like this. I'll be damned if I start selling pussy to pay the bills around here," Ruby said.

She was sipping from her Mimosa cocktail.

"We can always open up that clothing store," Sunny suggested.

"Yeah, we gotta do something fast, or get another hustle. Or we might just have to rob another bank," Maria said.

She gave her friends a stern look.

On the other side of the door, Billy Boy backed away from the door. He could not believe the words that just came out of his sister's mouth.

CHAPTER 12

"WHAT'S WRONG WITH hitting another bank Sunny?" Maria said in a demanding tone.

"If we have something sweet, we might as well run with it while it's good!"

Sunny gave her a sad look.

She said, "See, that's what I mean Maria. How long will this shit stay sweet? All I'm saying is we just need to get into something and keep this money flipping for us. So we don't have to hit another bank and take any unnecessary chances. Every time we go up in one of them joints, we are rolling the dice like a muthafucka. We're bound to crap out. You hear me?"

"What you think Ruby? All of a sudden, people act funny when they get a lil money," Maria playfully said.

She was thinking, *"Before we had a dollar to spend, this bitch was ready to rob every bank in the world! Now she's faking after getting a little bit of bread!"*

"I understand where both of ya'll are coming from," Ruby said.

"Sunny has a good point, but like you said Maria, if it ain't broke then don't fix it. You know I'm with whatever, so I say let's do the muthafucka. Why should we stop now with all that money inside them joints waiting for us to take it?"

"You know what Biggie and nem' said, Mo-Money, Mo-Problems," Sunny spoke up.

"I honestly think we should quit while we ahead and get into another profession."

"Okay Sunny, I feel where you're coming from. Right now we ain't hurting for any money. We'll lay where we at for now and chill out on robbing banks. But if something comes along that's too sweet and can't be passed up, we going to hit it, agreed?"

"If we do this, It will be our last robbery, agreed?" Sunny said quickly.

"Whatever ya'll decide is cool with me," Ruby said.

"Well, check it out bitch," Maria said.

She was looking directly at Sunny.

"Since you want to have the last word so much, we'll deliberate on this issue if it comes up again, agreed?"

The three of them laughed out loud after Maria's remarks.

"Where is that damn Billy Boy at with my damn car? He should've been back here by now. He know he don't have no damn driver's license. I'm already taking a chance by letting him drive it around."

"He's probably at the pool room hustling. You know how he feels about being the main provider around here," Sunny said.

"Don't remind me gurl. I can't be too mad at him. I let him work me for the car a few months ago anyway. He's been driving my shit like it's his now so I'm jive used to it.

C'mon ya'll. Let's get dressed so we can meet Shooter and Black at The Spotlight. You know Rare Essence up there tonight."

"Go on and get your freak on. Heey-Heey-Heey!" Ruby sang.

She started dancing like she was inside the Go-Go. That made the girls laugh.

"Cold blooded slut right there," Sunny joked.

"Thanks for the compliment, ho!" Ruby fired back playfully.

That caused them to howl with more laughter.

"If Billy Boy ain't back by the time we finish getting ready, we can all ride together in Ruby's ride."

"Sounds like a winner to me," Ruby said.

She rushed off to the bathroom to take a shower and get ready for the GO-GO. Maria and Sunny headed to separate ends of the house to handle their business as well.

$ $ $ $ $

AT THE SAME TIME, Billy Boy was pulling his dick out some young lady's mouth inside the pool hall's bathroom. She had been wanting to get with him every since he'd been coming around in the latest expensive fashions and playing big like he had a million dollars.

She growled and yanked back on his dick with her pouty lips. She took him deeper and deeper. She was sucking the shit out of his dick. That caused him to moan with pleasure. He gripped the back of her head and started fucking her hot-wet mouth with hard strokes. In, Out, In, Out, and Way In!

"Mmmmm."

She gagged a little over his plunging pole. She was trying to jerk him off faster so he'd hurry up and climax. If she knew she was sucking a youngster's dick who was still in high school, she'd never forgive herself. She had a son around Billy Boy's age.

She'd been captivated after seeing him hanging around the pool hall like a stick pin. He beat everyone that came through to play pool.

"Damn, Jackie! You about to make me Nu-Nuuuuu Arrrrghhhttt!" He groaned.

A gust of hot semen exploded down her throat. She nursed on his spewing rod until she milked every drop.

"Here you go. Don't spend it all in one place," he said.

He threw a $100 bill at her before leaving the restroom. He had to finish off his opponent in a game of One Pocket. He was playing Zap-Out, a young hustler from Northeast who was known for beating a lot of dudes in pool all over the city. When he heard about Billy Boy kicking ass, he came out to represent his talents.

"Damn Slim. I was about to roll out on you. I thought you got scared for a minute," Zap-Out smirked as he chalked his pool stick.

"Never that Slim. I was just draining the lizard, you dig."

Billy Boy laughed inside. He thought about Jackie's bomb head.

"You want to break, or you want me to break 'em?" Billy Boy asked.

"You can go 'head, cause if I break dem' rocks, you might not get a shot Cuzzo," Zap-Out told him.

"If you insist, but don't get too mad at my work. What we playing for?"

"Make it light on yourself."

"How about a hundred a ball? Is that cool?"

"C'mon Slim. You don't have no confidence in your game? Make it three-hundred a ball," Zap-Out said.

He pulled out a huge wad of money and placed it on the pool table.

"It's a bet. Say no more," Billy Boy said.

He broke and went to work.

By the time Billy Boy missed a shot, they were on their fourth game of One Pocket. Billy Boy really hit Zap-Out's pockets for a little over $16,000. Zap-Out was mad as shit, but the player in him respected the hustle. Now he knew Billy Boy was a first rate pool shark. It cost him a lot of money but now he knew.

"Slim, I tried to tell you. My shit is way serious on this shit," Billy Boy said.

He passed Zap-Out a bottle of Remy that he'd bought.

"I'm hip. It cost me a rack of money to find out. Help me out soldier. Throw me a few G's back to get back on my feet."

"I'ma look out for you this time Slim, but next time the favor's on you."

"You got that soldier. You lucky bastard."

"Not luck homez'," Billy Boy grinned.

 "Pure skillz. Pure-d' skillz," Billy Boy said.

He tossed him $2,000 back.

"A'ight, let's play a few more games, so I can get my money back."

"C'mon, Slim, how you gonna gamble with the money I just gave you?"

"I'm tryna get back Billy Boy, simple as that. You know how that shit goes. A'ight fuck it, let's shoot some bones then."

"Zap, I don't have a problem with letting you get a chance to win your money back but I need to get out of here. I had my sister's car all day. I know she's wondering where I'm at. I'll tell you what I'll do. I'll bait one of these other lames in for you. That'll give you a chance to win some of your money back."

"A'ight Slim. I guess I'ma have to flow with that. You a lucky mu'fucka."

"C'mon, I told you before it wasn't luck Slim. It's in my motherfucking bloodline to be a pool shark. I've been doing this shit since I was a kid. I think my great-great grand-dad was a pool player," he joked.

That caused Zap-Out to laugh and forget about the idea of robbing the youngster for his money back.

He had respect for a young nigga. Billy Boy could knock the color off them pool balls like he was an old-timer. He earned his respect.

Zap-Out beat some guy that Billy Boy hyped up to play him for $1,350. After the way Zap-Out ran through him, he blew his cover and nobody else wanted to play him.

"Since ain't shit else to do around here, what you about to do the rest of the night?" Zap-Out asked him.

"Shit."

"Listen, I know where there's a card game at tonight. Me and you can be partners and rape them peoples. They'll be playing poker. We can just keep raising the pot to chase everyone off. Then one of us can just fold and take the pot. We can split up everything at the end of the night. I played in there before. They got some thirsty niggaz that always chase down pots. If you got that bread they'll haul ass."

"Damn Slim. If it's that sweet, why do you need me?"

"Cause you got all the damn money! Slim, I'm not tryna' play you or nothing in no way. I just feel like you and me would make a good team. Besides, this is a sure way to get something for nothing. This here don't deal with luck or taking a ride on the Wheel of Fortune by chance. This has to do with knowing the cards, bluffing good, and bullying the pots."

"Slim, I gotta' get my sister's car back."

"Then again, you right. I don't know shit about shit. But I know this, I bet your sister's not tripping about you having her car."

"She might be Slim, I had this joint all day. I been 'spose to took the joint back after school."

"So what's a few more hours going to hurt?"

"Look Zap, I don't know. If I can get the car from her again, where you be at so I can come through and scoop you?"

"I'ma start coming through here at the pool hall. I usually hustle all around town just to eat. I can't afford to look sweet like you," he said.

He was referring to Billy Boy's fresh Prada sneakers and hitting-ass Versace' workman Jumpsuit.

"Fuck outta here Zap! You ain't saying nothing!" He giggled.

They both had to laugh.

"I'm serious Slim. I'ma stay here until this joints closes. If it closes, slide over my mother's joint around Brentwood to scoop me up."

"It's not a guarantee that I'm going to be able to convince her to let me use it again."

"I know Billy Boy. It's not certain that you'll pull it off, but dig it, if you do, you know where I'll be at."

$ $ $ $

*"T*hat was Shooter on the phone** just now. He said him and Fast Black will meet us at the club because something came up. He didn't want to talk about it on the phone. He did say it wasn't anything unpleasant. He said that he would explain everything when he sees us at the club," Maria told the girls.

"I'm glad it wasn't anything messed up or any unacceptable news."

"No Ruby. It wasn't anything of that degree, but it does look like we're going to use your car."

"That's cool with me unless you want to ride in Sunny's Nissan."

"Aw bitch. What? Chu' tryna' be funny?" Sunny snapped.

Her comment caused Maria and Ruby to laugh.

"I bought that Nissan because it would have looked real crazy for all of us to suddenly break out with fly-ass expensive rides. The feds might've been right on our asses like a motherfucka! Like a got damn hound dog!"

"Ease up Sunny. We just playing with you, damn!"

"Yeah, we was just bullshitting," Ruby added.

"But ya'll know I speak the truth."

"You're right Sunny. We hold high regards for you because you use your brain for all of us."

"Maria, I'm not upset about that. That bitch Ruby was just jonin' as always."

They all laughed.

"Ya'll bitches ready to get out of here? For some reason, I think Billy Boy is not going to show up anytime soon with my car," Maria said.

She headed out the door with the girls on her heels. They left the house dressed to kill. Maria sported an Yves Saint Laurent, fire engine red, leather pants outfit with a matching red lace bra. Her jacket had dime-size rhinestones on the cuffs of the sleeves. She showed off her pretty feet in some cross-strapped, high heel Jimmy Choos.

Sunny wore a Black D&G print, skin tight, leather halter dress with long sleeves that revealed all the curves of her gorgeous body. Her Manolo Blaniks peep toe pumps made her thick legs stand out more than anything else.

Ruby rocked some black, tight fitting, Fendi leather pants, a matching Fendi turtleneck, and a short black Fendi leather jacket that came up to her waist. Her black suede, high heel boots made her look like a sexy super hero.

They scrambled inside Ruby's car as Ruby got behind the wheel. Sunny and Maria sat in the front seat with her. As she pulled off, the girls started singing along with the Go-Go CD that was playing in the system.

$ $ $ $

"WHEN BILLY BOY ARRIVED HOME at the three story brick house, it was a little after 10 p.m. He parked in front of the house and got out. He noticed that Ruby and Sunny's cars were nowhere in sight. He walked up the four red brick steps that lead to the door, put the key in the lock, and entered the house.

He knew nobody was home because he didn't hear a sound.

He thought to himself, *"Damn! It slipped my mind that Maria told me that they were going out tonight. Today's Friday! Shit! I hope she don't be too pissed about me not coming straight home when I left from school."*

He went to the living room and made a bee-line straight to the kitchen. He opened the ice-box and removed some Neapolitan ice cream along with a carton of milk. He then went to the cabinet and removed a box of Capt'n Crunch cereal. Sitting everything down on the kitchen table, he started going to work. This was a habit he developed throughout the years. He liked eating ice cream and cereal together.

As he began to eat, he thought, *"Damn! Maria and them will be gone all night until the break of the wee hours in the morning. So I guess I will be hanging out with Zap. It seems like a good god damn scheme he has going on. I just hope he's for real about what he told me. Niggaz always scheming on a quick way to stack some money. The only thing I'm worried about is them motherfucking po-po stopping me late at night and asking for my driver's license. They stay trying to pull anybody over on the late night; especially if they driving a sweet-ass, expensive car. I'm not going to trip about that shit too much. It's only a $100 fine to get out. I just hate giving them motherfuckers my hard earned money I hustled all day for. Fuck it, if it will keep me out of jail, they can get that. Shiiid, while I'm waiting, I might as well lay back and smoke me a j' of this Hydro. Maria don't like it when I be smoking this shit, but what she don't know won't hurt her. Yeah, that's what I'ma do. I'ma smoke this chronic and put on that Jahiem CD. The one that* *got all the ghetto fly R&B shit on it. That'll kill some time until I'm ready to go pick-up Zap-Out."*

Billy Boy finished eating and went into the living room. He proceeded to his room that was on the second floor facing the back part of the house. His room was layed out with elegance. He had the Z-Box 325 surround sound entertainment system with X-Box and Playstation-3. His system always had the whole house jumping. Since the CD was downstairs, Billy Boy decided to go back down there and chill. Plus he liked listening to the Bose Acoustic wave music system the girls had installed down there. It played everything in a real mellow tone. That made you feel like you were at an actual live concert.

Billy Boy put the Jahiem CD on. He sat down on the couch and lit the weed. He took several long deep tokes as his favorite song came on.

"Cops Shut Down The Party, We Drag Low, Blow Smoke Outta Dutches, You Know We Fabulous, Oh Yeeeaaahh!"

He sang along with the song fucking up every verse as he got high as a kite.

"Damn, it's 10:35 now," he thought.

He looked at his watch.

"I'll leave around midnight to pick up Zap. It won't take me long to reach his mom's house from here."

Zap-Out lived off his hustling reputation. The two men were bound to cross paths. Zap-Out and Billy Boy clicked so well together. They were like brothers after their encounter. Billy Boy figured it wouldn't hurt for them to play on the same team together and get some money. What made it even better, they could go for brothers. Zap-Out was a brown-skin kid who wore his hair in a short cut with a razor shape up. Both of them had wavy hair.

Billy Boy stood 6'2". Zap-Out was a year older with an escalated height of 6'3" and a half all wrapped in a lean muscle toned frame.

Billy Boy called Zap-Out and told him they were on for the night.

128

$ $ $ $ $

RUBY DROVE HER CAR DOWN 15th Street then turned on Benning Road. It was a straight shot to get to Georgia Avenue. Once she made it to Georgia Avenue, Ruby made a right and sped up on Georgia Avenue which was a straight shot to The Spotlight Nightclub.

"Maria, did Shooter say he'll meet us there?" Ruby asked.

"He said him and Black will be together. They should be waiting on us outside. That's what he told me."

"I'm glad it's not that cold for it being October," Sunny said.

"Yeah, you right Sunny," Ruby blurted.

" If it was a little colder, we might be freezing our asses off in this leather shit!"

"Duh! This is the time of year when you 'spose to wear leather!" Maria cracked.

That caused Ruby to suck her teeth like she was mad.

"I think it's more the way the weather is as long as it's not frigid cold," Sunny said.

She was playing referee knowing Maria and Ruby's attitudes were bound to clash if she didn't intervene.

"I know. I was just fucking with Ruby. Anyway, the real reason I said we 'spose to wear this leather shit is because I told Shooter and them that we'll be wearing this. They 'spose to be waiting on us outside."

"You know when there's a rack of black muthafuckaz together, they instantly draw heat. We might be burning up in all this leather shit!" Ruby said.

They all laughed their asses off.

Ruby stopped the car near a light near the Silver Spring Metro Station. When the light changed, she turned off Georgia Avenue and made a left down the quiet street leading to the club to find a parking space. Parking several spaces from the club, Ruby and the girls exited the car. They made their way towards the club.

It was a warm night for November. It was around 56 degrees. A lot of people both young and old, were out on the town that night. They were all trying to get inside to hear Rare Essence. The men gave wolf calls and loud whistles of approval as the girls walked by. The girls looked at each other and smiled. They never lost their strides. Ruby threw an extra switch in her walk. That made a few dudes grab their dicks through their clothes. They secretly were wishing they could spend the night with her.

They got five feet from the club and spotted Shooter and Fast Black amongst the pack of young people that were standing in the crowded line. Unbeknownst to the girls, Shooter and Fast Black had robbed another bank earlier in the day. They came off with a nice amount of $45,000. The caper was so sweet that they couldn't resist. Truth be told, Shooter was addicted to robbing banks like an addict addicted to drugs.

"What'up ladies?"

He greeted each of them with a kiss on the cheek after they reached him. Fast Black did the same and sneakily palmed Ruby's soft ass when he kissed her.

"Don't start nothing you can't finish," she whispered to him while licking her pouty lips.

"I hear you," he said.

Maria gave Shooter a long hug.

"What was so important that you couldn't talk about it on the phone?"

"First Maria. Let me say how good and sexy ya'll are looking right now with them leather outfits on. Ya'll gon' make me and Black catch some bodies fucking with ya'll," he giggled.

"This is what's going on. I want to give you this before we go inside the club."

"Give me what?"

Shooter went into his pants pocket and pulled out a silk green scarf that was folded in a box sharp. He grabbed Maria's hand and put it in her palm.

"What's this Shooter?"

"Open it up," he smirked.

Maria unfolded the scarf and opened the small box. She couldn't believe her eyes. She had a big smile on her face.

She said, "This is the most gigantic diamond I've ever seen! It must be worth thousands!"

Sunny and Ruby looked in Maria's open hand.

They said at the same time, "DAMN! That's a jumbo joint!"

"I know jewelry. That piece gotsta' cost some loot for real!" Ruby said.

"I received it in a package deal," Shooter said.

He went in his pocket again. He pulled out twin rose gold, lady Rolex watches. There were four diamonds going around on the four main hours of the watch. He passed one to Ruby and the other to Sunny.

"Them watches are from me and Fast Black. We bought them as a token of our appreciation for the fine job you ladies did on that demonstration.

"Thanks Shooter and Fast Black," Sunny and Ruby cooed cheerfully.

The three of them hugged and kissed Fast Black and Shooter.

"Ya'll always treating us so special."

"Maria, our love for ya'll is special, that's why," Shooter told her.

"I know Shooter. You don't have to spend all your money on us; even though we appreciate the gifts."

"That's what the money's for. It's made to spend. Besides, three beautiful ladies like ya'll deserve to have the best."

"Shooter, you're definitely a girl's dream come true," Maria said.

Everyone laughed.

"We should be getting inside this joint. It's getting chilly again out this muthafucka," Fast Black said.

"Boy, you don't have any blood!" Sunny cracked.

They all laughed again while walking inside the nightclub.

Shooter spoke to the doorman. He was a big football linebacker looking guy.

"Listen Slim, I'm paying for us five to get up in here."

He turned and looked at them.

"Everything's on me tonight. Enjoy yourselves."

"Shooter, you're doing a lot of spending," Ruby said.

"You know you don't have to do that."

"Don't worry about it shorty, I'ma hustler," Shooter capped.

He was thinking about the Cassidy classic song that became a hustler's anthem nationwide.

"If it's money to be made, I can always get it, you dig?" He said.

He drew more laughter from them as they walked deeper inside the dimly lit nightclub.

CHAPTER 13

*T*HE SPOTLIGHT WAS COMPRESSED WITH YOUNG SCANTILY CLAD FEMALES. They were dancing everywhere. Several guys followed the women's moves while staying glued to their asses. Rare Essence had the party slow-jamming to their version of Anita Baker's classic, Sweet Love. They went to the bar and ordered a few drinks to get them in a festive mood before the band really got to cranking.

The five of them departed from their bar stools and started walking on the dance floor. They were mingling and dancing. Maria, Ruby, and Sunny felt hands grabbing and touching all over their bodies as they made their way towards the center of the dance floor. Maria hated this part of the GO-GO. She hated niggaz touching all over her like they had free access to her goodies.

"I'm the King of the GO-GO Beat!" The lead mic talker for the band chanted.

That caused everyone to get hype and rush towards the floor. They knew he was about to really get the party started.

"And my crew is R-E! Yeeeaaahhh! So when my band go chick-chigga-boom-chick-chigga-boom. I'M LOOKING FOR MARINDA!" He yelled.

That signaled the band to break down in a hard hitting break down. That had everyone dancing hard like it would be the last party on earth.

Maria, Sunny, and Ruby were shaking their bodies all over the dance floor. Maria and Sunny made a human sandwich with Shooter.

They were wiggling their bodies against him. Fast Black and Ruby were a few feet away from them in a dark corner doing more than just dancing. The way Ruby was working her body against Fast Black, you would have thought she worked in a strip club. Her tight leather outfit and the way she worked her body aroused so much excitement in Fast Black. He hiked her dress up a little and started playing with her pussy.

"SSS! AHHH BLACK! STOOOP!" She hollered over the music.

He slid two fingers inside her wet box to finger her. She now regretted not wearing any panties.

"I thought you wanted me to finish what I started?" He whispered in her ear.

He smoothly pulled his dick out his pants. He slid his hardness between her ass-cheeks while she kept dancing. She leaned back and kissed him passionately while he played with her pussy. He was getting her primed and ready for his penetration.

"I SAID I'M SEARCHING FOR MARINDA! I SEE YOU BIG SHOOTER!" The lead talker shouted.

He was putting Shooter on display as the band broke down.

Fast Black took this opportunity to enter Ruby's tight, wet pussy. She screamed out in pleasure as he fucked her in rhythm to the GO-GO sounds.

"Yeah Baby, right there, fuck me like that. Just like that. Mmmm-MmmmMmmm. Ssss, damn this dick is good," she moaned while bending over a little.

She was taking all of his granite-hard pipe. He grabbed her waist and pulled her back to meet his stabbing thrusts. He was going deeper and deeper and deeper.

"Ahh-Ahh-Ahh! Mmmmm! Shit Boy! I'm Cumming Already!" She screamed.

He slammed his dick in her harder and harder. The band kept playing. It looked like they were just doing a lot of dirty dancing to the naked eye, but Fast Black and Ruby were doing a mating dance that had him ready to explode.

"Cum with me Black. Cum with me Boo," she huffed.

She rotated her hips. She was taking all of his jack hammer. She looked back at him over her shoulder.

"I know you can do it. C'mon, you Big Dick Moth---

AHHHHHH!" She gasped.

She exploded in a leg shaking climax while releasing her love juices all over his sawing dick.

He plunged deeper inside her throughout the breakdown routine. He exploded inside her gripping, tight fuck box right before they went into another tune. They stayed that way in the dark until his dick slid out of her tight wetness.

"I'll be right back Baby. You so nasty," she giggled mischievously.

She excused herself to the bathroom to clean up.

Fast Black did the same thing. They met back up on the dance floor in ten minutes. They wanted to make it seem like they never left the dance floor. They made it back just in time. The band broke down in another slow jam, **R-Kelly's 12-Play**.

Sunny departed from the dance floor to sit down. She was giving Shooter and Maria their space. She watched Fast Black and Ruby dance along with Maria and Shooter. She suddenly felt sad that she didn't have a man to share times like these with. Right then, Sunny made up her mind. She knew what she had to.

$ $ $ $ $

*I*T WAS A LITTLE AFTER 12:30 a.m. when Billy Boy deviated from his house. He was on his way to pick up Zap-Out. He cruised down East Capitol Street with extreme caution. He was trying to stay out of the way of the police.

"Shiiid', if I can make it to Zap-Out's house without them motherfucking pieces of shit-ass cops stopping me, that will let me know that Lady Luck is on my side. Especially, if me and Zap make it back on the other side of town without any trouble from them so called peace keepers," he thought as he drove.

He knew he'd have a good chance of playing poker without losing any money.

"Man, let me stop thinking that way before something lousy happens," he mumbled.

He was getting a little closer to Zap-Out's house. Billy Boy got off at East Capitol Street and hit Benning Road, before speeding off towards the northeast. After floating Maria's car for ten minutes, Billy Boy made a right turn onto Rhode Island Avenue. He drove towards Zap-Out's projects in Brentwood. As he arrived in front of Zap-Out's building, he tooted the horn. Zap-Out's head popped out of his mother's apartment window after hearing the horn.

"I'll be right down Cuzzo!" He yelled.

Billy Boy hit the horn again.

Zap-Out grabbed his .40 caliber and his leather jacket out of his closet. Just as he was about to leave, his mother, Ms. Cecelia AKA Ms. CC came out of her bedroom.

"Boy, where are you taking your butt this early in the morning? You just brought your ass in here."

"Aw CC."

He called his mother by her nickname with the greatest of ease. They had a cool-ass relationship. She was extremely over-protective of him.

"I'll be back in a minute. I have to go and handle some business."

"What business can you possibly have at one o'clock in the morning? And what have I told you about calling me CC?"

"Chill out Ma. I ain't doing nothing but handling some business."

"Business my ass! Boy, you better not be going out there getting into no trouble. I looked out the window and saw that boy driving that expensive car. I hope you not out there stealing no damn cars!"

"CC don't worry. That's my partner Billy Boy. That's his sister's car."

"Yeah okay. You just make sure you stay your black ass outta' trouble. Be back in this house before sunrise. I'm telling you now if you get locked up, I'm not coming to get your hard-headed ass. I done told you now."

"Ain't nobody getting locked up CC," he said.

He kissed his mother on the cheek.

He ran out the apartment in haste. Ms. CC locked up behind her son. She made it back to the window just in time to see him getting inside the waiting vehicle.

"What's up Billy?"

"Ain't shit, you tell me," he said.

They pulled off.

"I'm just glad I made it safely over here, that's all."

"Slim, don't even trip on the small shit. We're about to be straight tonight, you hear me? I can feel it. Anyway, after you left me at the pool room, I caught me a few fresh suckers coming through and spanked their asses in Nine Ball. I got back about forty-five hundred."

"Hold up Zap. Tell me that shit later. I'm driving this car. I don't even know where the fuck I'm 'spose to be going."

"Oh, my bad Billy Boy. I thought you knew where the joint was at. The spot over there by your end. It's about five blocks from your house in fact."

"Okay, now I know where I'm going. You can finish telling me what happened."

"Ain't shit to tell. I worked a few niggaz outta' that paper. Now I got close to $7,500. Along with all that paper you won from me, we should be able to roll up in there with $20,000 or better. We can straight rough the pots off. That should be more than enough to rape a poker game; unless they're playing strip poker," he said.

They both laughed.

"Shiid'. The only way I'm playing strip poker is if they got some bad-top flight bitches in there playing. The ones who don't be faking when it comes time to come outta' their clothes and handlin' their business."

"Yeah, no bullshit. I like when them bitches be sitting in their panties. They be having that kind of pussy that's so fat and pretty. It looks like a strawberry ice cream cone ready to be licked all over."

"Ease up Slim. You jive making my dick hard as a motherfucka."

"Go ahead with all that freak ass shit Billy Boy! I'm not concerned with your dick. Freak ass nigga. I got my own!"

"You're a freaky dude too," Billy Boy said.

He hooked a left on New York Avenue. He then took the expressway back towards his side of town.

"That's the best way to be when it comes to them ball busters. That's what them bitches want. They need a nigga like me that will lick their pussies and asses real good. Have them going crazy over you trying to kill God to be with you."

"Slim, I said you're a freaky dude. I take that back. You're fucked up in the game Slim. You a straight grotesque muthafucka!"

"Man fuck you!" Zap-Out said.

That caused them to laugh during the trip on the expressway. They joked around and laughed for the rest of the way.

It didn't take long for them to arrive at the place where the card game was being played. Billy Boy parked. They immediately exited the car and headed for the back door of the house. They knocked twice on the door. An older lady answered. She was a light skin woman with grey hair. She looked to be about 50 years old. She was very attractive and sweet looking for her age. The boys could tell that she took good care of herself.

"Hey Zappa-Dappa. How you doing baby?"

She greeted him with a hug.

"C'mon in," she said.

She let them both inside the house.

After they entered the house, she asked, "Who's your friend? He looks more like your brother."

"Ms. Brooklyn, this is a good friend of mines. His name is Billy Boy."

Billy Boy acknowledged her with a head nod. That caused her to smile at him.

"I knew a handsome dude named Billy Boy in my younger years.

He was charming just like you," she said.

She smiled and gave Billy Boy a wink.

"You boys came to play cards? I'ma let you know now. The cards are so hot tonight they're leaping off the table like frogs."

"So that means people are winning?" Billy Boy asked.

"You can take us to the poker table now, please," Zap-Out said.

"You sure you boys want to play poker? They're betting real big over there at the crap tables," she pointed.

They followed her finger and spotted about ten dudes crowded around the huge crap table.

"Ms. Brooklyn, now you know all I play is poker when I come in here."

"You know they betting $50 dollars just to be dealt in."

"That don't make a difference to me and Billy Boy. We got plenty of cake. You hear me?"

"Okay. It's ya'lls choice," she said.

She escorted them over to the poker table. Two players had just got up from losing all their money they had on them.

They moved closer to the table.

Zap-Out whispered in Billy Boy's ear, "You know that old bitch told me the exact same thing when she first met me. Talking about she knew a handsome dude named Zap-Out in her younger years that looked like me. That old bitch got some game you hear me? You got to respect it though."

They busted out laughing and Ms. Brooklyn frowned at them real strange. She knew something had just played by her and she didn't catch it. The room they entered had four round tables where they played cards. All four of them were occupied. Zap-Out and Billy Boy sat down at the table where the two players had just left. Zap-Out knew one of the guys sitting at the table. He was much older than Zap-Out. Zap-Out knew his name was Big Bugg. That's all he knew about the guy. That and the fact that every time he came to the gambling spot he was up in there in the same seat.

"Damn Slim. I see you staying true to the hustle. It seems like every time I come through here, you be up in the same spot."

"You know I do what I do Young'n."

"You jive on this poker shit hard huh?" Zap-Out asked.

He knew that he would be one of the main challengers to the scheme he and Billy Boy had mapped out.

"I'm on money hard Young'n."

"Man! You are a sucker for this game!" Zap-Out cracked.

"Oh Yeah? Well, you just make sure when the cards are dealt, you have a winner's hand. We'll see who the real sucker is for this poker shit when you come up short Young'n."

"You ain't said nothin'. If it takes all night for me to take your money, then that's cool with me," he said.

He purposely left Billy Boy's name out of it. He didn't want Bugg or anyone else at the table to know they were together.

"However you want it Youngster. Don't talk about it, be about it. Me and my man Gaye come to play poker. Let's get this shit on the road," he said.

That alerted them to the fact that he probably had the same idea that Zap-Out had. That had them second-guessing their plan.

Zap-Out grabbed the cards and began shuffling them. After his third shuffle, he let Bugg cut and then started dealing. Billy Boy picked his hand up off the table. He spotted a Royal Flush from the break.

"Bet fitty," Billy Boy said.

He tossed a $50 bill onto the table.

"That's a bet Youngster," Bugg called.

"What about your man Gaye? He ain't betting shit?" Zap-Out taunted.

"All day Youngster. I'm just calculating how long it's going to take me to win your money," he grinned.

He tossed his money into the pot.

"Since you put it like that, I'ma come clean. This is my man, Billy Boy. I'ma bet an extra $100 on top of his $50."

"Bet," he said.

Everyone except Bill Boy went through three rounds of drawing cards and betting more money.

Zap-Out folded just before the last round. He had done his job in getting the pot up to $12,000. Now all he could do was hope for Billy Boy to have the best hand.

Billy Boy raised his bet to another $2,000. That forced Gaye to fold. Bugg called the bet. He was not afraid of whatever was to come. He was that confident in his hand. He had Poker-9's, a sure-fire winner. The only thing that could beat him was Billy Boy's hand.

After all the betting was done, Bugg didn't waste any time laying down his hand and reaching for the money.

"Hold up Poppa," Billy Boy said.

He laid his hand down to reveal the Royal Flush. That made Zap-Out whistle loudly.

"I think that bread belongs to my man, Old Timer!" Zap-Out laughed.

Billy Boy scooped up the large pot of crumpled bills.

Gaye dealt the next hand and the luck started off good for Zap-Out. He had Poker Jacks and decided to drag the pot out for as much as he could. He kept raising and raising until everyone folded except him and Gaye.

Zap-Out triumphantly laid his hand down on the table, "Read em' and weep fellaz! Poker Jacks!" Zap-Out said.

Gaye threw his hand down angrily.

"I had a boat and still couldn't beat that shit!" Gaye fumed.

Zap-Out took the last of their bank roll.

Most of the money they had hustled off other guys the whole night was gone in two quick hands. All they had was some small shit left. They knew the youngsters were going to try to bully the pot.

"Well Billy Boy, looks like we caught us some dogs in the dog house, you hear me?" He joked.

Billy Boy couldn't help but snicker.

"Go ahead and deal Billy Boy. You know how shit goes Zap. It ain't over til' it's over," Bugg said.

He had an angry tone.

That alerted Zap-Out about how he truly felt about losing.

"You right Big Boy. Anybody can get a lucky hand from time to time. But like you said, it ain't over til it's over," Zap-Out said.

Billy Boy dealt the cards.

"But I think tonight's our night to be doing the fucking at this table. So before sunrise, we will be the last ones standing. You hear me?"

The card game went on until the early hours of the morning. Zap-Out was very crafty with the cards. Unbeknownst to Bugg and Gaye, whenever it was his turn to deal, Zap-Out would set the card in a way that only Billy Boy would get the best hands. Billy Boy peeped what Zap-Out was doing the second time he dealt and just rolled with the flow. He was winning big every time.

$ $ $ $

*I*T WAS 3:45 IN THE MORNING when Maria, Ruby, Sunny, and Shooter along with Fast Black, vanished from the Spotlight Nightclub.   Shooter and Fast Black went in unconnected territory. They made preparations with the girls to meet back up later. It was 4:20 a.m. when the girls made it back home.

Sunny and Ruby were in the living room bundled up on the couch together. Maria was balled up in the big soft leather convertible lounge chair.

Sunny was the first to speak.

"Maria, I think Billy Boy was here earlier. When I went into the kitchen, there was a bowl in the sink. I know I cleaned all the dishes before we left. I know wherever he's at, he's okay."

"I don't know why he hasn't called any of us to let us know what's up."

"Maria, you know Billy Boy is a big boy. He knows how to take care of himself," Ruby said.

"He is cautious when it comes to making decisions. Don't worry, he's okay. He probably came home, seen we wasn't home, and went back out. He's probably somewhere playing pool."

"Ain't no pool rooms open at five in the morning," Maria

countered.

"You know they have them after hour spots where they betting real big on the sides after the pool room closes. My brother be doing the same shit," Ruby said.

"Okay, I have confidence that he's alright after talking to ya'll. Anyway, this ring is the motherfucking bomb, ain't it?"

"Yeah that joint sweet," Sunny said cheerfully.

"I know right," Maria grinned.

"I know this joint had to cost about five grand or better."

"Maria, I told you I know jewelry. That diamond you have on your finger is a high price joint. You must've really laid that pussy on him gurl."

"Bitch, stop playing," Maria retorted playfully.

"For real, you say five grand? I got it being worth more than that. Girl, you looking at every bit of ten G's or more sitting on your hand. These two Rolies he gave us are worth anywhere between six to eight g's. Somebody somewhere is mad as shit right now after these joints got snatched from their jewelry store. He had to rob the store for these joints. The reason I say that is because my brother be robbing them joints. He be coming off with watches and rings like this. That's why I know real expensive shit when I see it. I learned about that shit at an early age," Ruby boasted.

"It was very nice of Shooter to give us this jewelry," Sunny said.

"I think you got him open on the pussy too. You can tell by the way his eyes radiate every time he's around you."

"It has to be something! The pussy, the head! Something has to be good for a nigga to just up and give you a precious diamond like that! That costs alot of damn money!" Ruby added.

"Even if the ring is hot, he went through a rack of shit to get it. That means you put that hot pussy on him girl."

They fell out laughing at Ruby's statement.

"No, it wasn't the pussy. I got that bomb shit that's brown on the outside and cherry red on the inside. That makes niggaz want to taste the rainbow. I don't think that has anything to do with the way he feels about me. He fell in love with me from the first moment he saw me. That's what he told me."

"Bitch! All that sounds good. I know that pussy played a major role. You're forgetting that I'm a woman. I know how it goes. Black still comes back and wants to get this good pussy I got, even though we're not together."

"Ruby, if he's hooked on my pussy, it wasn't my intentions to do it. I didn't have some kind of designed scheme to hook the nigga. The shit just happened. I'm glad I met him because I like him a lot. He's been a big help to us."

"I really like the watch he gave us. I know Christmas is next month. I'm going to consider this watch as my Christmas present from Shooter and Black."

"You're right, Sunny," Maria said.

"Shooter has definitely been a big assistance, especially when my mom was living. I needed some money for her bills. He was there for me. I'll always remember that. Anyway, that's enough about that. I don't need to start thinking about my mother for the rest of the morning."

"We turned that Spotlight joint out didn't we?" Sunny asked.

She was trying to take Maria's mind off her thoughts.

"Hell yeah girl," Ruby blurted.

"All eyes were on us, especially when you and Sunny were doing ya'll thing with Shooter."

"And I was getting some dick from Fast Black," she thought. "Yeah, ya'll were shaking that body so much that them dudes had their eyes all up and down ya'll body. Ya'll fat butts was bouncing like crazy."

"Shiiid', you wasn't doing too bad yourself with a yard of dick up in your ass. I saw how Fast Black was digging up in your coochie," Sunny said.

She busted her out as Maria laughed.

"I knew you was a freak," Maria added.

"I couldn't help it. I think he slipped an E-Pill in my drink," Ruby snickered.

"Whateva' bitch. You got that white liver. Just admit it, nympho!" Sunny teased playfully.

"Oh, so you bitches find that real comical huh? Well, fuck you then. I wanted some dick and got some. It was as simple as that. Oh, did ya'll see that bama-ass-nigga trying to cut in on me and Fast Black?"

"Yeah, Fast Black damn near pushed that nigga out of the club!" Sunny said.

"I didn't see that," Maria said.

She was somewhat mad that she missed the incident. She knew if she would've seen some shit like that, she would've fell out laughing right there on the dance floor.

"What are you getting Shooter for Christmas Maria?" Sunny asked.

"You know what? That's a good ass question. What do I give a man that seems to have it all?"

$ $ $ $ $

BILLY **BOY AND ZAP-OUT** sat at the card table by themselves counting up all the money they'd won during the long, fought out poker game. They gave up a good fight, but like he prophesized, Zap-Out and Billy Boy were the last ones standing.

"Well Billy Boy, it looks like it's all good for us now. We're way richer than we were when we came up in this motherfucker," he said.

He passed Billy Boy a separate stack of money while he took the other.

"I heard that Slim. You jive put a nigga on to a sweet ass lick."

"I told you them suckers were sweet up in here. I'm talking cold-blooded anything, you hear me?"

"Yeah, they couldn't tell one time you were setting the cards up for me to get the best hands."

"That's why I kept doing the shit Cuzzo! Sweeeeet!"

They laughed their asses off while walking towards the entrance.

"The best part about the shit is they don't even know about us or how we be working. They're still lame to the game, you dig me? They don't have a clue. We can always slide through here and get them niggaz again. It's nothing personal. We're just hustling and that all goes with it."

"You ready to get the fuck up outta' here?"

"Yeah, cause I know my sister is wo--,"

Billy Boy's words were cut off by the sounds of the crashing door. Two masked gunmen stormed the house. Zap-Out didn't hesitate pulling out his gun and bussin' off shots. Billy Boy dove to the ground as the sounds of gunfire made him deaf.

After several seconds of shooting, Zap-Out took the two would be robber lives. He pulled Billy Boy up from the ground.

"C'mon Slim! We have to go! Now! We have to Go!" He shouted.

Billy Boy broke out of his trance. Ms Brooklyn laid in the corner trying to stop the blood from oozing out of her shoulder.

"You boyz need to get on outta here! I'll make sure everything is straight here."

"How you gon' explain all of this shit?" Zap-Out asked frantically.

He was now ready to kill her too. She was the only witness. He never left any witnesses. He kept looking at her and debating whether or not to kill her. His gut instinct told him to spare her.

"*I just hope this shit don't come back to haunt me,*" he thought.

She coughed and spoke,"Give me your gun. I'll tell the police the truth about these two here trying to rob me and got kilt' in the process."

She coughed as Zap-Out dropped the weapon by her leg. He ran past her and out of the house with Billy Boy right on his heels. Billy Boy doubled back and returned seconds later. He dropped $3,000 at her feet.

"I'm sorry Ms. Brooklyn, we didn't mean---."

"Get out of here!"

She winced in pain.

He took off running after Zap-Out.

When she was sure they were gone, Ms. Brooklyn crawled over to her purse. She pulled out her cell phone to call 9-1-1.

"Yes, I'd like to report a robbery. I've been shot. I just killed the two men who shot me."

"Sit tight Ma'am, help is on the way," the 9-1-1 operator said.

Several police cruisers were quickly dispatched to Ms. Brooklyn's house.

$ $ $ $ $

*A*FTER TEN MINUTES OF SPEEDING, Billy Boy looked over at Zap-Out who had his eyes closed like nothing had ever happened.

"Zap, what the fuck happened back there?"

"Shit, niggaz tried to rob the spot. I ain't letting em' get me like that," he said nonchalantly.

Billy Boy knew Zap-Out was on a whole different level than just hustling.

"You killed both of them?"

"Yeah, they would've got us. You hear me? So I just did what I had to do," he said.

Billy Boy left well enough alone as he drove Zap-Out back towards his house.

All the while thinking, *"I'm riding with a fucking killer and he seems to like my style for some reason. Yeah, Lady Luck is definitely on my side tonight."*

"Other than that bullshit, how you like winning all that dough Billy Boy?" Zap-Out said.

"Shit was sweet Cuzzo. Real Sweet!" He giggled.

They laughed and joked the rest of the way towards Zap-Out's house.

CHAPTER 14

AFTER DROPPING OFF ZAP-OUT, Billy Boy headed back home. He thought about the murders Zap-Out had committed and acted like it didn't faze him. Billy Boy blazed up a blunt of Hydro during the ride home to calm his nerves. He was working on the fifth blunt of the night.

"I'm smoking this shit like it's a cigarette. I deserve it because of the shit I've been through tonight with Zap-Out. He is a solid nigga for going out on a limb to save us from harm's way. He kept us from losing our winnings tonight. Damn, them niggaz at the poker table was so sweet that it's unbelievable. I wish they had some more money to give away. Fuck it, I'm way richer than before so I can't really complain at all. I'ma give half of this cash to Maria to help her out with some of the bills that we have," he told himself.

He felt bad that Sunny, Maria, and Ruby had been holding the fort down better than him.

Billy Boy knew they assumed that he didn't have a clue about what they had been doing for the last couple of months. He just hoped that they'd have limitations on what they're doing. He didn't want to see something bad happen to his sister or her girls. Especially Sunny, who he'd grown a soft spot in his heart for lately.

"I can't tell them how to live their life. I just hope they do the right thing," he thought.

He knew if something bad happened to the three of them, it would crush his whole world. As he inhaled the chronic fumes, Billy Boy dipped the Camry. He reflected back on a conversation he had one day in the pool-hall.

"Hey Youngster, if I knew how to shoot pool and play cards the way you do when I was a Young'n, I wouldn't have never ended up doing twenty-five years in prison."

"What the fuck you do to get all that time Grey-Top?"

"Robbed a few banks. I only got caught up and convicted for robbing two of 'em though. Yep," Grey-Top sighed.

"I went in when I was twenty-one. I'm forty seven now."

"Damn! That's a mean joint to swallow there Grey-Top. You ain't had no pussy in twenty-five years? Man, I think I would have found a rope and took myself out da' game. Fuck all that!" Billy Boy playfully said.

He meant every word. He couldn't imagine going two days without getting a shot of pussy; let alone 25 years.

"When you live that life, you have to be able to take whatever comes with it youngster. See, back then, people knew their place in the game. You had your killers, your thieves, your pick pockets, your hustlers, your con men, your pimps and your bank robbers. Now it's all fucked. You Youngins' fucked the game all the way up. You tryna' be something you're not. You tryna' do shit you have no damn bid'ness doin'."

"Not me Grey-Top. I know my lane Slim."

"I can see that Youngster. Listen here, I've been on parole for a year now. I have been hearing all kinds of bullshit about the robbing game. I even heard they got three broads robbing banks now."

When he said that, Billy Boy swallowed hard, hearing the old man confirm his suspicions about Maria, Sunny, and Ruby. He just remained silent. He was trying to see what else the old man knew.

"That's what I mean about ya'll fucking up the game. See, but you, yeah you definitely know what you know. I guess that's why I'm pulling you up. I know you probably saying, what the fuck can this old ma'fucka pull me up on? Well it's like this Billy Boy, " he said.

He then started breaking it down to Billy Boy on how to be so young he had a lot going on for himself as far as his hustling abilities.

"I like your style young nigga," Grey-Top confessed.

That made Billy Boy smile.

"So I'ma pull you up on some good game here."

He looked Billy Boy straight in the eyes.

Grey-Top told him, "You can be the best damn pool shark in this town. Hell, the whole damn world. You just have to keep at it. Do not go outside your lane. Plus, you can play any kind of card game like Floyd Mayweather defending his pound-for-pound crown."

"Thanks Grey-Top."

"I'm not finished. I'm just saying, you and that other bad youngster Zap-Out can make a real good team. Ya'll have to put that work in. They got ma'fuckaz playing pool and poker on TV for millions and millions of dollars these days. My point to you is never get side tracked and put a pistol in your hand," he warned.

"You got the skills to rob anybody you come across with your intellectual capabilities. Your brain is the most dangerous pistol in the world. You just gotta' know how to work that ma'fucka. You dig where I'm coming from?"

"Yeah, I follow you Slim."

"Yeah, so just stick to what you know best and fuck all that other shit. You have a sure-fire winner in your hands and brains. You can't lose!" Grey-Top smiled.

"I will not lose!" Billy Boy repeated like Jay-Z.

He looked up just in time.

"Aww Shit!" Billy Boy cursed.

He slammed on the brakes.

"Damn, I almost ran that fucking red light! I could've got killed," he thought out loud.

"I gotta stay focused and stop reminiscing," he thought.

He knew everything the older man relayed to him was pure law. When Billy Boy thought about Maria, Sunny, and Ruby. The older man's knowledge about the dirt they were doing always seemed to jingle in his mind. It didn't take long for Billy Boy to make it home.

Parking the Camry a few houses from theirs, Billy Boy walked down the quiet street. He entered the house at 6:15 a.m. like it was nothing. Maria and Ruby had been deviated from the living room and retired to their bedrooms. While they slept peacefully, dreaming of God knows what, Billy Boy spotted Sunny in the kitchen.

He studied her curvy frame clothed in purple panties, matching bra, and a sheer black Teddy with matching black slippers. She was cooking some pancakes with buttery fried eggs and fried ham. With her back turned to the doorway, Sunny never heard Billy Boy enter the house.

Standing in the kitchen doorway, Billy Boy grabbed his dick through his slacks. He openly lusted over Sunny's incredible chocolate body. Her long, black hair hung just past her shoulders. He was tempted to just walk up on her, pull her hair, and fuck her brains out right there in the kitchen.

"Damn, she's a phat lil' ma'fucka. A precious chocolate gem that I would love to wear out," he thought.

Startled, she suddenly turned around and jumped.

"BOY! Omi God! Billy Boy! You scared the shit outta' me!" She said.

She placed a hand over her chest and felt her rapid heartbeat.

"Boy!"

She sucked her teeth.

"Why you ain't let me know you was standing there?"

"Cause it would've ruined my shot of dat' ass," he thought.

"Girl, you better start paying more attention to that door when it opens. If I was a burglar, rapist, or serial killer, your shit would have been through booking!"

"Boy, whatever!"

She sucked her teeth like she didn't care.

"Yeah, okay, keep on acting tough. You was slipping and I could've roasted your pretty chocolate ass just like that ham you cooking!"

"Okay Billy Boy. I get the point. Where the hell have your little young ass been at all night? You had us worried about you. Especially when you ain't answer your cell phone."

"Maria ain't too upset with me is she?"

"No, she was just worried you. You didn't call to let us know that you were okay. Me and Ruby assured her that you was straight. We told her that you was probably out somewhere shooting pool."

"I know I should've answered my phone or called ya'll, but I did come home and nobody was here. That's when it hit me that ya'll said ya'll was going out tonight. I left back out and went to this after hour spot with Zap-Out."

"With who?"

"Zap-Out, that's my man from around Brentwood. He's a good nigga too. Anyway, we got caught up in this poker game."

"I told Maria that you came home."

"How you know?"

"I seen that bowl you left in the sink. So, who won big at the poker game?" She asked.

She was bending over to check on the toast she had in the bottom toaster oven. That gave him a nice view of her chunky camel-toe.

"Baby Girl, when it comes to winning money from suckers, you already know I'm the best!"

They both started laughing as he desperately tried to sneak in another peak of her pussy. Her thick thighs overlapped and hid her prize.

"You want something to eat Billy Boy?"

He wasn't used to seeing her beautiful half naked body. Billy Boy kept staring at Sunny. He never even heard her question.

Sunny finally turned around from the stove and noticed him checking out her butt with pure lust in his eyes. She slowly slid her hand on her waist and leaned into her right hip. Her curvy hip exploded from underneath the Teddy. That turned him on tremendously.

"Billy, did you hear what I said?"

She sucked her teeth as he looked up and down at her luscious body.

"I guess you didn't. Boy, you better stop looking at me like that.

Do you want something to eat or not?"

"Damn, my bad Sunny. I didn't hear you. My mind was on something else."

"Yeah, I can tell!" She said.

The sarcasm was evident in her tone.

"You know what Sunny? The only thing I want to eat this morning is you."

"C'mon Billy, I'm not in the mood for playing them games wit' chu'. It's too early."

She took the rest of the food out of the frying pan. She put it on a platter-sized plate where the other food was cooling down. She turned the stove off. Sunny turned around toward Billy Boy who was staring into her eyes. The sight of her body gave him an instant hard-on.

"Sunny, I'm not playing no games. I'm serious as a ma'fucka about eating you up for breakfast."

"Boy, no!"

She denied his request.

"We like brother and sister. Me having sex with you would be inappropriate."

After a few minutes of silence and watching her eat, Billy Boy cracked on the pussy again. He was letting the weed he'd smoked earlier articulate his thoughts and Sunny didn't have a chance.

"Sunny, you don't have to be scared. You know we meant to be. Come on and let me be the one who makes you feel wonderful. I got the right kind of plunger you need to open up that pussy between your legs. I know you clogged up, cause you ain't had no dick since God knows when."

"How you know?" She asked.

She was staring him dead in the eyes.

"I could be fucking. You'd never even know a thing," she stated saucily while spooning up some food.

"I know you ain't fucking because of the way you always walk around this house. You be glued to every word Maria and Ruby say about their sexcapades with their men. I can tell that pussy is tight as fish pussy."

Sunny blushed. She's always been eager to give him some pussy, but she wanted to make sure that he really wanted her first. She'd been praying to God that he'd come around and realize that she was the only girl for him.

"You need to stop fighting the feelings you have for me. Let me rock your world. Just gimme' a shot at making you feel like Heaven on Earth. That's how much I'm sure of myself."

Looking into his eyes, Sunny knew he wasn't little Billy Boy anymore. He was a young man after her body and heart. She stood up and put the plate down. She sat it on the stove and covered it with a pan. Before she turned to walk away, Sunny gave him the opportunity to view her again from behind. Turning around, Sunny walked over to him and grabbed his hand. She never said a word. She led him to her bedroom.

Once they were inside, Sunny shut the door. She commenced to take her Teddy off, dropped it to the floor, and moved to the center of the room.

"There's nobody in here but you and me. So what chu' waiting for?"

She challenged him as he walked over to her. They stood in the middle of the floor and faced off for a few seconds. Then he took off her bra while licking on her neck. She turned her back to him. She slowly turned her face toward him. They locked lips automatically and engaged in a passionate tongue-kiss. As their tongues intertwined in a hot mating dance, he worked his hands over her breast. He gently pinched her dark nipples and moved from her lips. He drug his tongue down her pretty chocolate back until he reached her butt-crack. That gave her body the shivers.

Billy Boy pulled her panties down around her knees. All the while licking and kissing all over her soft behind and the back of her thighs.

"Mmmm," she moaned.

He licked her thighs and calves until he finished pulling off her panties. Her eyes lit up with pleasure as he swirled his tongue between her butt cheeks. Contact was made to her slick coated pussy lips. As she moaned with delightful pleasure, he licked her pussy. He lapped at her juices then slowly licked back up her butt crack. He stopped at her puckered anal hole. He licked around her ass-hole for a minute. That blew her mind. Nobody had ever made her feel like that before. Pure Heaven!

Sunny slowly gyrated her hips as he licked her entire body back up to her neck. He worked his way around to the front of her body; which made her heart skip a beat. Getting wetter by the second, Sunny leaned into his mouth while he planted soft kisses on her chocolate, firm breasts down to her flat stomach. The pleasure from his mouth gave her the instant urge to let go of the orgasm her body had been holding hostage until this moment.

"UNNNGGGHHHH! I JUST Ca-Ca- OMIGOD!" She gasped.

She was trying to re-enforce her body as the thick love juices gushed out of her throbbing twat.

Billy Boy smelled the sweet aroma of her climax and lodged his tongue into her oozing pussy. He got harder by the second while sucking and licking around her meaty pussy. Still standing in the middle of the floor with her legs spread wide, Sunny slumped down on his swirling tongue. She was feeling so weak that she had to grip his shoulders for support. His oral skills were driving her crazy.

"Ssss! Damn Billy! Unnngggh!" She moaned.

She was biting her bottom lip and palming the back of his head. He made his tongue shake inside her wetness, which made her quiver with each and every vibration.

In a moment's time, Sunny felt his finger tapping her G-Spot. He sucked on her clitoris like a newborn sucking on a baby bottle. He was holding her still and pulling her closer to another climax. Before she could let out another sound, her knees shook uncontrollably as she came so hard that she cried tears of joy. Climaxing again right after the first leg shaking orgasm blew her mind so much that she couldn't stop quivering from the waves of pleasure.

Sunny's mind swirled about a million miles a second. She couldn't believe that Billy Boy's tongue was making her feel so good. She thought she was flying in Seventh Heaven. It was a wonder that she didn't wake up Maria and Ruby with her loud, breathless moans of stimulating passion.

Her pussy was drenched with wetness. A shiny sheen of love juices was left on his face and chin. He picked her up, placed her on top of his shoulders, and ate her pussy while walking her over to the bed. Laying her down on the king size bed, he slipped out of his clothes with the quickness.

Sunny's eyes lit up with desire when she saw his smooth, brown, thick manhood standing straight up in the air. The beauty of it made her want to suck it and ride it. When he crawled between her legs, she stopped him.

"Let me ride it Billy," she whispered.

She mounted herself on top of him.

She shocked him when she impaled herself and made her pussy muscles clench his beef stick. That left him laid back in a trance. His face balled up in an ugly fuck face. Sunny began moving up and down on his fuck pole. She braced herself on his chest. His stiffness ripped into her tightness. The pain soon turned to pleasure. She bounced on him violently and met his upward strokes. Moans of ecstasy escaped both of their mouths and echoed around the bedroom. She bucked like a wild horse. That alerted him to the fact that she was loving the dick.

"AAAH! AAH BILLY! UNNGGGH!" She screamed.

He grabbed a handful of her breasts while fucking upward. He was picking up the pace. He felt her walls closing in on him. They got tighter and tighter as her pussy lips contracted.

"AAAH! Mmmm Billy!" She cried.

The gratification of another orgasm gripped her body. After regaining control of herself, Sunny pushed off him. She got on all fours and tooted her ass up in the air. She was now inviting him to hit it from the back. Billy Boy didn't waste any time mounting her from behind. He started riding her hard and slow. He pumped her good pussy until she begged him to go faster and faster.

"Faster Billy! Faster!" She urged.

He spread her cheeks apart as he fingered her ass hole at the same time.

They rocked back and forth. They fucked at a rapid pace. The breathing got heavier as they raced for the climax of a lifetime. Billy Boy could barely stand her soft behind slapping up against his pelvic bone. His legs buckled with every stroke until he couldn't hold back his eruption any longer.

"Yesss! Give it to me Billy! Fuck Me! Fuck Meeee!" She howled.

She came again as he grunted and exploded his warm load. He shot it deep inside her oozing twat. They climaxed together so hard that they fell out on the bed from exhaustion. They laid in each other's arms. They both were amazed at the mind-blowing sex they'd just shared.

Billy Boy kissed her and said, "Did I rock your world? You damn sure rocked mine with that good ass pussy you got. I think I'm in love!" He giggled.

That caused her to laugh.

"I don't think I climbed the walls like you said I would," she said.

She reminded him of his declaration. That caused more laughter between them.

"Shiiid'! I ain't see nobody coming up in here taking me out in a straight jacket like you claimed neither!" He countered.

They both laughed again.

"But for real Billy. Fa-Real Fa-Real. You did make me feel marvelous. Boy, where you learn how to eat pussy like that? For a minute, I thought I was gonna' go crazy from pleasure. You truly lived up to your word Boo."

She kissed him tenderly.

"'Preciate the compliment. I'd like to talk to you about something."

"Billy, I'm not changing the conversation or anything like that, but "If it's about what you, Maria, and Ruby have been doing, I already know all about it Sunny."

"What are you talking about?"

"C'mon Sunny, don't play with me. I'm talking about them banks ya'll been hitting."

Sunny gave him a peculiar look. She was trying to act like she didn't know what he was talking about.

"Sunny, don't look at me like that. I been knowing about the shit for a minute now. I just didn't want to scream on ya'll about the shit. At the time I didn't feel like it was any of my business. Plus, ya'll were paying the bills. But after my mom's died, I gave it some major thought. I reconsidered that notion. I feel like ya'll are my business."

"Billy Bo---."

"No listen to me Sunny," he cut her off.

"Ya'll are my family.The only family I have. I must be concerned about what ya'll are doing. I couldn't stand to lose anyone else close to me again."

"Billy, I feel where you're coming from whole heartedly. You don't have to worry about us. We're through with that bank robbery shit. Well, let me express it to you like this, I'm hanging up my guns. Those experiences were enough for me."

"Thank God," he sighed.

She hugged him closer to her.

"But I don't know about Maria and Ruby. Your mom's passing has took a ferocious effect on Maria. It has changed her into somebody I don't even know. Now all she wants to do is rob banks. We don't need the money. We still have enough cash between the three of us to flip it into some kind of legal business."

"Yeah Sunny. I jive seen the change in Maria too. You know she really took our mom's death hard. I think she may imagine in her mind that she's doing it for our mom. Even though moms is gone, it started from our her predicament."

"So what are we gon' do Billy?"

"I have confidence that Maria will come out of that trance she's engrossed in before it's too late. With my assistance, along with yours and Ruby's, we should be able to bring her out of that captivation she's in."

"I don't think Ruby is hip to Maria's mind state. I'ma go talk to her right now so---."

"Hold up," he stopped her.

"Let me get some more of you before they wake up."

"Sounds cool with me! Don't get sprung boy!"

They laughed as he leap-frogged on top of her. That caused her to laugh uncontrollably before their lips locked in a passionate tongue-kiss. That started them off on another round of mind blowing sex. That eventually turned into three more rounds. Maria's mind state was the furthest thing from their minds. They had hot, buttery, passionate sex. They eventually fell out into a deep, coma like sleep from exhaustion and sexual gratification.

CHAPTER 15

SUNNY DANCED TO SOME SONG in her head while she stood in the kitchen. She was seasoning a few porterhouse steaks that she planned on frying for dinner when she got off work. When Billy Boy slipped up behind her, she jumped. He slid his hands around her small waist and hugged her lovingly. Sunny was nervous that Maria or Ruby might catch them, but very happy to be in his loving embrace.

"Hey Sunny! How was your dick last night?" Billy Boy asked while cuddling her.

"It was fantastic as usual. It only gets better and better every time coming from you."

She leaned back and smelled the Diablo' Armani Cologne on him.

"Mmmm, you smell good."

She was glad that they finally made love. She was also happy that he was mature enough to keep it a secret. They'd been going at it for a little over a week now.

"How about you and my sister? Ya'll talk yet?"

Sunny would have loved to tell him yes, but she couldn't. Maria had been avoiding her lately.

"Naw. We haven't been seeing each other lately. You know I be working and all that now. I be coming home chilling out with you. I haven't had time to see anybody, but you."

"So what? You complaining now?"

"No, but I'm just saying Billy, if you keep fucking me the way you're doing, you're gonna get tired of me," she hinted.

160

She just wanted to see where he was as far as them being together for the long haul.

"Mmmm," he moaned.

He cupped her ass with his huge hands.

"I'll never get tired of this. Matter of fact, where's everybody at?" He asked seductively.

She automatically suspected that he had something nasty on his mind.

"Maria went out with Shooter last night and hasn't come home yet. Ruby's still sleeping. Why?" She asked.

She knew that he wanted her.

He couldn't keep his hands off her every since that first night they had sex.

"Sex, right before work. Damn, this young nigga's bringing some much needed excitement to my boring world," she thought.

Billy Boy was squeezing her breasts from behind. That made her nipples get hard instantly. Billy Boy led Sunny to his room. He removed her business skirt, blouse, and thong. He then propped her knees up on the large sofa cushions that lined the far wall of his room.

Grabbing Sunny roughly by the waist, he slammed his rock-hard dick in her violently. That caused her to suck in a huge whiff of air. He spanked her ass while fucking her hard as he could from behind. She gripped the shoulder of the sofa while taking the brutal pain that his sweet dick gave her until it turned into nothing but pleasure.

"He probably knows that I like it rough," she thought.

She raised her ass up higher in the air. She was loving the pounding strokes of his thick boner. She groaned in enjoyment. She reminisced on their first sexual encounter and all the others they'd shared leading up to the one they were about to experience.

"Unnngh! Shiiittt! Sssss! Yeah Billy! Yesss! Gimme' Dat Dick Billy! Fuck Me Harder Billy! Harder Damnit! Harder!" She panted.

Her urging was driving him crazy. Pumping faster and faster, Billy Boy's knees buckled. He was putting in some serious work on her pussy as he raced towards an early morning climax. Grabbing her ass cheeks, he plunged deep inside her and held her in place.

"OOH! SUNNAAARRRRGGHHH!" He cried out.

He shot his warm semen all up inside her.

Sunny smiled with glee as he collapsed on top of her. She enjoyed the feeling Billy Boy gave her. Nothing compared to the sensation of lust and hard fucking between them. It seemed as though his dick spell grew even more powerful with each time they fucked. She never wanted to lose that feeling.

"Mmmm Billy. You make me feel so good. You're just the wakeup call I needed for work. I'm the luckiest woman in the world," she said.

She moved from under him. Sunny grabbed her work clothes and deliberately switched her way out of his room. She was showing Billy Boy that her hips and jiggling ass could hold a spell of their own. Billy Boy whistled under his breath. He knew what Sunny was trying to do: Entice him to go after her. He looked at Sunny's jiggling ass as she left the room and immediately started shaking his head.

Billy Boy retrieved a towel and wash cloth from his dresser drawer. He then headed to the bathroom to take a shower and get ready for his day.

$ $ $ $ $

*M*EANWHILE, ACROSS TOWN, Shooter had just got out the shower with Maria. His cell phone started ringing. Maria gave him a funny look and waited while he answered the phone. Having nothing to hide from her, Shooter pushed the speaker phone button.

"What's up?"

"Shooter?" The soft-spoken female voice called out.

That made Maria give him an evil glare. They'd been having sex for a while now. Quite naturally, Maria claimed him as her man. She didn't want any other woman trying to come between them.

"Fuck is dis?"

"Lee-Lee," she mumbled.

Shooter got excited at the sound of her name, but had to play it off in front of Maria. Shooter had many women who loved giving him the pussy and any other sexual fantasy he wanted, but Maria was his heart. She was the only woman who ever held his attention for longer than a month.

"Didn't I tell your ass to stop calling my damn phone?" He asked rudely.

He caught Maria's gaze that had softened up some.

"DIDN'T I?"

"But Shooter, please listen,"she pleaded.

"Naw. You listen. You gold-diggin'-ass bitch! I don't want you and don't have shit for your ass!"

"But Shooter, what am I 'spose to do? If my rent don't get paid, I'll be out on the street!" She cried.

They had sex several nights ago and Shooter promised to pay her rent. He was looking for her to give her the money. He saw her at the Go-Go with some drug dealer. She was hanging all over him like a groupie. Shooter decided to let the drug dealer pay her rent if she was so happy with him.

"Well, you should have thought about that while you was shaking your ass at the Go-Go with your man, Bozack!"

"Please Shooter! Just give me the money! I promise I'll pay you back. Please! I'll even suc---."

"Fuck I look like? A mu'fuckin ATM?"

He cut her off. He knew she was going to offer him a blow job for the money. He didn't want Maria to hear that shit.

"Bank of America? I ain't giving you shit! Don't call me no more geekin'-ass bitch!"

He hung up on her without giving her another chance to speak.

"Who was that?" Maria asked.

She was trying her best not to go off on Shooter, or show her jealous side. She kept her composure.

"Oh, that was this little broad I used to fuck with before we met," he told her the truth.

"She still thinks I owe her something."

Maria pretended like his confession didn't faze her. Her body language told another story. She harshly rolled her eyes at Shooter and balled her face out of place. Shooter waved the phone away with one hand like it was an irritable fly. He reached out to Maria with the other.

"C'mon Maria. She don't mean shit to me. You do and you need to know. I'm gon' be here for you until the end of time. You hold my heart in your hands woman."

Maria's anger cooled a little. His smooth words were quite the equalizer as she began to blush. Just when Maria thought this episode was over, Shooter reached out and pulled her in for a hug. He sucked on her neck. That stimulated her raging hormones. He moved to her lips while sticking his tongue in her mouth. He started sucking on her with a greedy hunger. Maria moaned with delight.

"Mmmm! Okay Boo. I get the point," she panted.

She pushed away from him. Maria felt bad for doubting Shooter's feelings for her. She just wanted her man all to herself. She felt that other women would take his attention away from her. That was something that she didn't want to happen, Ever!

"You know we really should start working on our family."

Shooter tried to slide in as they walked inside his bedroom to get dressed.

"Shooter, I don't want to talk about that right now," she admitted.

A whole rack of other thoughts were swirling around inside her head at the moment.

Shooter peeped how Maria always avoided him whenever he brought up the subject of them making a baby. His bedroom phone rang. He looked at the caller ID. Fast Black was calling.

He picked up the cordless phone and spoke, "What's up Black?"

"You ready? I got a real sweet move for us. You have to roll with me now."

Shooter listened attentively while Fast Black went on. Shooter learned that Fast Black was driving the getaway car in a bank robbery for another guy from Southwest. The guy got shot up pretty bad two nights ago while partying at the Go-Go. The job was set to go down today.

"I'm there Scrap, just hold on," Shooter said.

He hung up and then looked at Maria.

"I have to go out and make a move real quick."

"You talking about having a baby, but you stay in the streets more than you stay with me.

How you ever gon' have time? All you do is rip and run the streets!" She complained.

Shooter refused to argue with Maria. He took out a pair of black True Religion jeans, a matching wool turtleneck, and some black Nike boots from the closet. He dressed quickly, loaded fresh clips in his guns, and gathered his bank robbing bag.

Maria peeped what he was doing and wanted to go along. She understood the risks he took to make a way for himself in the world. Maria also thought he respected her for the go-hard woman that she was. She now realized that he didn't really respect her, because he would've asked her to roll with him. Maria just stood in the doorway. She was watching Shooter sit on the edge of the bed as he laced up his boots. She loved his taste in clothing and sense of fashion until that moment. She realized that she loved everything about him. They had a whirlwind romance built solely off of danger, drama, and excitement. She missed doing those dangerous things with him.

"You just gon' go on a move and don't say shit to me, huh?"

"Maria, this move ain't being planned by me. I'm very aware of the risks this entails. I'm far from stupid. I'll never put you in that type of situation."

"Problem is you don't know what I can handle. You don't know that you have a real woman on your side. You seem to want to protect me from danger. Did you forgot that's how we met? Hopefully, you'll be able to open up your eyes about me before it's too late."

Shooter had no reply. He stared blindly off into space. In his heart, he knew what Maria was going through. She wanted him to feel obligated to take her with him on a move he knew nothing about. It was just some spur of the moment shit. Shooter had a feeling that if he didn't invite her, things would never be the same between them.

"So you saying you tryna' go? Even though you don't know shit about the job?"

Maria stepped towards the bed and kneeled in front of Shooter. She pulled his face to hers while cupping his chin in her hands. She was infatuated with what Shooter did for a living. She wanted to be a part of every aspect of his life.

"You know I want to go. I can watch your back, just like you did for us," she said kissing him.

Shooter didn't know when it happened, but it did. He sensed that Maria was beginning to get addicted to robbing banks. That was a bad habit he'd picked up right after robbing his first bank.

$ $ $ $ $

45 MINUTES LATER, Fast Black parked the stolen Range Rover outside the bank in Chevy Chase, Maryland. Maria and Shooter got out. They walked cautiously towards the bank. They were more than ready to put in work. Maria was nervous. She couldn't believe that Shooter had actually brought her along on such short notice. Maria knew there was no turning back if she wanted to prove her worth to Shooter. Shooter surveyed the traffic in the bank as they were walking. The bank was extremely crowded.

"You ready?" He asked Maria.

He put on his shades and adjusted his dreadlock wig.

"Yeah, let's go."

Maria nodded while peeking around. She had on a strawberry

blond wig and a pair of mirror-tinted shades.

Shooter stepped towards the door and yanked it open. He brought up the 240 NATO Medium machine gun only to see Maria already disarming the guard in the corner.

Releasing a warning shot, Shooter ran over by the counter yelling out, "EVERYBODY ON THE FLOOR! NOW! NOW! NOW!"

From a distance, Shooter spotted a female reaching under the counter. She was probably going for the silent alarm. Shooter bolted over to her with his gun held high. He hopped over the counter and saw the blinking red light. He didn't have a clue how much time they had before the cops arrived.

Shooter pulled out a trash bag and started filling it with money from all six teller drawers. He was careful to stay away from the bait money and dye packs. The teller that hit the silent alarm thought she was safe, until she spotted Shooter running towards her.

"NOOO!" She screamed.

"Shut Up! Hot Bitch!" Shooter snapped.

He kicked her in the face and knocked out her two front teeth. He then leaped back over the counter with the loot.

Shooter and Maria ran full speed from the bank into the street while concealing their guns. They hustled over to the Range Rover where Fast Black had parked. Fast Black sped away down Chase Blvd. doing 60 miles an hour. Shooter and Maria tossed their disguises out the window while looking around nervously.

"Fuck happen in 'nere?" Fast Black screamed.

Several police cars sped towards them.

"One of the tellers hit the mu' fuckin alarm button!" Shooter said.

He was damn near lying on the floor under the back seats. He was scared to death of getting caught. He changed out of his clothes quickly while Fast Black drove.

Fear also filled Maria as she thought about getting caught. She wondered how Shooter knew the teller had hit the alarm. She missed all that and she had her eyes on everything at once.

"Please God! Don't let us get caught!" she said under her breath.
"You took my mother from me and Billy Boy. You can't take me from him too, please!" She silently prayed.

Her heart pounded vigorously from being totally shook up.

Fast Black drove while watching the approaching police cars. He slowed down a little as they passed him. He kept peeking behind him, using all his mirrors. Two police cars turned around. That made Fast Black extremely nervous. Fast Black got real paranoid as the police cars inched closer to him.

"Them peoples on my back Shooter!"

"Fuck you telling me for? Either you get us outta' here, or I'm bussin' my way out!"

Knowing what he had to do, Fast Black mashed the gas pedal. He pushed the Range Rover to over 100 miles an hour. His speeding confirmed the pursuing cop's suspicions. Seconds later, Fast Black made a dangerous turn trying to desperately get away from the chasing police cars.

Maria had a shocked expression on her face. She had no idea of knowing that Fast Black would try to flee without knowing the cops were actually chasing them. She looked back nervously as her heart dropped into her pussy.

"SCUUURRRR!" Came the sounds of the Range Rover's tires.

They screeched loudly as Fast Black slammed on brakes while making another quick turn. The sound of police sirens were deafening. Maria wanted this nightmare to end. Microseconds later, another police car appeared at the end of the block. It was racing full speed and approaching on a collision course.

"GO! GO!" Maria screamed.

Fast Black sped towards the cruiser. He was now playing a dangerous game of chicken.

Shooter looked up to peep out the scene. By now, the cop car was inches away from crashing into them. Shooter leaned out of the back driver's side window and fired the machine gun. He was peppering the cop car's front windshield. The police cruiser swerved out of the way to avoid being shot at again.

Fast Black continued on his escape route. He made two more quick turns. By now, only one car was chasing them from about a half a block away. The second car stopped at the scene where the shot up police car had stopped.

"Get the fuck outta' here Black!" Shooter urged.

The fear was now consuming him.

Shooter wondered if he'd killed the cops or not.

"Drive this joint Nigga! Drive!" Shooter said.

He slapped the back of Fast Black's seat. Thoughts of life in prison invaded his mind if he had indeed murdered a police officer.

Fast Black raced through several back streets recklessly. The police car stayed right behind them. Maria pressed her face into her hands and started crying hysterically. Her sobbing did something to him. Fast Black knew he couldn't let them get caught with Maria in the car. He had a new will to escape. Fast Black stomped on the gas pedal. He was gunning the engine even harder.

Nearing the corner, Fast Black started swerving from side to side. He was trying to confuse the police on which way he was going to turn: Right or Left? Faking to the right, then back to the left, and then back to the right. Fast Black got the police to take the bait. They swerved to the right behind him almost bending the corner. Fast Black cut the steering wheel hard to the left. He made a full turn and left the police a few feet back. Fast Black sped down the block and spotted two more police cruisers up ahead.

"SHIT! SHIT! SHIT!" Fast Black barked.

He saw the road block ahead. He made a quick left instead of driving straight into their trap.

"SHOW EM' WHY DEY CALL YOU FAST BLACK NIGGA! SHOW EM'!" Shooter yelled frantically from the back seat.

Fast Black made another quick right and jumped on Central Avenue. In the distance, Shooter spotted at least eight police cars behind them. When Fast Black made the right turn, he got the shock of his life. He saw two more police cars facing each other at the light. They acted as a road block. The cruisers blocked the escape route entirely.

Continuing forward with no regard or signs of giving up, Fast Black sped towards them. The cops aimed their weapons at the speeding vehicle. They were hoping to force the driver to stop. Right before impact, Fast Black cut the steering wheel hard to the left. He bounced over and then landed in the middle of the street. He then jumped into the on-coming traffic lane.

Shots from the police exploded just as the Range Rover swerved into on-coming traffic. The SUV rocked slightly as several bullets chined into the side doors and windows; shattering them on impact.

"AAAAAAHHH! AAAAAAAIIIIIEEEEE!" Maria screamed.

 She was terrified at being shot at.

Fast Black drove even faster out of fear that they were trying to kill them. He continued speeding on the wrong side of the street for several more blocks before jumping back onto the right side of the street. He was desperately searching for a quick getaway.

Peeking around nervously, Fast Black spotted a Baltimore/Washington Parkway exit sign up ahead. Looking in his rear view mirrors again, he knew he had a good enough lead on them to take the exit and get ghost.

"Ain't no way dey' catching us now!" Fast Black said with confidence.

 He took the exit quickly. Once he got on the parkway, Fast Black pushed the Range Rover to the limit. He created as much distance between them as possible. At the next exit, Fast Black got off the parkway and drove through several back streets in Riverdale, Maryland. There wasn't a police car in sight.

"Damn! That was close as shit Slim!"

Shooter released a burly sigh. He was relieved and happy about the outcome.

"Man! That shit was my rec'! You hear me? You know damn well dem' peoples can't fuck with me!" Fast Black boasted.

"What's my ma'fuckin name?"

"You did dat' Fast Black! You did dat'!" Shooter said with glee.

Shooter was setting Fast Black's props out.

 Maria just sat there quietly. She was wiping the last of her tears away. She was so scared that she couldn't even speak.

Fast Black drove them to safety.

"WOOOOOO! Damn I'm good!" Fast Black whistled.

He was replaying the hectic car chase in his head that he barely escaped.

CHAPTER 16

SHOOTER DECIDED THAT IT WOULD BE BEST that they all laid low for a minute just to make sure that they were in the clear. They got a little over $28,500 from the bank. That was a huge disappointment in Shooter's eyes. After breaking down the money three ways, they only got $9,500 and some change. Shooter felt it wasn't worth it, considering all the shit they went through to get away. Hours later, they all chilled over Maria's house.

Maria was sure that they were going to jail for bank robbery during the police chase. Memories of the police chase still had her shook up. She sat in front of the TV in her bedroom watching the news. She appreciated her freedom more, knowing she was close to losing it a few hours before.

Flicking through the channels, Maria paused on Fox-5 News. The bank they'd robbed was on the screen in the background while a reporter positioned herself in front of the camera. The TV screen also had a lot of news vans and police vehicles in the background.

"SHOOTER C'MERE FOR A SECOND!" Maria called him.

"BRING BLACK WIT' CHU' TOO!" She added.

Shooter came to her room in seconds.

"What's up?"

"Where's Black?" She asked.

"I think he's in nere' fucking with Ruby," Shooter informed her.

He flopped on the bed as the tall white female news reporter appeared on the screen.

"Good evening. I'm Shelly Tackett. Fox-5 is live on the scene here in Chevy Chase, Maryland where earlier a bank robbery took place at this bank you see behind me. It left one woman badly injured. Our sources tell us that the injured woman, who works in the bank, triggered a silent alarm. That alerted the authorities to the area," the reported said.

The screen flashed back to the scene in the bank. The surveillance cameras in the bank caught Shooter on tape kicking the woman in the face. Only his wig and shades could be seen from a high view.

"That ain't shit. Damn near everybody in the city got dreads," he thought.

He knew he was cool to walk the streets without having to worry about being arrested for that robbery .

"Why you do that lady like that Bo---."

"Hold up Maria, let me catch everything."

He cut her off as the screen flashed back to the reporter.

"I'm getting reports that the suspects fled the scene in a grayish Range Rover. An unidentified man, the same one in the bank footage you just saw, opened fired on an approaching police cruiser. He wounded the driver and his partner. The suspects took the police on a dangerous chase through the Chevy Chase streets. They were jumping onto the wrong sides of traffic just to evade capture. The police officers are listed in stable condition right now at Bethesda Naval Hospital Center. These violent suspects still remain at large. I'm Shelly Tackett. Fox-5 News. Now back to you Paul."

Maria changed the station.

She was trying to find any more coverage about their infamous crime. On another station, a large picture of her in the disguise along with Shooter's picture covered the screen. Maria's heart started beating twenty-million times per second. She couldn't believe that they had made the news. While they were in the car chase, Maria kept praying that nobody got hurt during their pursuit of freedom. Now that they had gotten away, Maria didn't care if the cops lived or died. Maria figured it was meant for them to get away being as though God took her mother away from her. She also took it as a sign that they should go on more robberies in the very near future.

"Listen Maria," Shooter whispered.

I'm sorry you had to go through that today. I warned you didn't I? I told you shit be gettin' hectic from time to time!"

"I know babe. We got away and that's all that matters right?"

Maria nodded a few times.

"You sumptin' else. You know that?"

"How scared were you today?" She asked him.

"I was jive scared as a mu'fucka for real. I just couldn't see myself going out like that, especially not over no punk ass ninety-five hundred!"

"That's all we got?"

"Naw, it was twenty-eight and some change. After the three way split, that's how much we got."

"Damn, I might need you to fuck me to sleep. I need to get away from this nightmare."

She smiled as she crawled up on the bed with him.

"You know I'm just da' nigga to do it too," Shooter laughed.

Maria went for his zipper. They made love for hours. Shooter gave her exactly what she wanted. As promised, Shooter fucked her to sleep, then he got up and left her house to go put his money away.

Inside Ruby's room, Fast Black explained the details of the car chase. He faked like he had his escape planned. Ruby listened in awe. She was doubting very seriously that Fast Black's tale was true. When he told her to look outside at the Range Rover, Ruby stared in a daze at the bullet riddled SUV. She knew now that he wasn't bullshitting her. As she stared at the Range Rover, Ruby felt grateful to Fast Black for making sure that Maria made it home safely. Even feeling obligated to give him some *"Thank You Pussy."*

At first, Ruby thought that he was just making the story up just to get in her panties. She was playing hard ball with the pussy when he first asked for some. It took nearly three hours and some change for him to convince her that his tale was true. The later it got, the harder to get Ruby played. After seeing the news about them, Ruby couldn't imagine how she would have reacted if Maria would have called her from jail.

Ruby got up and turned off the lights. She crept back to her bed slowly. Fast Black tackled her. They play wrestled and laughed for a moment. Then lust overtook them. It urged them on to have the best sex of their lifetime.

$ $ $ $ $

*T*HE NEXT **MORNING**, Fast Black walked out of their house and jumped back in the stolen Range Rover. He pulled off quickly as usual, with no idea that it would be the last time he'd ever see Ruby, Maria, Sunny, and Billy Boy again. While pulling off, Fast Black got a call from his cousin Bee-Bee. He started explaining to Fast Black how important it was that they meet up somewhere soon.

"What's so important Cuzzo?"

"Look, I'll tell you when I see you. You know I don't do too much talking on these phones."

"Look, I'm going over my mutha's joint right now."

"Bet. I'll meet you over there."

ONCE THEY MET, Bee-Bee informed Fast Black that he had a sweet caper that he wanted him to go on. He told Fast Black that he would break bread on the money 50-50. Not hurting for money, Fast Black sighed. He didn't really want to tell his cousin no, being as though they were real cool.

"Cuzzo, gimme' a few days and check back with me."

The rejection made Bee-Bee furious; yet he understood his cousin's wishes.

"Rrr-ight! I'm coming back in a few days too nigga!"

"Okay, geekin'-ass nigga! I'ma drive for you. Just gimme' some time to rest," he said.

He never told his cousin about the car chase that he barely escaped.

Bee-Bee gave his cousin a hug then left. He prepared himself to do more studying on what was about to take place in a few more days.

$ $ $ $ $

*R*UBY CALLED SUNNY AT WORK so she could tell her all about the details of Shooter, Maria, and Fast Black's infamous crime. Sunny had steam coming out of her ears while she listened to Ruby glamorizing Maria's episode.

"This bitch is crazy! Ain't nothing cute or funny about that shit!" Sunny thought.

She made her mind up to tell Ruby about herself soon as she got home. Then she'd step to Maria who was getting beside herself and give her a piece of her mind also.

"Ruby, I gotta' go."

"What?" Ruby asked kind of puzzled.

"If you forgot. I'm working!" Sunny replied.

Her response had a hard-edge dripping with sarcasm.

"Working my ass! Naw, you acting funny! Why?"

"Ain't nobody acting funny!" Sunny sucked her teeth.

"Yes you is! You need to come clean with me before you get off this phone!"

Ruby wasn't naive by a long shot. She knew when people were throwing her shade. Sunny's attitude wasn't making any sense to her. Ruby felt that Sunny wasn't really down for her like she was down for Maria. Lately, it seemed like she was purposely trying to destroy their friendship.

"C'mon Ruby. Don't do this. I'll talk to you later," she sighed.

She hoped Ruby would get the hint and let her go.

"Yeah, whatever. I just called you about our girl. You acting all funny and shit. I thought we was family, but I see you on some other shit. Every since you got that weak-ass job, you been acting like your shit don't stink!"

Ruby hung up on Sunny. That made her mad as shit.

Sunny looked at her cell phone in shock and fury. She could only imagine what Ruby was saying about her back home. She wanted to go and give Ruby a piece of her mind and fist if it came to that, but Sunny was stuck at work. She had a feeling if she left early without a valid excuse, she wouldn't have a job to return to. She returned to work; shaking her head from side to side. She hated the fact that Ruby got out on her over the telephone.

"What the hell is happening to us?" She asked herself over and over for the duration of her stay at work .

$ $ $ $ $

AT THE SAME TIME, Billy Boy walked out of his house and jumped into the passenger seat of Zap-Out's used dandruff hued Nissan ZX. Zap-Out pulled off quickly. Zap Out bought the ride right after the night of the murders.

The lady of the house, Ms. Brooklyn got off with 5 years probation for being in possession of an unlicensed firearm. Once the investigation confirmed her story, the D.C. prosecutor declined to pursue the indictment for 2 counts of murder against Ms. Brooklyn.

Today they were getting off to a late start. It was a little after 10 in the morning. Normally, they would have been in school getting into all types of hustles. Every since the murders, Zap-Out had been acting more arrogant and pressing people. Billy Boy wondered how far Zap-Out would go before he killed somebody else. Every time he watched Zap-Out and his actions, Billy Boy thought about the old hustler, Grey Top's lecture: ***Just stick to what you know best. Every time you go*** *outside your lane, disaster strikes!*

Zap-Out stopped at a traffic light on Benning Road and Minnesota Avenue. He dug into his pants pocket and retrieved a sandwich bag of Purple Haze and Hydro mixed weed. He gave it to Billy Boy. He almost shoved it in his face.

"Twist something up Cuzzo. We need to be nice and twisted before we reach our destination. I got some woods in the glove compartment."

Billy Boy found the pouch of Backwoods Sweet Cigars. He quickly rolled up three marijuana laced cigars. Zap-Out turned on the Satellite Radio.

It already had Nas', **Made You Look remix** playing, "And everything is real I see. Like my niggaz that just came home, but only have a jail I.D.! And I still buzz. Sumpin'-Sumpin-Sumpin. Cuz you know the flow's ill just like Will was!"

Zap-Out rapped along with Jadakiss's scorching verse. He was bobbing his head to the banging sounds.

"Ay'! Kiss dat' nigga Slim!" Billy Boy said cheerfully.

He was setting out Jadakiss's props before firing up one of the spliffs.

"Ay'! Where we going anyway?" He asked.

Zap-Out zoomed in the opposite direction of their school.

"The old broad, Ms. Brooklyn, wanted to holla at me and you."

"For what?" He asked puzzled as hell.

"I don't know, but she said it's important. I couldn't duck her, because she jive took a beef for a nigga, you dig."

"True dat!" Billy Boy said.

His mind flashed back to that scary night. It was a night he'd never forget.

"Ay' Zap. Maybe we need to really step it up on the pool shark tip," he suggested.

He passed Zap-Out the spliff. He took several deep tokes on the spliff. Zap-Out thought about Billy Boy's suggestion and all the negative things in life he was doing. Zap-Out also thought of the power that killing gave him. He loved that feeling and never wanted to lose it.

"Pool shark?" He asked sarcastically.

He exhaled the chronic fumes.

"Fuck playing pool Billy Boy! I got my eyes on a bigger prize," he explained.

He passed the spliff. Hearing that, Billy Boy got fidgety sitting in the passenger seat. He wanted to say something to show Zap-Out there's another way out. There was another way to get rich, but he couldn't seem to find the words.

$ $ $ $ $

*M*S. BROOKLYN OPENED THE DOOR FOR THEM. She had been out of business every since the night Zap-Out killed the two men in her spot. She didn't know where to turn. Most of her money was gone due to her mounting legal bills. Ms. Brooklyn would lose her house if she didn't do something fast to get some money. After all the drama, Ms. Brooklyn realized how much she put herself on the line. She had a son and a grandson in prison who needed her. She hadn't been able to help them since that night. That made her feel like a piece of shit.

As they entered her house, Ms. Brooklyn gave both of them a hug and a kiss on the cheek. Zap-Out and Billy Boy took a few steps into the spacious living room and found a spot on the sofa. Ms. Brooklyn sat down slowly to conceal her nervousness.

"Hey boys. What I wanted to see ya'll about. Well."

Zap-Out sensed the apprehension in her demeanor. His eyes were drawn to her trembling lips. He instantly sensed trouble.

"What's up Ms. Brooklyn?" He asked.

"I'm hurting boys. That thing you did really blew up my spot. I had something real nice going on here before that happened. I have people that depend on me to survive."

Billy Boy and Zap-Out watched her closely, trying to figure out where she was going with her words. They were trying to figure out if she was going to ask them for help or try to blackmail them.

"So what chu' tryna' say Ms. Brooklyn?" Zap-Out probed.

"Honey, it needs no explanation. I need for ya'll to get this place back up and running soon before they take my house from me. I'm three months behind on the rent."

She fanned herself while fighting back the urge to cry.

"For real-for real, I ain't nowhere like that on the cash tip, but I'll do what I can to help you out," Billy Boy volunteered.

"Thank you baby. I'ma really need your help."

Zap-Out hesitated. He didn't want to outshine his partner. He felt obligated to assist the woman who risked her ass to save his. Digging in his pocket, Zap-Out pulled out a wad of bills. He peeled off $500 and gave her the rest of his bank roll.

"That's like $5,700. I wish I had more to give you. I'm still scraping out here to survive, you know."

"Thank you so much baby! Thank ya' hear!" She smiled.

She clutched the money so tight that they saw her fingers turn white from the pressure.

After spending two hours with her discussing various ways to open her gambling spot back up, Ms. Brooklyn cooked them lunch. They wolfed down the fried chicken, collard greens, mashed potatoes, and Spanish rice like hungry slaves. The chronic they smoked gave them a serious case of the munchies.

"Here's my number and an extra house key. Just call me any time before you come over.

"You family now," she told them.

Zap-Out took the house key and phone number from her. Ms. Brooklyn started crying. Zap-Out nor Billy Boy could find the right words to comfort her. They spoke what was on their hearts.

"We won't never leave you out there," Zap-Out said.

"Yeah, we promise to make sure you get back on your feet," Billy Boy added.

They left her house and watched her as she stood on the front porch waving good-bye to them. Zap-Out felt the Glock-45 on his side.

He decided the only way to relieve Ms. Brooklyn of her uncomfortable living arrangements was to go hard. He knew doing dirt to help out Ms. Brooklyn was dangerous, but for some reason she was loyal to him. When one finds a woman who is loyal like Ms. Brooklyn, he has to aid and assist her because she'll always have his best interest at heart. Another reason Zap-Out wanted to help was because she lent him a helping hand when he didn't expect her to. He could no longer worry about what was right or wrong; nor who got hurt. What had to be, had to be, whether he liked it or not.

"Damn Slim. We really gotta' step it up now and help Ms. Brooklyn," Billy Boy said.

Zap-Out drove away from her house.

He thought, *"You took the words right outta' my mouth Billy Boy."*

CHAPTER 17

MARIA HAD JUST PUT THE FINISHING TOUCHES ON HER make-up when she heard the front door slam along with loud arguing. She was waiting on Shooter to come pick her up. They were going up to Georgetown to eat and hang-out for the evening. Maria didn't want no beefing going on in her house. She decided to go and intervene before things go too out of hand. Maria threw on her sandals and rushed from her bedroom.

Maria entered the living room only to find Sunny standing toe-to-toe with Ruby. They were looking like they were about to rumble.

"WHY THE FUCK YOU SAY ALL THAT SLICK SHIT THEN HANG UP ON ME?" Sunny yelled at Ruby.

"WE COOL BUT NOT DAT' DAMN COOL FOR YOU TO BE TRYNA' CARRY ME AND SHIT!" She snapped again.

Ruby snapped back at her. She was waving her index finger in Sunny's face.

"Sunny don't come up in here disrespecting me! I just spoke da' truth! If da' truth hurts, then oh well!"

Ruby rolled her eyes at Sunny.

"OH WELL WHAT? WHAT CHU' WANNA DO?" Sunny snapped.

She started taking off her earrings.

"You got me all the way fucked up! We can thump up in this bitch for real!"

"Fuck you Sunny. I ain't ducking shit."

Ruby spoke rather calmly. She was not backing down.

Maria intervened. They'd gone too far. All the things they'd been through together. Fighting each other should have never even crossed their minds.

"C'mon with dat' shit ya'll. We are family. Ya'll know that shit ain't right," Maria butted in.

"Naw, her fake-ass came at me first with dat' bullshit!" Ruby said angrily.

She waited for Sunny to make the first move so she could beat her ass.

Sunny turned on Maria and went off. She was putting her right in the middle of it.

"You shut up! This shit is all your mutherfuckin' fault anyway!" She spat.

"My fault?" Maria asked in a baffled manner.

"Yeah, if you wasn't out there still with dat' robbing banks shit, Ruby would've never called me at work about that shit! I wouldn't have no reason to be pissed off!"

Before Maria could say anything, the doorbell chimed several times. That put an end to the back and forth bickering. Maria gave Sunny and Ruby evil looks as she went to answer the door.

"That's it? You ain't got shit to say?" Sunny fumed.

"Sunny, not right now. I'm still gon' do what the fuck I wanna do. You not my mother, she's dead! You can leave me the fuck alone!" She insisted.

She then opened the door. Sunny rolled her eyes at Maria, but said nothing. Ruby walked away from Sunny. She was still mad, but played it off.

"Okay Maria. I'll see you later girl!" She said.

She was gritting on Sunny who walked off to her bedroom.

Shooter stood in the doorway holding a bouquet of long stem yellow, red, and white roses. He was sporting a dark green Armani Exchange polo shirt, a black leather jacket, some blue Moschino paper denim and cloth jeans, and some black-on-black Timberland Euro-Hikers. His understated look was set off by a huge diamond earring in his right ear and a jewel encrusted wrist watch.

"Hey Baby Gir---."

"KEEP ON FAKING RUBY, I'M TELLING YOU!" Sunny yelled. She cut Shooter off. She was not letting the look Ruby gave her go.

"Whatever Sunny. Gone get chu' some dick so you can stop being so emotional about everything!" Ruby teased her as Shooter entered the house.

Maria couldn't believe that they were still going at it in front of her man like that.

'SO YA'LL JUST GON' DISRESPECT MY COMPANY LIKE DAT?" Maria yelled.

"No disrespect to you Shooter, but we just going through a lil' sumptin'-sumptin' right now," Sunny spoke up.

Ruby slammed her bedroom door. She laid on her bed and started crying out of anger. She couldn't believe Sunny came at her sideways for putting her on point about Maria. Ruby thought she was doing the right thing. After going through that episode, Ruby vowed to never share any news or anything else with Sunny. That way, she'd never have to worry about coming to blows with her over frivolous bullshit.

BACK IN THE LIVING ROOM, Maria gathered up the roses and took them into the kitchen. Sunny followed her. Maria closed the kitchen door for privacy. She then put the roses in a jar of water.

"Look Sunny, I don't care about your fucking feelings, cause evidently you don't care about mine. The way you just disrespected my man was unacceptable. Like I said before, my mother is dead. I don't know who you think you is all of a sudden, but all this brand new shit you doing don't faze me at all. I seen the signs of you switching up, but I didn't want to believe the shit. You've been my girl since back in the day."

Maria paused and stared at Sunny who looked like she was about to cry.

"You can't forget about where we came from. Keep in mind what got us in this big ass house that we arguing in right now. You have left me no choice but to give it to your ass in the raw. Bitch! Don't Ever Forget We Family! The one game I don't play is switching up on family. You stay loyal to the end, regardless. Right or wrong!"

Maria broke Sunny down to pieces. Sunny rolled her eyes then leaned against the stove.

"Maria, you still out here robbing banks don't make no damn sense," she hissed.

"We have more than enough money."

"Enough is never enough with me. I'm not ever going back to living in them pissy smelling hallways in Southeast and not being able to take care of my family!" Maria told her before leaving the kitchen.

That basically was telling her: End Of Discussion!

Sunny stood in the kitchen's doorway looking mad as hell. Shooter escorted Maria out the front door. Sunny paced back and forth in the living room for a few minutes after Maria left. She then headed to her bedroom. She walked by Ruby's room and stood there for a minute just looking at the door. Sunny didn't want to go to bed without talking to Ruby.

Sunny knocked on the door really hard. She wanted to make sure she was heard. Ruby opened the door with an attitude along with a mean look on her face.

"What the hell do you want now Sunny?" She barked.

Her attitude reminded Sunny of how badly she felt for venting her frustrations and anger on the wrong person.

"Girl, just hear me out for a second. I got some shit to get off my chest," Sunny said.

She shoved past Ruby and then entered her room. Ruby allowed Sunny into her bedroom and watched her flop on her bed.

"So talk," Ruby demanded.

She folded her arms across her breasts. She had on an oversized H.O.B.O. t-shirt and some multi-colored ankle socks. That was her sleeping gear.

"Ruby, I'm going to apologize to you. I feel really fucked up for going off on you. Maria just pointed out some shit to me. That made me realize I was totally wrong. I was just so damn mad about hearing that shit she did coming from you. I just couldn't handle it. You was telling me like the shit was cute. That shit really had me twisted. I'm sorry Ruby. Can you please forgive me?"

Sunny didn't know how long Ruby stood there looking at her, but she didn't say a word. That made Sunny feel even worse than before.

"Ruby, I said I'm sorry."

"Sorry ain't gon' cut it Sunny. I thought we were cool and you said all that fucked up shit to me. You were acting like I was just some nothing-ass bitch out on the streets. You wanted to fight me!"

The tone in Ruby's voice was full of anger.

"Ruby, I was faking like shit. I never wanted to fight you," she answered truthfully.

The truth of the matter was Sunny was blinded by anger. She didn't really want to fight Ruby.

Ruby was surprised that Sunny came clean. She smiled when she sensed that Sunny's apology was indeed genuine.

"Now all you gotta' do is cook me something to eat to make it up to me."

"Ruby, I'm tired as shit for real. I'll go and cook you something to eat if it means that much to you."

She raised up off Ruby's soft king size bed and headed for the door.

"Girl, you ain't got to cook me nothing today, but you gon' cook for me."

Ruby gave Sunny a hug and squeezed her. They didn't say anything for a minute. They just held each other like loving sisters. When the hug ended, Sunny stepped out into the hallway.

"And for your info' Miss Thing, I be getting some Dick! Some Good Big Dick at that!"

"Oooh for real? Girl who?" Ruby laughed.

She found Sunny's statement rather amusing and farfetched.

Sunny didn't respond. She just stepped off and back pedaled towards her bedroom. She just stared at Ruby like she was offended about being asked to reveal her and Billy Boy's secret.

$ $ $ $ $

AN HOUR LATER, Shooter and Maria entered Smith's Point Bar/Club. The upscale restaurant/nightclub was crowded with preppy white and black men dressed in pressed khakis and sport coats. They were vying for attention from women in knee-length skirts and modest tops. Maria felt out of place around the usual conservative crowd. She was dressed in a pair of orange, tiger striped leather pants and matching leather top.

"Relax Baby Girl. What? Chu' ain't been around white people before?" Shooter asked jokingly.

They sat on the stools at the center of the main bar that was actually a huge fish tank. Maria could see the fish swimming through the counter-top.

"Pssst," she sucked her teeth.

"Boy please, I'm from Kentucky! Ain't nothing but white people out there!"

"Damn, I could've sworn that you was a city girl the way you be going and shit."

"Well, I came to D.C. when I was young. You can say the city rubbed off on me."

Maria and Shooter enjoyed each other's company as they were talking and enjoying drinks. All the while being surrounded by a small entourage of other couples, undercover homosexuals, and lesbians. Most club goers seemed oblivious to Maria and Shooter's presence. They just respecting their privacy.

"Ay'! What was up with Sunny and ya'll earlier?"

Maria didn't say anything. She just kept staring at him and continued nodding her head to the John Mayer song blaring from the speakers. She was enjoying the date too much and didn't want nothing to ruin it.

"It wasn't nothing. It was just some girl talk. We do it like that all the time," Maria lied.

She took a sip from her Moet/Mimosa cocktail.

"You sho' threw me off with that," he laughed.

"I thought that ya'll was tighter than that."

"We are. Right now I'm here with you. They shouldn't matter right?" She said.

She was licking her lips.

"So you might as well get them off your mind so we can finish enjoying the rest of our night," she added.

She pulled him on the dance floor. Within minutes, Maria was dropping it like it was hot. She was bumping and grinding her soft behind up against Shooter. Shooter stayed glued to her ass for a few minutes. He was trying to keep himself from getting hard, but it still happened.

When he got hard, Maria jumped a little, then turned on him and pulled him closer to her. Seconds later, Shooter felt her hand wrapping around his boner. She kept dancing and looking up at him.

"Maria, you know what chu' doing right?"

He palmed her behind so he could press up on her fully.

"Yeah, I'm trying to get some dick," she giggled.

She then kissed him.

She put his stiffness back in his jeans and zipped his fly back up.

"Meet me in the ladies bathroom in five minutes."

"Girl, you a freak!"

"Only for you though," she smiled.

She kissed him again before walking away.

Within minutes, Shooter was fast stepping right behind her to the ladies restroom. They found a stall and kissed for a few minutes. They were trying to get up enough nerve to have sex in public. Maria pushed him on the toilet stool as she eased her leather pants down. She stepped out of her right pants leg. She removed her peach colored thong and sat on his lap.

"Take it out for me Boo," she said in husky tone.

She was steady grabbing at his belt buckle.

Shooter lowered his pants until they were around his ankles. Maria began guiding his thick sword into her wetness. He stopped her when he heard the bathroom door open.

"Hold up for a minute," he whispered.

"Somebody's out there."

"So what? It makes it more exciting," she giggled.

She then lowered her wet pussy onto his upstanding meaty pole.

Maria slid her hips back and forth as she made slow, circular moves on the dick. Shooter palmed her soft behind. He was breathing heavy as he dug up inside her tight-sweet nectar.

"Ssss! Shooter! Unnggh!" She grunted.

She slowly grinded on his impaling shaft. They slowly fucked as numerous women entered and left the bathroom. Shooter sucked on her breasts through her leather top. It felt good, but not good enough. Maria removed her top and dropped it on the bathroom floor. Shooter sucked on her pouty hard nipples while raising her off his stabbing boner.

"Unnngggh Shooter!" She moaned.

She slid her pussy up and down on his pumping dick. She squirmed while he stroked her sugary walls.

"Do you want me to nut up in you?" He asked.

He was breathing heavily in her face.

"Damn it feels sooo good! I want chu' to, but we can't Boo. Not right now!" She explained.

Her body started to shiver. All the while she kept riding him, speeding up, and trying to make him lose control.

"Unnngggh! Sla! Slow down Boy!"

She bit her bottom lip and sucked in some air. He continued to pump her full of dick. The movements were fast and erratic.

Shooter tried to slow down, but her tight-contracting pussy felt too good. He was forced to pump faster and faster while trying to get his aching dick the release it needed.

"I can't! It's too GA! GOOOOD!" He bellowed.

His dick started to tingle. That alerted him that he was about to explode.

"Awww Fuck Maria! I'm about to nut!" He panted.

He slammed her down on his throbbing love muscle until his legs started to shake. Maria eased up off of him and squatted in front of him. She grabbed his stiff pole and started jerking it. She was licking the head vigorously in circular motions and loving the taste of her own juices which covered his dick.

"Ummmm Shit Girl! Awww Shit!" He moaned uncontrollably.

He was shaking, jerking, and shivering as she squeezed harder. That only made her jerk his dick at a faster pace.

"Cum for me Daddy! Cum for Mama!" She urged in a seductive tone.

She took him into her hot, wet mouth and began deep throating him. The first warm streams of his explosion landed on her tongue soon after.

"Mmmm! Yesss Daddy! Yesss!" Maria cheered.

She extracted his spewing dick from her mouth. She pushed it into the toilet and allowed him to spill his babies into the toilet water.

"AARRRGGGGGGHHHH!" He gasped.

She held his spewing dick in the toilet.

He leaned up and kissed her lovingly while she jerked the last of his love gunk from his dick.

"Let's go somewhere and finish this!" She giggled.

She was giving him a mischievous look.

"Okay, let's go. Hurry up and get dressed," he whispered.

He didn't want anybody hanging inside the bathroom to hear him. Maria stood up to put her thong and pants back on. Then she grabbed her top and kissed him on the lips.

"Thanks Boo. I needed that!"

"Girl, you just nasty. Get your ass offa' me."

He laughed at her. He pulled his pants back up while she fixed her clothes. He buckled his belt. Easing out the stall, he found several women staring at him with their mouths hanging open. Shooter nodded at the women politely and said nothing as he hustled from the ladies restroom.

Maria emerged from the stall seconds later. She smiled when she realized that the women knew what she'd just done.

"Sometimes I have to get it on the spot ladies. The dick is that good!" Maria told them.

She walked out of the bathroom. She almost fell in her heels as she tried to catch up to her man.

CHAPTER 18

*O*VER THE NEXT TWO WEEKS, Zap-Out and Billy Boy worked like slaves. They were doing all they could to get Ms. Brooklyn's after-hour spot back up and running. With such a hectic demand to help her, Billy Boy had very little time to spend with Sunny. The only time he would see her was when he came home in the morning. She would already be on her way out the door; heading to work.

Very few people showed up at Ms. Brooklyn's spot. Zap-Out and Billy Boy were forced to lose their money on purpose. They would take hours and hours to win it back just to keep gamblers coming around. Most of their winnings went to Ms. Brooklyn; so when Billy Boy did get some free time, he didn't have any money to do anything with Sunny.

When Ms. Brooklyn started selling fried chicken and fish dinners at her place, Billy Boy knew it wouldn't be long before she was back on top of the game. Billy Boy asked Zap-Out to cover for him tonight at Ms. Brooklyn's so he could chill out with Sunny.

"Yeah, I got chu' Slim," Zap-Out said.

He then hung up his cell phone. He had just robbed a few hustlers around Saratoga Avenue in Northeast a few hours ago. He had enough money to work the house and cover for Billy Boy. Billy Boy had no idea about the mischief that Zap-Out was into.

Billy Boy and Sunny were sitting on the couch watching the movie Love Jones. She suddenly fell ill and could no longer hold down her dinner. She hurried to the bathroom and wrapped her arms around her stomach. Jumping off the couch, Billy Boy followed her to see if she was okay. He attempted to enter the bathroom, but she locked the door.

"SUNNY!" He called.

He was knocking on the door.

"GO AWAY BILLY!"

He got worried when he heard that response. He also heard her gagging loudly, as if she was vomiting.

"SUNNY, YOU A'IGHT IN THERE!" He hollered through the door.

"Why you hollering up in here?" Maria asked.

She just appeared out of nowhere.

"It's Sunny. I think something's wrong with her!"

Just as Maria grew concerned, Sunny cracked the door open and peeped out at them.

"I'll be straight. It must've been something I ate, that's all. Can you excuse us for a minute Billy? I need to holla' at Maria right quick."

"Sunny, you know you ain't got to ask me nuffin' like that. It's not like I'm your man and you need my permission to talk and shit!" He said.

He was trying to play it off for Maria.

They didn't know how she'd take them being a couple. They felt it would be best to keep their relationship a secret, or so they thought. Apparently, Ruby found out about their secret one night when she ventured into Sunny's bedroom looking for some sanitary napkins. Ruby cracked open the door and spotted Billy Boy fucking the dog shit out of Sunny from behind. Ruby softly closed the door and walked off to the kitchen. She tried not to believe her eyes. Ruby also remained silent about what she knew. She had learned her lesson about telling other people's business. She didn't care how important it was for Maria to know her brother and best friend were sleeping together. All Ruby cared about was remaining true to her vow.

"I won't be the one to tell Maria about Sunny and Billy Boy's affair," Ruby told herself.

She never said a word about what she saw that night.

"Boy, shut up!"

Sunny sucked her teeth while faking anger for Maria's sake.

When Billy Boy walked off, Sunny pulled Maria inside the bathroom and closed the door.

Maria leaned on the door and looked Sunny up and down.

"Maria, I think I'm pregnant."

"WHAT THE FUCK YOU MEAN?" Maria said damn near losing her mind.

"By who?" She snapped.

Hearing Sunny's news was like hearing the world was coming to an end. Maria knew that there was no way she would be able to get Sunny to rob another bank now.

"This guy I been sneaking around with on the low-low."

Before Sunny could say anymore, Maria turned and started opening the bathroom door. She was trying to get out of the bathroom.

"I can't hear this shit right now!"

"Maria, I'm not for sure about it yet, but I'ma get a pregnancy test tomorrow!"

Her voice echoed in the narrow hallway and invaded Maria's ears even louder.

"MARIA!" Sunny called out.

She only heard a door slam. She knew her news had upset Maria.

Sunny brushed her teeth. She then headed back to the living room to deliver the news to Billy Boy. Sunny made it into the living room, but Billy Boy was nowhere in sight. That made her nervous. She thought the same disappearing act might occur once he learned about her pregnancy. She wasn't sure about being pregnant, however, her period was three weeks late. That put her suspicions on high alert. Her sudden sickness only added to her paranoia.

Sunny walked to Billy Boy's room to confront him. She knocked on his door. Billy Boy opened it with a goofy smile. He was as naked as the day he was born. Sunny's eyes dropped down to his swinging love muscle. She decided to tell him about her pregnancy after they got their freak on.

$ $ $ $ $

MEANWHILE, ACROSS TOWN AT MS. BROOKLYN'S GAMBLING SPOT, Ms. Brooklyn called Zap-Out to the side. She needed to tell him about the different ways that people cheated the house. They stood in the shadows. They were watching the crowds congregate while trying to win each other's money. It had taken them a minute, but they finally got the gambling spot back up and jumping just like she had it before the murders took place. Things were more lucrative now. People she had never seen before were coming through her spot. That forced her to hire several helpers.

After Zap-Out and Billy Boy helped get her back on her feet, Ms. Brooklyn decided it would be wise to offer them a partnership. Zap-Out still hadn't denied nor accepted her offer, being as though he still loved playing in the streets. Billy Boy told her that he would go along with whatever Zap-Out decided to do. Billy Boy felt that he had no right to decide on taking her offer unless Zap-Out took the offer first. Zap-Out was the reason that Ms. Brooklyn had entered into his life in the first place.

Now Ms. Brooklyn had the only gambling spot on that side of town. She owed it all to Zap-Out. She nor Billy Boy were aware of the many devious moves Zap-Out made just so she could be the only one to provide a service to the people who needed to gamble. All Ms. Brooklyn had to do was open the doors and supervise. Zap-Out, Billy Boy, and her other employees handled the rest.

Ms. Brooklyn assigned each person of her 7-man team to a table. The basement resembled a mini-casino adorned with 2 poker tables, 1 Black Jack table, 2 Crap tables, 1 Roulette table, and 1Georgia Skin table. The tables were bringing in thousands; even on slow nights. The men running the tables would bring her $650 off of every $1,000 the tables made. They were keeping $350 for themselves. The operation ran like clockwork.

Ms. Brooklyn opened the house at 9 p.m. on the dot and closed down at 7:30 a.m. six days a week. Her consistency in feeding her customers and providing a safe and non-drama type environment built up her clientele. It didn't take long for the gamblers to spread the word that Ms. B's spot was back and better than any after-hour spot in D.C.

Days after the house really started raking in money, Ms. Brooklyn told Zap-Out to hang around and help her count the money. She wanted so badly to keep him on her team. She showed him how much his hard work was paying off. She took the $15,600 of the night and gave it all to him.

"Naw, Ms. Brooklyn. I can't."

"Can't is never in a man's vocabulary Baby. You helped me out Sugar. I'm just showing you my gratitude. Now go on and take the money Chile'," she said with a smile.

He still refused. It took her all morning to convince him to take the money. Every since then, he played her house day in and day out to protect his investment. Zap-Out feared the house would get robbed or go hay wire without his presence.

"Niggaz smart Ms. B', but dey ain't stupid. You know." Zap-Out told her while studying the crowd.

"I know baby, I was just tryna' give you a lil' game," she laughed.

She gave him a tight hug. He reminded her of her son who was doing 45-to-Life in prison for a murder beef. That was the main reason she covered up for Zap-Out. She didn't want to see another young black man get swallowed up by the corrupt justice system that had already claimed the lives of her son and grandson.

"Boy, you need to stay your ass outta' trouble."

The look on her face told Zap-Out that she was serious.

"I need you to help me run things around here. You know I'm old."

"You only old as you feel Ms. B'!"

"Smart answer baby. Where's Billy Boy?" she asked.

"He had some things to handle tonight. He said to tell you to gimme' his cut."

"His cut?" She asked.

She looked somewhat shocked. She couldn't believe what she was hearing.

"We must be partners then, since he's asking you to pick up some money that he hasn't worked for."

Now Zap-Out understood the play. He assumed that Billy Boy and Ms. Brooklyn had conspired to force him into making a decision about being a partner in the gambling house. Her conversation, along with Billy Boy's sudden absence from work tonight, now made sense to him.

"Yeah, they ain't slick at all," he thought.

He gave her a funny look.

"Ms. B', I don't know what we are. I thought we was just cool. You helped me out a few times. I'm returning the favor. Same thing goes for Billy."

"Listen Zappa-Dappa."

She used the pet name that she gave him.

"If you don't work, you don't get paid. I'm not the Salvation Army, baby. I have people to take care of. I can't be giving away all my money unless it's for a purpose."

The look on Zap-Out's face let her know that he really wasn't feeling her answer. To Zap-Out, it felt like she was switching up and there was no way he'd allow her to do that to his partner, Billy Boy.

"I was going to wait and tell you when all of us was together, but we decided to take you up on your offer," he told her.

He refused to let this lucrative operation slip from his hands.

She snatched him into another bear hug, while he patted her back. He was watching everything in the house. In five minutes flat, a fight broke out and Zap-Out sprang into action.

"GET DA' FUCK WITH ALL DAT' BAMMA-ASS SHIT!" He shouted.

He pulled out his gun. The combatants already knew the routine. They raised their hands high in the air and prepared to be escorted from the house. After their departure, everything went back to normal except for one thing, Zap-Out and Billy Boy were now 50-50 partners in one of the most lucrative gambling spots in D. C.

CHAPTER 19

*F*AST BLACK SAT IN HIS BEDROOM, inside his mother's house on the Northeast side of town. He was tired from all the weed he'd been smoking. He laid down on his jumbo queen size bed and went to sleep. Fast Black supported his mother with the proceeds from all the driving he did during those robberies. He made sure that she owned the house that he went to chill in from time to time.

Fast Black wasn't hard-pressed for money at the moment. He still had a nice amount of money from the bank robberies that he drove the getaway cars in. He had enough clothes and shoes to give away to all the young boys that lived on his mother's block. He would still have an abundance of shoes and clothes left. Not to mention he had the best jewelry. The last robbery he went on with Shooter and Maria, he purchased a brand new 2005 Sportster motorcycle.

On Tuesday, October 27, 2005 at 7:30 in the morning, Fast Black's first cousin, Bee-Bee woke him up. Bee-Bee was the son of Fast Black's aunt. He was a year younger than Fast Black. They acted more like best friends than family. They had grown up together during their younger years. They spent time playing, fighting, chasing girls together, and having fun.

Bee-Bee did all the talking. Fast Black was half awake and trying to pay attention to what Bee-Bee was explaining to him.

"I'm telling you Slim, this shit is bonafide. You know I wouldn't bullshit chu'."

Bee-Bee strolled back and forth across the shiny polished wooden floor.

Now he was more aware from the half sleep.

Fast Black said, "Yeah Bee-Bee.You told me the same stankin' shit last time."

"Black, you know I explained the situation to you before. The dude had the days mixed up. That's why we only took ten grand out the joint instead of the fitty' grand that was 'spose to have been in there. But listen Slim, nobody gave me any info on this spot. I checked it out for myself and its sweeeet!"

Bee-Bee smirked before continuing.

"The nigga 'spose to make the drop at the bank at nine-thirty this morning. I been watching the nigga. I know for a fact that he gon' be dropping off anywhere between fitty' to eighty thousand dollars. Slim, the nigga do this shit every second Tuesday of the month."

"How the fuck you know how much money he gon' be carrying on him?"

"Look Black, I can't fake. I did get a little information from a friend of mines that works inside the joint."

"What kind of joint you talking 'bout anyway?"

"Man, it's this cracker that owns a liquor store. He's the one that's depositing the cake in the bank. He's an old cracker mu'fucka. I can blow on him and knock his old ass out. I can take this sonuvabitch Slim!"

"I don't know 'bout this shit Bee-Bee. I don't like fucking with that liquor store shit. Ain't no real money in that shit Slim."

"We ain't gon' rob no liquor store! We robbin' the owner! He won't even be in the liquor store when I get his ass!"

"I just don't know Slim."

"C'mon Cuzzo. Man do this for me. You said you got me, remember?"

Fast Black regretted promising his cousin that he would go on the caper with him the other day.

"Plus, it'll be 'bout forty grand a piece for us Black."

"I just don't know Bee-Bee. It ain't the money. I'm not aching for none. It's just I always get bad vibes about dealing with liquor stores."

"I done told you Cuzzo. I'm not robbing the liquor store. I'm just robbing the owner."

Fast Black saw that he was going to be persistent, so he just laid there and listened to him ramble on. Even if he wanted to, Fast Black couldn't refuse Bee-Bee, being as though he was his favorite cousin.

"A'ight Bee-Bee, you beat me down again. But I'm telling you, this is the last time Slim."

"Damn Cuzzo. I knew you wouldn't let me down. All you gotsta' do is drive. I can handle the rest."

"Bee-Bee, don't be geeking and shit when you take the nigga off. Whatever you do, make sure that before you rob his ass, you shake em' down for any weapons."

"Don't worry Cuzzo. I got this."

"Another thing Bee-Bee, you jive caught me at the wrong time. I don't keep any stolen cars on hand," he said sarcastically.

"So this is what we gon' do. I'ma park my car outta' sight. I'll be waiting for you right there."

"That's cool with me Cuzzo. I know the perfect spot where nobody will see your car too."

$ $ $ $ $

AT 8:20 A.M. Fast Black and Bee-Bee foot-stepped from the house to the front porch. All they could see was the gloomy weather.

"Damn, this is a misty rainy morning! On top of that, it's bone chilling cold out this muh'fucka! Bee-Bee, you better be lucky that you're my favorite cousin. I'd prefer to still be in my warm bed sleeping."

"Ease up Cuzzo'. It's been raining like this all morning."

"You said the cracker 'spose to drop the cash off at the bank 'round nine-thirty?"

"Yeah."

Fast Black adjusted the collar on his Hugo Boss double breasted, glossy black, leather duster trench. He pulled it up around his neck.

"A'ight let's go. First I gotta' get something to eat," he told Bee-Bee.

He started walking to his car. Minutes later, Fast Black pulled up in front of 7-Eleven. He told Bee-Bee to grab him a cup of coffee and a ham and cheese sandwich. When Fast Black tried to give Bee-Bee the money for his stuff, Bee-Bee waved him off.

"I got chu' Cuzzo. I mean, dat's da' least I can do for you for assisting me on this move right here," Bee-Bee smirked.

He then got out and rushed inside the store. Fast Black glanced at his cousin's back while he entered the 7-Eleven. Then he started looking at the rain drops covering the windshield.

In an instant second, Fast Black zoned out all the while thinking, *"Fuck is I'm doing out here off da' early morning fucking with Bee-Bee's crazy ass? And the whole thing that's really crazy is I don't even need the money. He's lucky he's my favorite cousin, cause if he wasn't I would've never got out dat warm-ass bed to do this shit! Dat's what da fuck I get for promising his ass something in the first place over a week ago.* I just hope everything goes smooth, so I can get back to my bed."

At that time, Bee-Bee opened the car door and the cold chilling air interrupted his thoughts.

"Here you go Cuzzo. This coffee is hot as shit! I put some cream in it, but left the sugar out. I didn't know how much you put in your shit. I brought you out 'bout fifteen packs so you can dress it up just like you like it. Here's your ham and cheese too," he said.

He gave him the items. He then went on about how the man in the store tried to tell him how to cook the sandwich.

"I told that Al-Qaeda looking-ass nigga to lay on back, cause I know what my Cuzzo wants. I put the shit on two minutes for you

Cuzzo. It's nice and steaming hot."

"Thanks Bee-Bee."

"Anything for you Cuzzo," Bee-Bee said.

Fast Black put the coffee in the cup holder on the side of the door panel before pulling off.

Driving with one hand, Fast Black started wolfing down the ham and cheese sandwich like a Cambodian refugee.

"So where we going Bee-Bee?"

"Oh? I ain't tell you?"

"Yeah, I jive think you did mention something 'bout it at the house, but it slipped my mind," he said.

He glanced over to see Bee-Bee gobbling down a jelly doughnut.

"Damn Slim! That's all you eating is a doughnut off da' cherry soda? I don't see how you do that shit off da early morning Slim. You always had some fucked up eating habits."

"Man, Ma-Dukes cooked for a nigga this morning. I had some fried eggs off da' more pork sausages. Mom puhleeeaaasssseee!" He joked.

"Yeah, moms jive be doing herself something in the kitchen every morning before she goes to work. She makes sure her baby eats too. So I made me two sandwiches before I left out the house."

"Oh yeah?"

"Yeah, but anyway lemme' tell you 'bout the spot. You know where the bank at down there on Seventh and Pennsylvania Ave.?" Bee-Bee asked.

His question made Fast Black choke on his food from the rush to get his words back out.

"Man, 'da fuck is wrong with you! You must be lunching like a motherfucker if you think I'ma go down there to rob anything with all them police running around that muh'fucka! That's more than insane! That's just plain old stupidity! Fuck is you smoking on Slim?"

"Ease up Cuzzo. I done told you that it's sweet! Real Sweet!" Bee-Bee conned.

He knew that his cousin was a sucker for anything concerning what he told him. Bee-Bee always used that to his advantage; like now.

"I know the lay-out and everything on my man. I checked the joint out way before hand. I'm talking 'bout way before I even came at chu' with this shit. I already know the ins and outs Cuzzo," he assured Fast Black.

"I'm telling you now Bee-Bee. You better know what the fuck you doing. We going down here fucking 'round with all them police. On everything I love, dis' da' last time I'm fucking with chu'. I mean dat' shit for real!"

"Aw Cuzzo. Just ease up."

"Man, fuck you! Don't ease up Cuzzo me! You better have your shit right fucking with these peoples. I said what I said!" Fast Black snapped.

He drove his sleek looking ride towards the downtown area from 2nd Street in Northeast. He eventually zoned out during the ride.

"If anything happens to his lil' ass, my Aunt Toni will never forgive me," Fast Black thought.

He looked over at his cousin who had a goofy grin plastered on his face.

Bee-Bee didn't know anything about hustling like Fast Black. Fast Black had the techniques and ability to triple his worth anywhere he went on Earth just by knowing how to do certain things. Bee-Bee wanted to make Fast Black believe that he knew a thing or two about the robbery game and hustling, which he didn't have to do. Fast Black would love him regardless, but in Bee-Bee's mind he wanted to make himself seem bigger than what he actually was to his cousin. He knew his cousin was doing things on a bigger scale than he could ever imagine at his age. Fast Black had a compassionate heart for his cousin. He would do anything for him and Bee-Bee abused it every chance he got.

The car turned off 7th Street and onto Pennsylvania Avenue. Fast Black didn't take long to reach their destination. It had just turned 9:16

when Fast Black parked his car on a side street where it wasn't busy. There were plenty of people walking back and forth. After waiting for a few ticks, Bee-Bee checked the chrome .45 caliber inside his leather jacket. He was trying to pump himself up to do the deed.

"Listen Cuzzo. It's nine-twenty now. The dude should be at the bank in ten minutes. I'm outta' here."

"Make sure you be careful Slim."

"I told you to relax Cuzzo. I got dis," Bee-Bee smirked.

"Taking this money is like smelling the sweet aroma of perfume. That's how sweet this target is," he said.

He pulled the black skull cap down low to keep the chill of the cold air off his ears. Bee-Bee gave his cousin some dap and exited the car.

"Cuzzo, gimme til' five minutes after nine thirty," he said.

He started walking off to his intended target.

Fast Black wanted to stop his cousin. He wanted to tell him don't do it, reconsider. Bee-Bee was already five feet away by the time Fast Black could announce the words.

"Damn Bee-Bee. Be careful Slim," Fast Black mumbled.

He had a bad feeling rumbling in his gut about the stick-up.

Bee-Bee watched the bank about twenty feet away from around the corner. His head swiveled back and forth. He was looking out of place and plain right in the wrong. Nobody noticed being as though it was cold and raining. People just wanted to get to work and out of the bad weather. It didn't take long for the mark to show up.

Just as Bee-Bee predicted, the mark was right on time. He was moving along with the traffic of people that were trying to get somewhere in a hurry. Bee-Bee didn't care who seen what or who was in the way. All he cared about was the money he was going to take from the mark in the bag. Creeping up on the mark from behind, Bee-Bee stayed incognito so the mark couldn't see him until it was too late.

"You know what da' fuck it is cracker!" Bee-Bee hissed.

He jabbed the .45 in the mark's back.

"Gimme dat' muh'fuckin money!"

Bee-Bee quickly reached for the overnight bag in the mark's hand. Not saying one word, the mark let Bee-Bee take the money. Bee-Bee was surprised that the mark gave up the money so easily. He took off running towards the direction of the car where Fast Black was parked. Bee-Bee never had a clue that the mark was chasing behind him. He never looked back to see where the mark was.

Bee-Bee also didn't hear the mark yell, "STOP RUNNING BEFORE I SHOOT! I SAID STOP! FREEZE!"

Bee-Bee made a critical mistake. He never did what Fast Black told him to do far as patting the mark down for any weapons. Bee-Bee appeared at the car as Fast Black was looking out of his rear view mirror. He could see the mark running behind his cousin with a gun drawn.

"Bee!"

Fast Black's warning was cut short as the marks' gun erupted with a barrage of deadly missiles. The slugs from the marks' 357. Magnum found their target. Bee-Bee's chest was blown out. The force of the penetrating bullets knocked Bee-Bee face first onto the ground right beside Fast Black's car.

"Noooo! Bee-Bee! Noooo!" Fast Black shouted.

He moved frantically to help his cousin. Sliding across the seat, Fast Black opened the passenger door and leaned out the car. He pulled Bee-Bee inside under the duress of more gunfire. Still alive, Bee-Bee winced in pain while he scrambled inside the car still clutching tightly to the bag of money.

"No Bee-Bee! No! How the fuck did this happen?" Fast Black said sadly.

He pulled away from the curb. Before he could disappear out of sight, more gunfire exploded and found its target once again. This time, several bullets cut through the back window of Fast Black's car. The window shattered and Fast Black was hit in the left shoulder. The force of the impact slammed him into the steering wheel.

"Ahhhhh!" Fast Black yelped in traumatizing pain.

Neither Bee-Bee nor Fast Black had any idea that the liquor store owner was an off-duty D.C. police officer. Soon as the gunfire sounded in the area, all officers in the vicinity rushed to the scene immediately. With their guns out, they approached the off-duty cop cautiously.

"Drop your weapon now!" One officer demanded.

"I'ma cop! I've just been robbed and the suspects are getting away."

Somewhat puzzled, the officer told the off-duty cop to show some identification.

"Do it slowly!" The officer warned.

He kept his gun aimed at the off-duty cop's head. The off-duty cop reached slowly into his jacket and pulled out his badge and explained what had happened again. Some officers took off after the suspects. The other officers radioed in the model of Fast Black's car.

It wasn't before long before a squad car spotted Fast Black's car. Fast Black noticed them and put his skills to work. The chase was on. Inside the car, Bee-Bee was laughing weakly while coughing up blood.

"Damn Cuzzo. I forgot to shake dat' cracker down," he said as he took his final breath.

Those were the last words Bee-Bee uttered before dying with his hand still holding onto the bag of money. Fast Black never realized that Bee-Bee had died on him.

"Hold on Cuzzo. I'ma get chu' up outta' this. Just hold on," he said.

Now he was gunning the engine. With the gas pedal all the way down to the floor, Fast Black sped along the streets trying to get away from the police cars in hot pursuit. There was too much blood pumping from his gunshot wound. The dizziness began to cloud his vision. Fast Black couldn't really focus on driving.

Weaving through traffic, Fast Black made a dangerous left turn onto 9th Street and drove on the wrong side of traffic. He still couldn't shake the pursuit.

"It won't be long now Bee-Bee. We gettin' up outta' here. You know my name right? Say my name Cuzzo. Get me hyped! Get me hyped!"

He talked to his cousin as if he was still alive. Fast Black never saw the traffic police officer directing the traffic due to the cold, gray rainy morning. He kept having light, misty black outs. Dozing again, Fast Black swerved a little and woke up just in time to see his car smashing into the traffic cop with tremendous impact.

Blood from the cop's mouth splattered the front windshield as the cop stayed glued to the front end of Fast Black's car.

"OOOOHHH FUCK! I'M SORRY! AWWW SHIT BEE-BEE, I JUST HIT A COP! WE GOTTA GET AWAY NOW CUZZO! CUZZO? CUZZO YOU OKAY?" Fast Black yelled frantically.

He jumped back on the right side of the street. When Bee-Bee didn't answer, Fast Black looked over and saw his cousin's eyes wide open and staring up at the ceiling of the car. Fast Black automatically knew he was dead. Soon as he turned to focus back on the road, Fast Black saw himself barreling down on the Metro Bus that was only inches away from him.

"AAHHHHHHHHHHHHH!" He yelled.

He suddenly released the steering wheel out of reflex of being surprised by the sudden appearance of the bus. Upon impact, he went flying into the back motor of the Metro bus.

"BOOOOOOM!" Came the sounds of Fast Black's car exploding on impact into a mushroom of flames.

Fast Black never had a chance. He died instantly.

CHAPTER 20

SHOOTER PARKED HIS ESCALADE IN FRONT OF THE **GIRLS HOUSE**, and jumped out of the truck. He galloped towards the door. He was trying to escape the cold, brisk, first day of November. It had been about five days since the tragic turn of events that led to Fast Black and Bee-Bee's deaths.

Ruby opened the door with a smile as he entered the house.

"Hey Shooter. What's going on?" She greeted him.

He never acknowledged her words.

"What the hell is his problem," Ruby thought.

He asked, "Who home wit' chu'?"

"Me, Maria, and Sunny. Billy Boy left early this morning for school."

"Listen, I need for all three of ya'll to come in here so I can holla' at cha'll," Shooter told her.

Ruby went over to the stairs and started hollering for Maria and Sunny to come down stairs. Shooter went into the living room and took a seat on the sofa. Ruby joined him seconds later.

"So where's Black at Shooter? You know I ain't heard from his ass since the day ya'll hit that bank out in Maryland," Ruby said.

She was totally unaware of what had happened to Fast Black.

Shooter looked up from the couch with a pitiful expression and sadness all in his eyes.

Ruby sensed that something was wrong as soon as she laid eyes on Shooter. Sunny and Maria entered the living room at the same time.

"Hey Shooter," Maria and Sunny said in unison before taking a seat.

"Listen up ya'll," Shooter sighed.

"I have some very bad news. "

The girls looked around at each other and then back at Shooter. They were trying to figure out the bad news.

"The other day Fast Black was in another high speed chase after a stick-up. Something fucked up happened with him running over a policeman. Then he crashed into a bus and got killed."

Ruby put her hands over her mouth in shock. She couldn't believe what she'd just heard.

"No not my Black. It can't be. It just can't be," she thought.

They watched him lower his head in sorrow.

Maria moved closer to Shooter on the couch to give him a comforting hug. She rocked with him back and forth. Sunny tried to wipe the tears that welled up in her eyes. All of them loved Fast Black in their own special way.

"Ha-how did this happen? I mean what?"

Ruby's voice cracked. She was trying to get her question out. She felt sick inside like a part of her had died at hearing the news.

"About five days ago. From the lil' shit I've been hearing, Black's cousin Bee-Bee was with him. They hit some liquor store owner who turned out to be the feds. A rack of crazy shit happened after that," Shooter sniffled.

He was trying to hold back his tears.

"The police started chasing Slim. You know how Fast Black do. They'll never take me alive!" Shooter sang out loud.

He was remembering the vow Fast Black said to him one night before they robbed their first bank together.

"And Slim didn't fake it. He went all out on them peoples. He slaughtered one of them pig's with his ride before he crashed. I don't think he would've got caught but they said it was raining real heavy that day."

Ruby just sat there crying softly. She felt like the world was going to end for her. Maria sensed the pain Ruby was experiencing. She'd already been through it with the loss of her mother. Sunny, on the other hand, felt bad for Fast Black's family over their loss. He could never be replaced.

"Slim's mother told me that Black and his cousin got burned up so bad in the explosion that they could only identify them by their dental records."

"Damn! That's some fucked up shit!" Sunny said.

She was trying to see through a haze of tears.

"Fast Black was a real cool muh'fucka. Damn, that's some bullshit," Sunny vented.

The tears rolled freely down Ruby's cheeks. She knew Fast Black the longest. She felt closer to him than anybody else in the room. Now she regretted getting his baby aborted. At least she would've been able to have something to remind her of him every day for the rest of her life. Now she didn't have anything and it was crushing her.

"And ya'll ain't even know Black had a tattoo that said I Love You Mom on his right leg. That part of his body ain't burned up too bad. That's how his mother really knew it was him."

"So Black was driving his own car?" Ruby asked weakly.

She had tears still running down her face.

"Yeah. From what I hear, he was."

"Something ain't right. I been knowing Black his whole life. He always stole a car before going on any move. Yeah, something is definitely wrong with that picture there," Ruby said.

She was wiping tears from her face.

"I don't know. You knew Slim longer than me. When I heard his cousin Bee-Bee was with him, I knew that was a mistake right there. You know Slim always had a soft heart whenever it came to the lil' punk."

"Oh my God! That's who was with him?" Ruby gasped.

"I know him. Fast Black loved him like a little brother. He would do anything for him."

"That included driving his own car in a stick up on a rainy day." Shooter finished her sentence for her.

"I'm thinking it had to be on some spontaneous shit for Black to go out the house like that with Shorty."

"Damn! That don't sound like Black at all," Sunny added.

"It sure don't," Maria agreed.

"Ya'll just don't know the relationship Black had with his cousin," Ruby sobbed.

She then got up and walked off to her room in a daze.

$ $ $ $ $

TWO AND HALF MONTHS HAD PASSED SINCE FAST BLACK'S DEATH. Fast Black's mother was so disturbed after her son's death that she held a private funeral for only immediate family members. Ruby, Maria, Sunny, Shooter, and Billy Boy were highly upset that Fast Black's mother would do something like that to prevent them from attending the funeral services. Ruby eventually found out where Fast Black was laid to eternal rest. He was out in Harmony Cemetery. It was somewhere out Maryland.

Shooter, Billy Boy, Maria, Sunny, and Ruby went to his grave site to say their personal good-byes. After that day, Ruby started visiting Fast Black's grave site every week. She talked to Fast Black about everything that was going on in her life. His death really pained Ruby to the point where she felt like a part of her had died.

Truth be told, it was the guilt of killing Fast Black's baby and cutting off any chances of his legacy to keep on living that made her go to his grave site. She was searching for forgiveness.

CHAPTER 21

*T*HE FIRST DAY OF FEBRUARY HAD ARRIVED ON A FRIDAY NIGHT and everybody in the house was getting ready. They were taking Billy Boy out to dinner for his birthday. Zap-Out and Shooter also came over.

Sunny changed jobs over the last two months. She now worked like a slave at Macy's near Pentagon City mall in Arlington, Virginia. She still was having sex and making love to Billy Boy every chance she got. Her pregnancy turned out to be a false alarm. After that close call, Sunny always made sure they used protection. Nobody in the house except Ruby knew about Sunny and Billy Boy's secret relationship. They did a really good job at concealing their love making and feelings for each other; or so they thought.

Ms. Brooklyn's house was raking in megabucks. Billy Boy and Zap-Out had to be at the spot six nights a week. Now that they were partners with Ms. Brooklyn, they were making more money than an average crack dealer on a good day.

Ruby still suffered from depression over the loss of Fast Black. She continued visiting his grave site weekly. She prayed to God to grant her the grace to be strong and move on with her life. Most of Ruby's time was spent lounging around the house and watching soap operas. She often thought about Fast Black and his child that she aborted. When Ruby would get intoxicated to clear her head, she didn't have anything else to think about. She started smoking weed more and more every day. She tried to escape her depression and the haunting memories of getting an abortion. When the weed no longer provided the escape she needed; Ruby took it up a notch and started smoking P.C.P.

Maria and Shooter spent most of their time together. With such a loving man giving her all the attention she could want, Maria had very little time to think about robbing any banks. However, the thoughts always came up from time to time. So when Maria overheard Shooter planning another bank robbery, she wanted to be in it to win it.

Days after overhearing Shooter, Maria stepped to Ruby.

"Ay'! You still tryna' hit the caper with me right?"

"What type of stupid ass question is that? You already know I'm down for whatever," Ruby said.

She was still somewhat intoxicated from the P.C.P. she'd smoked the previous night.

"We can go on that shit right now far as I'm concerned."

"Yeah okay. I'ma wait for the right time to holla at Sunny being though she's tryna' do the legit thing for the moment," Maria said.

She knew Sunny had been burying herself in her work lately. Maria decided to wait on the right time to ask Sunny about going on the move with her and Ruby. Everyone gathered in the living room.

Sunny walked in and started talking up a storm.

"I hope ya'll is ready to go. Ya'll know I still have to be at work by ten in the morning."

Sunny twirled around and revealed her dark wool Calvin Klein knit pullover dress. It looked like it had been painted on her curvy frame. Her Giuseppe Zanotti calf high, 6" heels made her look like a long legged model. Sunny complimented her ensemble with a dark blue fox-fur coat.

"Aww' Girl. You been going crazy about being on time every since you got that damn job. It ain't like you really need to work. We still got plenty of cake put away," Ruby said.

She was looking fly as ever in a dark pink, silk blouse with matching draw-string pants by Jessica Mc Clintock. Ruby's blood red, ostrich skin, high heel boots and trench coat had her outfit looking like something straight out of a high fashion magazine. Ruby had a deep love for dark pink and reddish colors. She made it known every time she put on something to wear when it came to going out on the town.

"Ruby, you know I love working out there, so don't even start none."

"Then again, a little extra money can't never hurt the stash," Ruby said.

She smiled at Sunny.

"Y'all bitches ready to go and take the birthday boy out on the town?" Maria blurted.

That caused Billy Boy to snap his neck and give her the evil eye.

"Maria, I done told you before. I hate it when ya'll be calling each other the B-word," Billy Boy snapped.

Everyone in the room could sense the seriousness in his tone.

"Okay Baby Brother, Damn!" Maria giggled.

"It's your night tonight. Your wish is my command."

Maria gave him a hug and kiss on the cheek. Maria sported all black. She had on a Louis Vuitton v-neck sweater, skin tight leather Marc Jacob pants, suede Chloe calf high boots, and a Louis Vuitton suede jacket.

"Shiiid', he damn sure don't look like my little brother. There damn sure ain't no blood involved," Ruby cut in.

She licked her lips. She openly flirted with Billy Boy just to see Sunny's reaction.

"Then again, he looks like a candy coated brother that I wouldn't mind licking all over ."

Okay Ruby. Damn! You needs to quit all that shit. You acting like you tryna get in my baby brother's pants on his birthday," Maria playfully said.

Ruby caught the evil look that momentarily creased Sunny's face. It vanished as quickly as it had appeared.

"Maria, stop calling him a baby," Sunny spoke up.

"He ain't no damn baby no more."

"I don't care how old he gets or how big he gets, he'll always be my baby brother. Ain't that right Billy Boy?" Maria asked in a big sister tone.

He nodded in agreement. Maria and Billy Boy hugged again.

Sunny thought, "*I don't know what type of time Ruby is on, but she'll never get none of that good dick that Billy Boy be slinging up in me! Not as long as I got breath in my body.*"

"Ay' Shooter. This my man, Zap-Out. Zap, this Shooter. He's a pretty good dude," Billy Boy introduced them.

"We already met while you was in the back trying to get your outfit together," Shooter said.

He wore a two button, golden brown, Hugo Boss suit with brown Mauri lace-up crocs and a brown Ralph Lauren Purple Label suede, three-button, knee length coat.

"Oh, that's my bad then. Are you and Zap-Out ready to go? Maria and nem' is tripping. They want to stay up in here and talk all night for real-for real!"

"Aww' boy shut up! We ready!"

Maria sucked her teeth.

"Yeah. We ready to roll," Shooter and Zap-Out said in unison.

Zap-Out wore a dark grey, four button, Brooks Brother's suit with a black and white Ferragamo dress shirt. His black leather Cole Haan, side zipper, ankle boots went nicely with his outfit and dark grey wrap around coat.

"Then let's go," Billy Boy smirked.

He brushed imaginary lint off his dark blue Giorgio Armani suit and matching silk Gucci shirt, which he had open at the neck. A pair of black leather Gucci slip on ankle boots and dark blue Gucci trench coat high-lighted Billy Boy's outfit. He was basically declared the fashion guru of tonight's outing.

They departed from the house.

Ruby said, "You know ya'll should take my Seville since it matches my outfit."

"Ruby, you really think you the Queen-B or some shit huh?" Sunny joked over the sounds of everyone's laughter.

"Naw bitch! I don't think! I know I'm like that and then some! You need to find out what Ruby means for real!" She cracked.

That caused everyone to crack up with more laughter.

"I'm sorry Billy Boy for using the b-word, but you know how we be playing sometimes," Ruby said.

She did not want to hear Billy Boy's mouth.

"Yeah okay. I'ma let chu' slide on that one, but that's the last time Ruby."

"Okay Billy Boy. I kinda' like using the word bitch. It's empowering for me and very liberating."

"And only you can see it that way!" Billy Boy joked.

Everyone had to laugh as they headed to the cars.

Billy Boy drove Ruby's car and Ruby rode shotgun. Ruby got a kick out of Sunny pouting from the back seat while sitting beside Zap-Out. Maria and Shooter followed Ruby's car in his Escalade. It didn't take them long to reach the restaurant where Sunny had made reservations earlier that week. They all sat at a long round table with roses and candles resting at the center of it. Soft sounds of smooth jazz oozed from the speakers surrounding the table.

Billy Boy sat at the head of the table. Everyone else found spots around him. They drank champagne and cognac while waiting on the waitress to bring Billy Boy's birthday cake.

When the waitress came back to the table, she produced an all-white, triple-tier cake decorated with red roses on the side with each year Billy Boy had lived in red cursive icing. The top of the cake had even more red cursive icing which read:

HAPPY BIRTHDAY
BILLY BOY
WITH MUCH LOVE

"Happy Birthday Billy!"
"Aww' for me?" He joked.

All five of them sang Happy Birthday to him.

"Happy Birthday Billy Boy. Happy Birthday to you."

"Now blow out the candles so we can crush that joint," Zap-Out joked.

"Don't forget to make a wish," Sunny said.

She winked at him.

"I won't," Billy Boy said.

He closed his eyes to blow out all seventeen candles on his cake.

"I would like to make a toast," Billy Boy said.

He blew out the candles and raised his drink.

"Speak Chile'!" Maria joked.

Everyone stood up with Billy Boy and raised their glasses.

"To all my beloved friends: Zap-Out, Ruby, Sunny, Shooter, and my lovely sister Maria. I appreciate this wonderful party ya'll gave me. I don't know if heaven has a paradise up in the sky like a lot of people think. I sure hope so. If it gives me the same marvelous feeling I get whenever I'm around you guys then it must be a helluva' place to be. Even though' I'm not in a rush to see it," he said.

That caused everyone to smile.

"But on some real shit. I love all ya'll from the bottom of my heart. I will never forget this night for as long as I live. Ya'll gave me this from your heart and that's what family and friendship is all about. Love, Loyalty, Trust, and Honor! So here's to Family and Friendship!"

Billy Boy started drinking his champagne. All three girls rushed to his side and started kissing him all over his face.

"Happy Birthday Billy Boy! We love you so much!" They said cheerfully.

They kissed on him while smearing cake icing on his nose and lips.

"Lemme get that for you," Sunny said.

She started licking the icing off his nose and lips in a seductive way. Seeing that caused everyone to look on in awe.

"Sunny you better stop playing before you make me get real excited up in this muh'fucka," Billy Boy said in a playful tone.

He was trying to throw everyone off to what he and Sunny were doing behind closed doors.

"Aww' boy shut up wit cho' nasty ass! I told you before. You ain't ready for this good pussy!" Sunny said following his lead.

"Shiiid'! The way this going, I can't wait for my b-day to roll around! I need to get all that love, you know," Shooter told Zap-Out.

Maria couldn't help but hear him.

"Awww'. The poor baby is feeling left out ya'll," Maria said.

She put her hands on her hips.

"Shooter, it don't have to be your birthday for me to kiss all over your face. Far as I'm concerned, every day is your birthday. Now go ahead and get in your birthday suit," she playfully said.

She walked over to where Shooter sat.

While Sunny and Ruby returned to their seats, Maria reached Shooter and wrapped her arms around his neck from behind. She bent over and kissed him passionately. She then wiped her lipstick from his lips.

"Aww'. My Shooter-Pie jealous, hmmm? Jealous cause you ain't get no wet kisses."

She talked to him like he was a baby.

"You know I have plenty of kisses for you Baby. Cause you Mama's Shooter-Pie."

"Sit your freak-ass down ho!" Ruby joked.

"Hurry up before you get us put out this joint. You acting all nasty and shit."

"Why don't chu' mind your business ho!" Maria fired back.

"C'mon Sis."

Billy Boy interrupted them.

"I know ya'll just playing, but I don't like ya'll calling each other them words. Let's just finish having my party okay."

"Okay Baby Bro'," Maria said.

She smiled and took a seat beside Shooter.

After that, they made a few more toasts. They got their drink on and partied well into the night. They had a ball.

"Ay' Billy Boy. I heard you and Zap-Out like taking chances shooting in the dark?"

Before Billy Boy could respond to Shooter's question, Zap-Out said, "What chu' talking 'bout Moe?"

"The toss of the dice! What else could I be talking about?" Shooter responded nonchalantly.

That put Zap-Out at ease.

Zap-Out was the type to always be on the defensive, even when he didn't need to be.

"Yeah Slim."

Billy Boy cut in.

"We jive be doing our thing on the craps, but we really into shooting pool. We like other shit like playing cards. We can get a lil' crap game going if you tryna' lose all your money tonight."

Billy Boy challenged in a playful manner.

"Naw Slim. I'm cool."

"Ay' Shooter. Why you ask me that anyway?" Zap-Out inquired.

He was still somewhat suspicious over Shooter's sudden line of questioning.

"Naw. I was jive thinking since it's Billy Boy's b-day; I know this all night gambling spot that's set up like a small casino. I wanted to hit that joint. I'll rape 'em for a few thousand and give it to Billy Boy for his b-day."

"It's still early. That sounds like a winner to me," Ruby said.

She was still sipping on her drink.

"It sure beats going to the Go-Go and running into some unnecessary bullshit."

"If everyone is down with it, then I don't have a problem with it," Billy Boy said.

In the back of his mind, he hoped Shooter wasn't talking about going to Ms. Brooklyn's spot.

"I got a few grand I'm tryna' blow tonight. You dig me?" Zap-Out said.

He was looking over at Maria.

"What about it Maria? You down with the get down?"

"I don't care. Whatever makes my Baby Bro happy tonight. I'm with it."

"Me too Billy Boy," Sunny added.

"Anything you want on your birthday, I'ma give it to you."

She had to throw it out there. She let it be known that she was flirting with him.

"I shouldn't have a problem with getting up in the morning and getting to work."

"Alrighty' then. Let's roll," Billy Boy said.

Shooter dropped a few hundred on the table to pay for everybody's meal. That included the tip for the waitress.

REACHING THEIR DESTINATION SOMEWHERE OUT IN OWINGS MILLS, MARYLAND, Zap-Out walked around the small casino in awe. Seeing all the traffic and money being tossed around, he felt like the operation he had going on with Ms. Brooklyn was elementary compared to this professional spot. Zap-Out bought $5,000 worth of chips.

"Slim, they jive doing the muh'fucka out here," Billy Boy told Zap-Out.

The $5,000 worth of chips was a present from Shooter.

"That's letting us know that we bullshittin'. I mean, we doing a'ight, but we have to step our shit up starting tomorrow at our spot."

"I feel you Zap. I feel you," Billy Boy said.

He walked off with Zap-Out to see what they wanted to get into first.

Shooter bought over $10,000 worth of chips for him and the girls. They then went over to the crap table.

By the time they got there, they heard Billy Boy talking to the table-man.

"I'm tryna' buck the dice Slim!"

"Hold up Youngin'," the beefy table-man said in a nasty tone.

"Don't chu' see I got a player here trying to buck his point? Just wait cho' turn. The dice gon' rotate."

"What's his point then? I like em'!" Zap-Out called out from behind Billy Boy.

"Nine! Put up or shut up!" The table-man said in a challenging tone.

"I bet two hundred he nine or five."

"That's a bet young nigga!"

"Oh, I like em too! I like em' too!" Ruby shouted.

She was trying to get on the bandwagon. She didn't have a clue as to what she was doing.

"That's a bet Sweet Thang. Put your money on the table so Daddy can pick up," the table-man said.

He winked at Ruby.

All of the bets were placed. The player, a dark skinned man with short dreadlocks, shook the dice repeatedly.

He looked over at Ruby.

"I know I'ma hit this muh'fucka now since you betting with me! Beauty can't never lose! Beauty always tame da' BEAST!" He bellowed.

He tossed the dice. They seemed to sail through the air in slow motion. One of the dice rolled several times while the other spun on one of its edges.

"NINE! We have a winner! We have winner!" The table-man said.

He pushed all the money towards the player who nobody in the room knew except Ruby. They did this at many casinos on many occasions. They were brother and sister. They knew by eye contact when to bet and when not to bet on his hand.

Ruby had seen him while walking over to the table and decided to surprise him by yelling out a bet. She was hoping that he'd catch her voice, which he did.

"Place your bets now! Place your bets! Player is coming out with a new point!" The table-man said.

Ruby's brother gave her the eye to bet on his come out. Ruby dropped the $400 in chips she'd just won on the table.

"Thanks for believing in a true WINNER!" Ruby's brother shouted.

He was tossing the dice and snapping his fingers.

"SEVEN! Another winner!" The table-man said.

You could hardly hear over the roar of cheers.

"Place your bets! Place your bets! Get in where you fit in!"

The table-man urged the crowd.

Ruby's brother rolled a ten this time on the dice. That was somewhat a hard point to hit on the dice.

Everyone started betting against him on the dice; except Ruby. She only bet $200 in chips on his point.

"I'ma teach you muh'fuckaz 'bout my hand! Get em' girls!"

He talked to the dice while throwing them. They landed on the total number of eight.

"Eight plus two."

He shook the dice and smiled around the room.

"Equals ten all Dizzay in the Pizzaint!"

He threw the dice again and came up with the total number of five.

"You five more off Big Dawg!" Shooter teased.

He had bet $1,000 in chips that the dice wouldn't strike on the number ten.

"Don't worry! I'ma hit cha' real nice and QUICK!"

He bellowed as he tossed the dice.

"SEVEN! WE HAVE A LOSER! WE HAVE A LOSER!" The table-man announced.

He scooped up all of Ruby and her brother's money.

While the table-man paid everyone at the table, Ruby told Maria that that was her brother.

"For real? He's kind of cute girl."

"Oh yeah? You bet not let Shooter hear you saying no shit like that!" Ruby playfully said.

She stepped off to go see her brother. Shoving her way through the thick crowd, she reached her brother and gave him a hug.

"Lionell! Su'p Boy! Why you ain't hit that damn number? You making me lose like dat'!"

"Dat' muh'fucka ain't wanna' jump up fo' a nigga. You see all them thirsty ass people jumped on the ten?" he smirked.

He then got all big brother on her.

"Who you up in here with anyway? That's why I probably lost. All of you damn minors all up in my bid'ness."

"C'mon bro. Don't start that bullshit. You know I'ma big girl and can take care of myself. I been doing it for the last four years."

"So what! I asked you who you up in here with?"

"Lionell. I'm here with my friends Maria, Sunny, and a couple more dudes. You met Maria and Sunny when I brought them over to the house. They helped me move, remember? They the same two girls I live with boy. You needs to stop tripping and shit; tryna act like my father!"

"Ain't nobody on no geeking ass shit like that. I'm not tryna' be or act like your father. I'm just concerned about my little sister. That's all. You way out here. It's a lil' hump from the city. I just wanted to know who you was rolling with."

"I don't see nothing wrong with that. Well, Lionell, we out celebrating for Billy Boy's b-day. He's Maria's little brother."

"Okay. Ain't nothing wrong with doing the muh'fucka for his b-day. You ain't fucking him are you?"

"Boy, don't make me slap your ass! NO!"

Ruby sucked her teeth.

"He's got a lil' girl on the side. You want to hang out with us? That way you can meet Maria's brother and the rest of my friends. Since you so concerned about my well being and haven't met them yet," she said in a sarcastic tone.

He hated when she carried him like that.

"It sounds like you got a posse of muh'fuckaz wit' chu'."

"No Boy!" Ruby smiled.

"It's only six of us. There are three boys and three girls."

"It jive sounds like a party mob to me sis."

He looked around the room.

"Anyway Ruby, I don't have time right now."

"You ain't never got time to hang out with me Lionel!" She whined.

"Now you know it ain't like that Sis. I just have to handle a few things then go meet some people. That's the only reason why I'm up in nis' joint. I'm just killing some time before I go handle my business."

"Mmm hmm!" She pouted.

"Don't make me the bad guy. Besides, I trust your word that you're in good company. Then again, I know it's good company whenever Maria and Sunny is wit' chu'."

"Boy, you so full of shit."

Ruby sucked her teeth.

"You make me sick sometimes!"

"But I love you though."

He smiled and gave her a hug.

"Ay.' I'm 'bout to roll out. Do you need any money?" He asked.

He started reaching in his pocket.

"No I'm fine."

"Here, take this," he insisted.

He handed her a little over $1,500.

"I don't need no money bro. I got some," she said.

He just stood there holding out the money for her to take it. Ruby knew if she didn't take the money, he would persist until she took it.

"Here girl. You already know I ain't going nowhere until you take this damn money."

"Maybe I won't take it. That way you can hang out with me."

"Ruby stop playing. C'mon now. I have to go."

"Give it here boy!" Ruby said in an angry tone.

"But I done told your ass I don't need it!"

"Well, give it away to charity or the homeless. I don't care what chu' do with it. It just makes me feel good giving it to you."

"A'ight, since you put it that way."

She smiled as he gave her a kiss on the cheek.

"I'ma see you later on. Make sure you stop by the house and see mama."

"I will. I'ma tell her I saw your ass out here acting all grown and shit too."

"Okay Daddy!"

They both shared a laugh before Lionell left to go handle his business.

Ruby made her way back through the crowd and over to the crap table where her friends were. They were all crowded around Zap-Out and Billy Boy. Billy Boy held the dice in his hand. He was letting Maria and Sunny blow on them for good luck. Billy Boy was just coming out the stall for his point when Ruby reached them.

"Where's that fine-ass brother of yours?" Maria asked.

"He said he had to go and meet somebody. I tried to get him to come and chill with us. You know how it is when niggaz be ripping and running."

"SEVEN! WE HAVE A WINNER! WE HAVE WINNER!" The table-man shouted.

He slid Billy Boy a pile of casino chips. Maria, Sunny, and Ruby started jumping for joy after hearing that Billy Boy had won.

"Place your bets folks! Place your bets! Player is coming out now!" The table-man announced.

Shooter and Zap-Out, along with the girls, dropped down thousands on Billy Boy's hand.

"Nine is the point! Nine is the point! Place your bets folks!"

"I like 'em nine or five for this money right chea'!" Shooter said.

He dropped half of his chips. It was a little over $8,000.

"House will take that bet. Anymore bets?"

"I like the straight nine for all this money!" Zap-Out said.

He dropped all of his chips on table. It was close to $13,000.

Zap-Out was the win it all at one time type of guy or go home broke. He knew Billy Boy had an okay shooter's touch when it came to craps. That's why he bet so heavy on him.

"That's a bet soldier," the table-man said.

Maria, Sunny, and Ruby looked at each other and then dropped all their chips into the pile with Zap-Out's and Shooter's.

"What's your bet ladies?"

"Whatever they said. We just going with a winner," Maria said.

She was smiling at Billy Boy. It added a little pressure, but it was pressure that he liked coming from his sister.

"Okay Youngster. Go 'head and shoot em'!"

"Kiss these for me Sunny," Billy Boy told her.

She did just that with a loud smack.

Billy Boy shook the dice a few times then tossed them high into the air. He was letting them fall for it all.

"I see five," the table-man said.

He slid Shooter a stack of chips.

Maria jumped up and down while smiling at her brother. Shooter gave her a stack of chips.

"Your dice again Champ. Try again."

Billy Boy blew on the dice and threw them like a behind the back pass.

"That's an eight. You getting hot Champ. You 'bout to break the house if you hit this number here," the table-man playfully said.

"G'head and try your luck Youngin'."

Turning to his sister, Billy Boy gave her the dice.

"I want you to roll the dice for me Maria."

"What the fuck! C'mon with that bullshit Billy!" Zap-Out thought.

Maria took the dice and started to shake them.

"Billy, I don't know what I'm doing. I never shot dice before."

"Hold up before you shoot them," Billy Boy told her.

"Now just relax and keep shaking them until you feel like it's the right time to throw them. It's not hard at all."

"Get they ass Maria!" Sunny cheered her on.

"Make em' pay girl!" Ruby added.

Maria shook the dice while looking nervous.

"Shit ain't hard Baby Girl. Gon' and get that money," Shooter said. He gave her ass a soft pat from behind.

"Mmmph!" Maria moaned playfully.

She then threw the dice on the table.

"NINE! NINE! NINE! WINNER-WINNER-WINNER!" The table-man shouted over the roars of cheers.

Maria saw everyone jumping up and down and shouting like they were crazy. At first, she thought she had lost everyone's money. She lowered her head in shame and was about to cry, until Billy Boy hugged her.

"You did it Maria! You did it Sis! We won!"

"We won?"

"Yeah! We won!" Billy Boy laughed.

"AAAAAHHHHHH! WE WON!" Maria shouted joyfully.

She jumped into his arms.

"WE WON!" She screamed.

Billy Boy began twirling her around in the air.

They gambled until 3:30 in the morning. Everyone won some money while betting on the group of teens. Even the people that were having a bad night won something. Sunny and Billy Boy got their freak on once they reached the house. Maria went home with Shooter. That left Zap-Out and Ruby all alone.

Zap-Out knew about Ruby's feelings for Fast Black so he didn't crack on the pussy. He did let it be known that he liked her though.

"I'm just not ready to see nobody yet Zap. I hope you can understand that."

"Yeah I feel you. Just don't forget who's first in line whenever you come out of your slump."

"Okay, I got that," she said.

She gave him a hug before going off to her bedroom. Zap-Out was left in the front room to sleep on the couch.

CHAPTER 22

A WEEK AFTER THIER FESTIVE NIGHT ON THE TOWN, all Maria did was contemplate robbing another bank. At the beginning, Maria considered the tragic incident that happened to Fast Black and his cousin, but it was only at the beginning. She didn't reflect on it anymore. She was ready to take some more money.

As Sunny was preparing for work, she looked at the clock and noticed that it was 7:30 a.m. She had to be there at 9:00.

"Damn, I'm running late. I'ma have to start leaving Billy Boy's nasty ass alone at night," she told herself.

She was smoothing down her pencil skirt.

Sunny walked over to Maria's room to make sure she did the grocery shopping while she was at work. Entering Maria's room, Sunny was happy that Maria was lying in bed awake.

"Ay, I'm getting ready to roll out. Don't forget to go shopping. We need some chicken and some more shit for the fridge."

"Okay, I got chu'."

"A'ight then. I'ma see you later on."

"A'ight Sunny, but before you go, I need to holla at chu'."

"What about Maria? You know I'm already running late as it is."

"Naw, I just wanted to know if you still tryna' hit that last bank joint with us?"

Everything in the room stood still for a minute as Maria's words invaded Sunny's ears. Sunny took a deep breath and hoped Maria

228

wouldn't get offended by what she had to say.

"Look Maria, on some real shit, we really don't need to rob anymore banks. I'm doing pretty good at my job. Billy Boy's bringing in some money every night. I think that will keep us ahead of the cash that's sitting in the stash. The answer is no. I'm not tryna' to go on anymore moves."

"Sunny, you already promised you'd go with us. That little bit of money we got in the stash is going to run out sooner than you think."

"Well, if all of us get a job that money won't have to run out."

Sunny sighed.

"Listen Maria, I'm not tryna' to make robbing banks my lifestyle."

"Ain't nobody said you had to rob banks for a living. Look, we already talked about it. You said you was going. Our word is all we got Sunny. C'mon Sis, this will be the last one."

Sunny just looked at Maria like she had lost her mind. At that moment, Sunny knew that Maria wouldn't take no for an answer, so she did what she thought was best.

"Maria, I can't talk about this right now. I'm running late for work. The only reason we kept robbing banks in the first place was to take care of your mother's hospital bills. She's gone now Maria. She's gone. We don't have a reason to rob any more banks."

Maria didn't comment about what Sunny just said. She just laid in bed and watched as Sunny left the room and slammed the door.

She went outside and waited for her car to heat up.

Sunny thought, *"I hope Maria will stop thinking about robbing another bank. Ain't no reason for it. She's just asking for trouble. We done got away too many times to go back. I know when to quit. That shit is over for me for real."*

Back in the house, Maria eased out of her bed and decided to go talk to Ruby about the conversation she'd just had with Sunny. Entering Ruby's room, Maria saw that Ruby was still sleeping peacefully. Maria tip-toed over to Ruby's bed and then dove on top of her. Ruby woke up swinging wildly. After the swinging episode, she wiped the cold out of her eyes.

"And why you up so damn early anyway?"

"Bitch don't be coming at me with all that grouchy ass shit. I ain't got time for it."

"Well, if you ain't got time for it then why the fuck did you wake me up outta' my sleep? I was in the middle of fucking Shooter's fine ass on the hood of my car."

"Ruby, don't get fucked up in here," Maria said.

She had a serious tone.

"The reason I woke your ass up is because I just finished talking to Sunny. Now she's faking about going on the caper with us."

"For real?"

"Yeah, so that's why I woke you up. I just wanted to know is you still down to hit the joint?"

"You woke me up to ask me that? Bitch I should beat your ass. You know I'm still with you. We've been talking about that shit off and on for the last few weeks. DUH!"

"Naw. I just thought since Sunny had second thoughts you might feel the same way."

"Maria, I told you before I'm with you on whatever one hundred percent. Why are you tripping?"

"Cause Sunny is faking on us like she's too good to be a part of what we tryna' do."

"Listen Maria. People grow and fall in love. "

"Who the fuck she in love with? Ain't no nigga been coming 'round here for her ass," Maria vented.

"Maria," Ruby sighed.

"Sunny has a thing for your brother. They been fucking for a minute now. I think Sunny has fallen for him."

Maria was mad for about ten seconds. Then she felt like if her brother was going to be with any woman it might as well be Sunny.

"So you see Maria, we can't press her into something she don't want to do, especially now that she has some dick in her life," Ruby giggled.

That made Maria smile.

"I guess you right about that Ruby. Fuck it then. When the time comes, me, you, and Shooter gon' handle it then. You cool with that?"

"Bitch, stop worrying about nuffin'. We have it under control. Now get the fuck outta my room before you drive me crazy about this shit," Ruby said.

She threw a pillow at Maria before burying her head back under the covers.

Maria left Ruby's room to go confront Billy Boy about keeping secrets from her. She entered his room only to find an empty bed. Maria called him on his cellphone.

"Sup' Maria?"

"You and Sunny. That's what! Why you ain't tell me ya'll was fucking?"

"Cause I didn't think it was any of your business. That's why."

He got smart just to mess with her.

"Boy, don't play with me. Sunny's like our sister."

"No she's not. She's like your sister. C'mon Maria. You know me and Sunny was bound to get together the way we kept sex playing all them years."

"So you ain't cheating on her are you? She's a good woman."

"Sis, stay outta my bid'ness," he laughed.

"But naw, on the real, I'd never cheat on Sunny. I jive dig the way she makes me feel."

"Aww', my Baby Bro is in love," Maria cooed.

That made him blush on the other end of the phone.

"Bye Maria. I'm gone," he smirked.

"Okay.Okay. I'm sorry," Maria giggled.

"Listen Maria. Don't go making a big fuss about this. Sunny thinks you gon' be mad at her for us being together. Let's just make her think it's still a secret. Matter of fact, how you find out anyway?"

"Now it's your turn to say stay outta my bid'ness baby bro. Love you. Bye," Maria said.

She ended the call and she could still hear Billy Boy yelling her name repeatedly before she ended it.

Maria smiled. She knew Billy Boy would be puzzled all day about how she found out about his relationship with Sunny.

With that in mind, Maria suddenly turned and ran back towards Ruby's room. She needed to know how Ruby found out about Sunny and her brother before she did.

"RUUUUBBBBBY!" She yelled.

She rushed back towards Ruby's bedroom.

CHAPTER 23

*T*WO DAYS LATER, Maria and Ruby laid in bed watching TV and smoking weed. They waited on Shooter's arrival. Billy Boy had taken Maria's car and driven it to school earlier that morning. Sunny was busy at work making that legit money.

Maria passed the spliff.

Ruby said, "You know, after this stick-up I think that's gon' be it for me."

"Yeah Ruby, I'm wit' chu' on that. We should give up our bronco days after this joint," Maria said.

She then took several tokes on the spliff. She exhaled some of the chronic fumes and passed the spliff back to Ruby.

"Ay', you know I been working on Shooter. He 'spose to have something ready for us soon."

"Whatever he finds, I hope it has a rack of loot inside like the first joint we hit together."

"So what are we going to do without Fast Black and Sunny?"

"Maria, I'm really not tryna' think about Black and what happened. That was some real fucked up shit. Every time I think about it, it hurts. It hurts bad."

"I feel you girl. I be feeling the same way. Black was a good nigga for real. He was like family. I loved him just like my brother."

"So do you think we need somebody to take their spot or just roll without them?"

Right now Ruby, I can't say. I'm still at a standstill on that topic. I guess when the three of us determine how the joint we gon' hit looks, then we can decide on how to go about things. I just wish Sunny would stop faking and fuck with us. We jive need her for real."

"I doubt if she's gon' change her mind Maria. You know how stubborn she is."

"I know, but we should be able to handle all the details. It ain't like we haven't done the shit before."

"Yeah, but we two people shorter this go round," Ruby pointed out.

"We can do the muh'fucka, but this time it's gon' be without Black and Sunny."

"Like you told me Ruby, don't worry. We'll be okay."

"Yeah whatever Maria. Now can you get the fuck outta my bed so I can play with my pussy in peace? You know how freaky I get when I gets the weed up in me."

"Nasty bitch!" Maria jive snapped.

She jumped out of Ruby's bed.

"I mean, you can stay if you're into that type of thing. I just thought that since your husband is coming over you'd want to spend a little private time with him instead of me."

"Bitch fuck you!"

They both laughed before Maria left Ruby's bedroom.

It was a little after 1p.m when Shooter knocked on the door. He knocked for about three minutes before Maria answered the door.

"Hey Boo."

She greeted him with a kiss.

"Ain't shit. Sup' wit' chu'?" He asked.

He slid past her into the house. Shooter took a seat on the couch. Maria flopped on his lap. They shared another kiss before Shooter broke it up.

"Where's everybody at?"

"Sunny's at work. Billy Boy's in school. Ruby is still in the bed."

"Still in bed? Don't she know what time it is?" Shooter said.

He was glancing at his Rolex Yacht Master. He noticed that it was a little after 1:30 in the afternoon.

"She was up after Sunny went to work. We was waiting for you. Then we got twisted and she went to sleep on me," Maria said.

She refused to tell him the real reason why Ruby had fell asleep. It was from the exhaustion of the climax she had after playing with her pussy.

"Oh yeah?"

"Yeah. So what brings you by here so late in the afternoon anyway?"

Maria stated in a sarcastic and playful tone.

"Stop playing with me Maria. You know why I came over here. You been pressing me to come over here with the lick for over the last two weeks now. So you can stop with all that faking."

"Aww', my baby mad at his mama?"

She cooed and gave him a kiss.

"Naw. I ain't mad. It's just that I don't be playing when it comes to business. I think I have a joint for us to hit."

"For real?" Maria asked.

She moved slowly off his lap to listen to what he had to say.

"Yeah, I been talking to a friend of mines who works in the bank. We're real cool."

"How cool Shooter?" Maria blurted.

She was unable to control the jealous streak that zipped through her body.

"Chill out woman. The only woman that has my heart is you."

"Mmm, umkay you can proceed."

Shooter shook his head behind Maria's statement.

"Like I was saying before you rudely interrupted, she's real cool with me and she's been giving me the layout of the spot. She's mad about not getting a raise or some shit. By the middle part of the month, they should have about three point eight mill up in the spot."

Maria whistled in delight. She was thinking about all the things she could do with that money.

"Damn, that's a lot of money Shooter. That could put us on easy street for life Boo."

"Who you telling?" He responded.

Shooter smiled as Ruby walked down the stairs in a short tee-shirt and some skimpy boy shorts. Shooter glanced at Ruby's thick body on the sneak tip before focusing back on Maria.

"Who you telling what?" She asked.

Maria relayed everything that Shooter had just ran down to her to Ruby.

"Damn, that's a helluva' lot of bank there. That shit can put us in retirement for real. I'm talking 'bout hang the guns all the way up. You hear me?" Ruby said excitedly.

"Now we ain't got dat' much time left to hit this joint. As soon as they get all that loot, an armored truck will come and scoop it up two days after that," Shooter told them.

"So how many people work in this bank? What's the security like?" Ruby asked.

She was ready to hit the bank immediately.

"Yeah? Who is this woman that gave you the inside info? You sure she's straight up?"

"Why you asking me questions like I'm some type of amateur?" Shooter said.

He gave Maria a funny look.

"She's cool with me from way back. She's a trooper from the old school. You ain't got to worry 'bout dat. And to answer your questions Ruby, there's only one guard. He's a real old muh'fucka that slow as E-Muh'fucka! You can take the gun up offa' him soon as you enter the bank. That's how sweet this old cracker is. We don't have to worry 'bout no funny shit jumping off on the security tip."

"Naw Shooter. I wasn't thinking like dat'. I was trying to figure out how the split on the loot gon' go between us three after we break your inside connect off with some cake," Ruby said.

"What chu' mean by only three of us? What's up with Sunny?"

"Shooter, Sunny don't want any parts of this caper," Maria spoke up.

"Why not? We jive need her on this joint Maria. Ya'll can't talk to her?"

"I tried. She ain't going for shit," Maria told him.

"She gon' have to go for something. I mean with Fast Black outta' the picture, the four of us gon' have to come together on this caper. Besides, I don't have anyone else to assist us in pulling this thing off. Ya'll have to make her change her mind," Shooter pleaded.

"I don't know Shooter. Sunny seems like she's standing firm on what she wants to do."

"Well, we have to come up with something fast. We don't have much time left before that money drops and the truck comes to take it away."

"Why can't the three of us pull this off?" Ruby asked.

"Sunny is a good driver. This is the real reason why we need her. I know for sure we'll have at least a few days to come up with our decision. Damn! Why the fuck is Sunny doing this shit to us?" Shooter barked.

"Don't worry Boo. You getting upset over nothing. We'll come up with something good for us."

"I sure hope so Maria. I sure hope so."

"Don't get all bent outta' shape Shooter. We gon' make this shit work.

Shiid!' For three-point-eight mill, I know we can find some kind of way to get that shit!" Ruby said.

They sat in the living room. They were deep in their own thoughts of the upcoming caper. They were wondering how they were going to pull it off with only three people.

CHAPTER 24

ON THE MORNING OF FEBRUARY 14th, an extreme cold front swept through the nation's capital. While a lot of people were staying inside trying to avoid the very cold morning, Maria, Ruby, and Shooter were planning to go out in the cold to rob a bank.

They all stayed over Shooter's house the night before. They came to the conclusion that they would rob the bank the very next morning. Shooter paced back and forth going over the plans again.

"So ya'll with me on this right?"

"Yeah," Maria and Ruby said in unison.

"Okay, let's go over this for the last time," he sighed.

"Do ya'll know what to do once we hit the bank?"

"While you hold down the floor, we will go get the money just like we did the last time," Maria said.

She then added, "The only difference this time is I'll be driving the getaway car once we get outside the bank."

"So what do you do once we get to the bank?"

"I leave the car running, so we don't lose precious seconds once we come up outta' the bank," she answered like student in class.

"Ruby, what's your position?"

"To follow Maria's lead and be the second one in and outta' the bank."

"Good. Good. Ay', don't forget that I can help ya'll out with the money if the shit gets too heavy for ya'll to carry. I'ma be the last one out the door watching ya'll backs too."

"Damn Shooter!" Ruby blurted.

"We been over this shit a hundred times already. We know what to do. Let's get this shit on the road."

"No bullshit," Maria agreed.

"Shooter, I'm with Ruby on this one. Stop procrastinating and let's get on with this mission."

"Excuse the hell outta' me! I was just making sure everything is in order. Ain't nuffin' never wrong with doing a double check."

"Okay. Is everything on the up and up? I mean, to your satisfaction?" Maria asked him.

"Yes Maria. Everything is on key. If ya'll ready, we can roll out," Shooter told them.

He made sure to grab his pistol grip pump shotty. They left Shooter's apartment and got in a stolen, dark green Porsche Cayenne. Once inside, Shooter grilled them as Maria pulled off. Shooter continued to grill them until they arrived at the bank around 9:15 that morning.

Maria parked on the side of the bank. They sat on a quiet street that looked like it could be somewhere in middle America. Fallen leaves from trees covered the ground with left over traces of snow peppered all around. Looking around like he was on the run, Shooter looked at the bank and then back at both girls with widened eyes.

"Ya'll ready to do this shit?"

"We about as ready as we ever gon' get!" Both girls said in unison.

They exited the car. Maria left the car running as instructed. Soon as the three teens entered the bank, they noticed that the old guard wasn't on duty. There were two younger guards standing at the door. That didn't stop Shooter though. Already locked in on the mission, Shooter went straight for the guards. He disarmed them without anyone noticing.

Two youngsters were walking down the street heading to school. One of them noticed the exhaust fumes oozing from the car that Maria left running.

"Ay' Slim! Look at that joint!"

The young dark skin boy with a wild afro told his friend. He was known as Tips. He was a wild juvenile who had been into everything but a coffin before reaching the age of fourteen.

"Yeah that joint jive hitting Moe!" His partner Coffee said.

Coffee got the name due to his dark skin. Coffee was more laid back and smoother than Tips.

"Naw. Look stupid nigga! Somebody done left the keys in that joint!"

Tips pointed out. They ran up on the car to get a better look.

"Slim, they slippin' like shit! They just begging for a nigga to snatch this joint!" Coffee said.

Tips looked inside the bank before moving towards the driver's side of the Porsche.

"C'mon Slim! This is right here!" Tips said before easing inside the car.

"Man, you's a wild muh'fucka," Coffee smiled.

He followed his partner and jumped inside the passenger seat.

The teens sped off in the stolen car. They had no idea that they just put three bank robbers in a bad predicament. Back inside the bank, Shooter was making the guards lay down on the floor. After disarming them, Shooter put their guns inside his pants and gave Maria and Ruby the eye signal to move out.

"A'IGHT! EVERYBODY GET THE FUCK ON THE GROUND! YOU KNOW WHAT TIME IT IS! DON'T MAKE THIS ROBBERY TURN INTO A HOMCIDE!" Shooter yelled.

All the people in the bank started laying on the ground.

"Everybody just remain calm and nobody will get hurt!" Shooter said in a firm voice.

He was waving the shotgun over the crowd cringing on the floor.

"YA'LL HURRY UP! YOU ONLY GOT EIGHT SECONDS LEFT!"

By this time, Maria and Ruby were already inside the bank's vault grabbing the first bags of money they saw. Seeing that it was filled to the brim with cash, both girls picked it up and launched the bag across the bank counter to Shooter.

Still clutching the shotgun in one hand, Shooter picked up the bag and flung it across his shoulder. He was looking like one of the actors in the movie HEAT.

"Let's Go! Four Seconds Left!"

Hearing that, Maria and Ruby gathered up as many money bags as they could and jumped back over the bank counter. As they ran towards the door, everything went haywire. A monkey wrench was thrown into their plans. Unbeknownst to them, two U.S. Marshalls were inside the bank on this morning trying to make a withdrawal before heading off to work. Soon as they reached the door, both Marshalls went for their service Glocks. One of the Marshalls rose up on one knee and took aim at the fleeing teens.

"FEDERAL MARSHALLS! FREEZE AND DROP YOUR WEAPONS!" The Marshall kneeling on one knee yelled from a shooting position.

Shooter noticed them a second too late. He couldn't believe what he'd just heard.

Thinking of Fast Black's motto: They'll never take me alive! Shooter turned quickly on the Marshalls and pulled the trigger.

"BOOOOOOOOM! BOOOOOOOOM!" Came the sounds of the pump shotty erupting in the massive bank.

That sent people scurrying for cover and yelling at the top of their lungs. During the confusion, several buckshot's emptied from Shooter' weapon hitting Federal Marshall Tom Roberson in the legs and shoulder. Being as though he was about thirty-five feet away from the initial blast, the buckshot's didn't really hurt him, but he felt the burn.

Dropping on his stomach, Marshall Roberson returned fire along with his partner. Shooter fired the shotgun until it emptied hitting nothing but plastered walls and the bank counters. Dropping the shotgun, Shooter went in his waistband for the two Glocks that he took from the bank guards. Shooter wasn't able to get them out fast enough before the Marshalls had advanced on him. They fired rapidly.

Being experts in the field of shooting and disabling criminals with lethal force, the Federal Marshalls moved with quick precision. They proceeded to dump several bullets into Shooter's body.

"NOOOOOOOOOOOOOO!" Maria screamed.

The first bullet hit Shooter high in the chest. That caused blood to explode from his body. Even though he got hit badly, Shooter still went hard. He blasted the two Glocks like a frantic Marine who was in the middle of a firefight with insurgents somewhere in Iraq. Shooter never felt the pain from the chest wound. All he could feel was the fear of being caught and taken to jail. Shooter continued firing until a few of his bullets hit their mark. One of them slammed into the Federal Marshalls right arm.

"Tom! I'm hit got damnit!"

The Marshall screamed and fell to the floor while clutching his bleeding arm.

Marshall Roberson took careful aim and smacked Shooter right between the shoulders.

Shooter kept firing like a madman in a trance. His bullets hit the Marshall on the ground in the abdomen as the he raised his gun and fired. That last shot from the wounded Marshall hit Shooter in the forehead. He was killed instantly.

"AHHHHHHHHH! AHHHHHHHHHHHHHH!" Maria screamed.

You could hear the cries and wails of other people shouting over the exploding gunfire as Shooter fell dead.

During the commotion, the two younger bank guards went for their ankle weapons.

Ruby and Maria saw what was happening. They were momentarily stunned by the ambush. They moved behind the beams in the bank. They pulled out a .380 and 9 mm. that Shooter had given them a long time ago during their first robbery with him.

Taking aim at one of the guard's hearts, Ruby fired rapidly. She remembered how her brother showed her to shoot. Just as she pulled the trigger to pump lead into one of the bank guards, his partner was able to sneak up on Ruby like a thief in the night.

Without hesitating, the bank guard fired two .38 caliber slugs into the back of Ruby's head. She never felt the second bullet penetrate her skull. She died instantly. Her brains exploded from her head. The bank guard was sprayed with blood and brain fragments.

The bank guard dropped his weapon out of shock after witnessing the gruesome sight he had committed. He'd never killed anyone before. It messed him up mentally. As Ruby's body fell to the ground, blood flew everywhere. Maria saw everything.

Maria felt like even in death, Ruby was able to disarm the guard. She decided to get him back for her friend. As Maria fired her weapon at the unarmed guard, visions of Ruby, Sunny, Shooter, and Fast Black all together with her having fun flashed before her eyes.

When Maria saw the guard go down from an arm wound, she continued firing and moving towards the door. The Marshall started shooting in her direction. That forced her to find cover behind a beam. Realizing that both her friends were dead, Maria wasn't going to let them kill her without taking some of them with her. She fired a few more times. Her gun jumped back. It was alerting her that it was now empty.

"SHIT!" She huffed.

She threw down her weapon in frustration.

The Marshall kept firing at Maria.

She ducked behind the beam without a clue of what to do next.

"Hold Your Fire! Hold Your Fire!"

The bank guard yelled out to the Federal Marshall. The bank guard knew that Maria was wounded. She was concealed behind the beam looking like a deer caught in the headlights of an oncoming car. All the customers in the bank looked at Maria from behind the bank counter. They were fearing more bloodshed.

The Marshall lowered his weapon and ordered Maria to come from behind the beam with her hands up.

"I'm not going to ask you again! Give it up! You don't have a chance in hell of making it out of here alive!"

Maria contemplated for several seconds while leaning her head against the wall. She made her decision.

"Okay! OKAY! I'm coming out! Don't shoot me!"

"I won't! Just come out with your hands in the air where I can see them!" Marshall Roberson ordered.

Maria did as she was told. Once she was out in the open, Marshall Roberson leveled his gun and aimed it at her chest. Maria glanced down at Shooter and Ruby's bodies and wanted to cry. She felt like their deaths were all her fault because she pressed them to rob this bank.

"LAY DOWN ON THE FLOOR, SPREAD YOUR LEGS, AND STRETCH OUT YOUR ARMS WHERE I CAN SEE THEM!" Marshall Roberson ordered.

The bank guard knew that Maria was shot in the arm. He jumped to his feet and reluctantly picked up his gun. With his hands shaking, he covered Maria with the gun he had dropped while Marshall Roberson rushed towards her to handcuff her. While they restrained Maria, one of the bank tellers hit the silent alarm. That signaled to the police that a robbery was in progress.

"You watch her! Don't take your fucking eyes off her for one second!" Marshall Roberson told the guard.

He ran over to check on his bleeding partner. When Roberson reached his partner, Roberson saw him trying to hold in all the blood pumping from his stomach. It looked like a waterfall.

"Hold on Edwards. I got cha' partner. Just hold on man. Help is on the way," Roberson said.

They could hear the blaring sirens getting louder and louder.

"Just relax and breathe, you'll be fine," Roberson said.

He comforted his partner who felt weaker and weaker from his gunshot wounds. Just as he was blacking out, a crowd of DC police and paramedic workers stormed the bank.

"OVER HERE! OFFICER DOWN! OFFICER DOWN!" Roberson yelled.

The other officers secured the crime scene. They made sure that no other suspects were in the crowd of customers standing behind the bank counter.

"Damn, this shit looks like a St. Valentine's Day bloodbath," one officer commented.

Maria was being escorted in handcuffs out of the bank. Being as though she was the only suspect alive, she was rushed to the First District Police headquarters downtown. They charged her with all kinds of felonies. They hit her with bank robbery, attempted murder on a federal officer, kidnapping, and endangering the lives of others during the commission of a felony. On top of that, Maria got charged with three counts of murder while armed.

She didn't know that by law if you commit a crime with another person and they are killed by someone else or any law enforcement during the commission of that crime, by law you can be charged and held responsible for that person's murder.

Maria's bloody massacre was being played all over the news by the time she got fingerprinted and processed inside Central cell block. They kept Maria locked up there all night without a phone call. She was handcuffed and shackled like a slave. The very next morning, Maria was escorted by several armed Marshalls across the street to Federal Court. She got arraigned in front of District Court Judge, the Honorable Albert Breckenridge.

The court clerk called the proceedings to order. That made Maria cringe.

"This is the matter of the United States versus Maria Vernelope Valentine!"

Billy Boy and Sunny were there along with Vicky and Cindy. Once Sunny got the news from Billy Boy, she contacted Cindy because she didn't know who else to call or what to do in the situation concerning Maria.

Somehow Maria had managed to persuade a male officer to let her make a telephone call last night from Central cell block. When Billy Boy answered the phone, Maria started crying.

"I already saw it all over the news Sis. Just stay calm. I'ma get chu' outta' this okay?"

"I don't know Billy. I don't know. It's not looking too good," Maria sniffled.

She looked over at the officer who gave her a hurry up signal with his finger.

"Billy I have to go. I need for you to come down to the court building tomorrow. Find out where I'm at and what's happening."

"I'm on it. Me and Sunny."

"Okay, I Love You."

"Love you too," Billy Boy told Maria.

The line went dead.

Now Sunny felt somewhat glad that she did contact Cindy. Being as though Cindy was majoring in criminal law at Howard University. The only reason Vicky was there was because Cindy had caught her while she was at home from college out in California. Vicky attended USC, but she returned home to help her father out because he was very ill. Now that he was doing okay, Vicky felt like she could leave him home alone to go back to school.

On her way out the door, the phone rang. Vicky turned to answer it. It was Cindy.

Cindy told her everything that Sunny had told her that had happened to Maria, Shooter, and Ruby.

"Oh My God!" Vicky gasped.

She covered her mouth.

"Tell me about it," Cindy said.

"I'm on my way down to the court building now just to make sure they don't try and railroad Maria."

"I'll meet chu' there," Vicky said.

She then hung up. She headed out the door to go see about her old friend.

The judge glared down at Maria from the bench. He presented himself as a menacing figure in her eyes. Maria just lowered her head while the judge read the police reports and witness statements.

"This is a very serious case. What does the government have to say in this matter?"

"Your Honor, I'm Rachel Patterson representative for our great nation and I think this is a very heinous, gruesome, and frightful case. The government asks that the defendant be held without bail. It's evident that she's a menace to society."

"What's the defendant's position on this issue?"

Maria's court appointed attorney stood up and cleared his throat before addressing the court, "Your honor, I see no need to keep this young lady in jail while awaiting trial. She has to care for her sick brother. She has no prior criminal record. The defense respectfully asks that a bond be set in this case. To add Your Honor, Maria Valentine is a lifelong resident of the district. She has never been outside of Washington, D.C. in her life."

Cindy looked on feeling good about Maria's chances with the court appointed attorney that represented her. But to be on the safe side, Cindy decided to help Maria out on her case as much as she could.

The Judge nodded his head like he took everything into account on both sides.

After several seconds that seemed like an eternity to Maria, the judge began talking,"Well, given the circumstances surrounding this case and seriousness of it, this court sees no other option but to refuse bail at this time. Maria Valentine will be remanded back to the D.C. jail until the next status hearing on, let's say, May eighteenth."

"That's fine Your Honor," the prosecutor spoke.

She began gathering up her briefcase and papers.

"Thank you, Your Honor," Maria's lawyer said.

He then told Maria what just happened. He also told her that he would come over to the jail and see her in two days to go over a few things in her case.

Maria just nodded and lowered her head as a Marshall escorted her from the courtroom. Sunny broke down in tears and had to be comforted by Cindy and Billy Boy. Billy Boy, Sunny, and Cindy all took turns going to see Maria after that day in court. Sometimes they all went to see her together. On other days, they rotated going over to the jail to see her.

Vicky went back to USC to finish up in school. She always wrote Maria and allowed her to call her on the phone. Vicky even sent Maria a $3,500 check to assist her with her legal bills.

Time seemed like it moved at a snail's pace to Maria while she remained locked down in the D.C. jail. Since her arrest, only three months had passed. She had only been back and forth to court once for a status hearing. The judge denied her bail again and gave her another court hearing six months down the line. During that time, Cindy got with Maria's lawyer and filed numerous motions. They brought Maria back and forth to court on different proceedings. The judge kept denying Maria's bail because her name stayed in the Washington Post headlines. The high profile case got Maria locked down in segregation inside D.C. jail. That really made time seem to stand still. She also missed out on Ruby and Shooter's funerals. Billy Boy sent her pictures. That only made it harder on her while in jail.

Shooter and Ruby had their funerals together. Everyone showed up to pay their last respects and show love to them. It was a very sad and heartfelt funeral. Ruby's brother took care of all the expenses for both of them; being as though Shooter didn't have any family.

Sunny had tried to give him all of Ruby's belongings and Ruby's car. He declined and told Sunny to keep them.

"You sure?" Sunny asked through a haze of tears.

"Yeah, Ruby loved ya'll so ya'll might as well keep a part of her too."

Close to a year later, Maria finally got her day in court. She was ready along with Cindy and her lawyer to do battle. The Federal Prosecutor's office sent two of their most extreme prosecutors who were known for not losing, to handle Maria's case. Jamie Lopez, a 5'8" French vanilla complexioned woman who could give Halle Berry a run for her money in the looks department. Her jet black hair hung just above her small waistline and her curvaceous body made men's mouths water. At only 30 years old, Jamie Lopez had put away more criminals than one federal penitentiary could hold.

The other prosecutor went by the name of Thomas Rosenbloom. He was an old, tough cat that's been in the court system for many years. He knew a lot of tricks. When it came to the law, Rosenbloom was considered a modern day Shakespeare. He was a master of the game. Lopez was studying under the 5' 5" portly man with olive dark skin with a head full of blondish gray hair. In his late fifties, Rosenbloom's cold, steel, gray eyes told a story of a man that had seen and did a lot in his lifetime.

Maria definitely had a fight on her hands. One that she wasn't going to throw the towel in on so quickly like her court appointed lawyer had suggested she do.

CHAPTER 25

Soon AS THE PEOPLE ENTERED THE COURTROOM FOR THE JURY SELECTION PROCESS, Maria stood up and raised her hand.

"Yes, young lady?"

The appointed judge for the trial asked.

"Um, I'd like to fire my attorney due to conflict of interest," Maria stated just like Cindy had schooled her.

Maria's court appointed attorney gave her a disbelieving look like she just committed the ultimate betrayal. He knew that it would be a black spot on his unblemished record. The attorney spoke up and tried to rectify the situation.

"Your Honor, this is a first for me. I see no conflict in this case."

He glared at Maria and then back at the judge.

"There is conflict Your Honor. I recently found out that I could have a paid attorney to assist me in my defense instead of one provided by the state. I'd like the best defense possible. My life is on the line here."

Maria spoke from the heart.

Cindy and a slender black man with curly short hair carrying a briefcase; stepped up to the defense table.

"If I may add Your Honor."

"And who are you?" Asked the 5' 4" judge.

He had a head full of white hair with a bald spot in the middle. He was known throughout the court system as Judge Robert Louis Stevenson; the Hang 'Em High Judge with 30 years under his belt on the bench. Maria learned through the prison grapevine that she needed a paid attorney to even have a fighting chance in Stevenson's courtroom.

Just so happened, days after Shooter's and Ruby's funeral, Sunny, Billy Boy, and Zap-Out went over to Shooter's apartment to clean it out and get his stuff. During the packing, Sunny found Shooter's stash inside his closet tucked away neatly inside several shoe boxes.

After packing up all of Shooter's things, they put them inside his Escalade and drove it back over to the house. Once they reached the house, Sunny told Billy Boy about what she found and they sat down and counted up all the money. Shooter had well over $650,000 hidden in those shoe boxes.

"Damn! I guess hitting dem' banks do have its benefits!" Billy Boy said playfully.

Sunny had to hit him in the chest.

"Ouch! What? I'm just saying, damn!"

"Boy, don't play like that!"

Sunny jive snapped on him.

"Ain't no benefits in that shit. They died because of that money. They couldn't get enough of it."

Sunny stepped off and went to her room. She locked herself inside and cried herself to sleep.

While looking at all the money sitting on the table, Billy Boy called Cindy to ask her about obtaining a lawyer for Maria.

"That's gonna' cost a nice piece of change Billy," Cindy told him.

She was doing her nails. She was getting ready for a date with some hot shot banking attorney that she met at the mall.

"Listen Cindy, money ain't a thing. My sister's life is on the line. Whatever the cost gon' be, I got it. I don't care if you have to go and unbury Johnnie Cochran. I want the best lawyer in this city at my sister's trial."

"I'm on it first thing in the morning, but here's what I want you to tell Maria to do."

Cindy started telling him everything that she wanted Maria to do right before the jury selection process in her trial. The very next day, Cindy shopped around in the yellow pages until she found a lawyer for Maria. An attorney by the name of Christopher Rainey, a 190 pound, George Washington University of Law Graduate. He had ten years of practicing criminal law in the Metropolitan with only two losses under his belt. His only losses were the result of his clients choosing to take plea deals at the last second. Prosecutors feared the 33 year old Rainey whenever he stepped into a courtroom.

"I'm Christoper Rainey. I am the attorney for the defendant," he spoke.

His swagger put Maria at ease like she could take on the world with him defending her.

"Is this true young lady?" The Judge asked.

He was staring at Maria.

"Yes Sir, I mean, Your Honor," Maria answered.

That caused a few people in the crowd to giggle.

"Alright Mr. Rainey, you may proceed, but I hope you're ready for trial because I'm not postponing this thing," the judge said.

He then moved forward with the jury selection proceedings. Maria ended up with seven women and five men on her jury.

After the court clerk announced the United States verses Maria Vernelope Valentine docket number: F-1968-05, both prosecutors stood up, announcing their presence, "Good morning. Your Honor. Jamie Lopez and Thomas Rosenbloom on behalf of the United States."

"Good morning, Your Honor. Christopher Rainey representing Ms. Maria Valentine."

"You may sit," the Judge said.

He then turned on the jury.

"I need to make a few remarks to you, the jury, before these proceedings begin. It's for the benefit of those of you who have never sat on a jury before in a criminal case."

He told them exactly what the government needed to prove its case beyond a reasonable doubt. Then he told them that they'll hear from the defense lawyer who only has to prove doubt.

Jamie Lopez was the first to rise and approach the jury box for her opening arguments. The five men sitting on the jury couldn't believe their eyes as she approached the jury box with a runaway model walk. They all were lusting in their own way over her curvy frame clothed in a tight, dark blue pencil skirt and white silk blouse. Her dark blue pumps highlighted her thick legs and calves. That was exactly the effect she was looking for.

"Good morning, ladies and gentlemen of the jury. This is the case of Maria Vernelope Valentine. I, along with District Attorney Thomas Rosenbloom will show, no I'm sorry," she smiled.

"We will prove beyond a reasonable doubt, that Maria Valentine, the woman sitting behind me, did in fact commit the offenses she's being charged with today. They are armed bank robbery, three counts of first degree premeditated murder, and ten counts of attempted murder."

She paused to let the horrible charges linger in the air.

"Yes, we will prove that Maria Valentine with malicious intent, did in fact, participate in this brutal crime that caused several deaths. She's definitely responsible and needs to be brought to justice. It's your job to make sure that justice is served. So people of the jury, please pay close attention to all the facts surrounding this senseless crime that was committed by that woman."

She turned and pointed at Maria.

"When we rest our case, you will have no doubt in your minds that the woman sitting over there is the culprit responsible for the crimes committed and deserves everything she gets," Jamie Lopez stated.

She walked back to the prosecutor's table.

As she gave up the perfect runway walk, the men in the courtroom watched her with fascination. They were enchanted by the way she moved her thick body.

Sunny, Billy Boy, along with Zap-Out and Cindy sat in the back watching the prosecutor while she made her opening statement.

"Who the hell do she think she is? Jamie Cochran?"

Cindy whispered to Billy Boy who giggled softly.

"Mr. Rainey, you may proceed."

"Yes, thank you, Your Honor."

He stood and walked over to the jury box.

"Good morning everyone. I hope everyone is feeling fine. I'm representing the defendant in this case. I won't take up all of your time with a bunch of legal mumbo-jumbo. I will highlight the fact that the prosecutor just said some very, very terrible things about my client," he sighed.

"Terrible indeed. You know the beauty of it all. They're going to have to prove to you beyond a reasonable doubt. Remember the words, reasonable and doubt. They will have to prove that in every single charge that said defendant is on trial for. All I will prove to you is that Maria did not murder anyone in that bank. If my client is guilty of anything, it may be attempted bank robbery. Remember, ladies and gentlemen of the jury, reasonable doubt. That's what the government can't show you involving any murders that my client is being charged with. This is a very serious matter that needs your undivided attention. A woman's life is on the line here. I implore you to watch this case very closely and listen to every detail to make sure the Government proves beyond a reasonable doubt that Maria Vernelope Valentine is guilty of murder," he smiled.

He gave up a sly wink.

"I think you see that is not so. Thanks for your time and assistance in this sensitive matter," he said.

He walked back to the defense table.

Maria sat at the defense table sporting an all-white, Virgin Mary, ankle length Christian Dior dress. She looked more like an innocent Catholic school girl instead of the bank robber/murderer that the prosecutor had painted her out to be.

The Prosecution called their first witness to the stand to testify about the events that happened inside the bank on the morning of February 14th.

"Can you state your name for the record please?"

"Geraldine Thompson."

"And what is your occupation?"

"I work as a bank teller."

"Okay, can you tell us and the jury what happened on the morning of February 14th?"

"Sure. I was working in the bank. I was getting the morning monies together when, " she said.

She told a very gruesome version of what transpired in the bank.

"No further questions," Jamie Lopez stated.

She had a triumphant smirk plastered on her face.

Even Christopher Rainey had to admit that Prosecutor Lopez put on a brilliant performance. As he approached the witness stand, his main focus was showing flaws in the witness testimony.

"Okay. You said you were ducking behind the counter when the shooting started. Correct?"

"Yes."

"So it's possible to say that the defendant could not have fired the gun that killed those people."

"Yes."

"Did you see the defendant with a gun during the robbery?"

"No."

"Did you ever see the defendant with a weapon during the bank robbery?"

"No," the white lady said lowering her head.

"No further questions Your Honor."

He turned and winked at the Prosecutor. He then headed over to Maria to explain to her what had just happened.

During the nine day trial, Thomas Rosenbloom and Jamie Lopez put on brilliant performances. They were trying their best to get Maria convicted. Maria's attorney, Christopher Rainey, fought hard like it was his life on the line. That made the jurors really weigh out the evidence on both sides.

During the closing arguments, Maria's attorney explained to the jurors that Maria didn't pull the trigger that lead to the bank guard's slaying. Therefore, she could not be held responsible for the crime.

" I'd also like to add that Maria didn't fire the bullets that killed her friends. The authorities did. So it's evident, and I mean, even Stevie Wonder can see that Maria Vernelope Valentine isn't responsible for the crimes she's being charged with," he said.

He walked back and forth in order to study the jurors.

"Remember I asked you before to remember two words; reasonable doubt. The government failed in proving this in the murder and attempted murder charges. They failed miserably, so all the defendant asks is that you the jury give her justice. Thank you."

The prosecutor got up and rebutted the defense's closing, which was basically useless because most of the jury had already made up their minds.

The jury went into deliberations for two days and six hours. On the third day, they came back with a unanimous verdict. During that time, Maria's attorney visited her over at the CTF facility. He talked to her about what to expect.

"I think we are looking pretty good. I just don't want them to find you guilty of murder. If we can just get around that hurdle, the robbery is nothing. Most likely, I'll get you out within eighteen months on that charge."

Maria sat at the defense table holding her lawyer's hands as the jury entered the courtroom.

"This is it Maria," her attorney whispered.

She looked at the jurors who didn't look at her.

The foreman of the jury handed the bailiff a sheet of paper. The bailiff gave the paper to the judge. He read it and looked at Maria and then back at the jury.

"Will the defendant please rise," the judge told her.

He then looked at the jury.

"How does the jury find the defendant on the counts of premeditated murder in the first degree?"

The foreman looked at Maria and looked at the ground.

That scared Maria. She just knew they were about to convict her of murder.

"Not Guilty!" The foreman said.

That caused Maria to cry tears of joy. She knew she had a chance at gaining her freedom again.

"And how do you find the defendant on the counts of attempted murder?"

"Not Guilty. However, we do find the defendant guilty on the bank robbery counts in the indictment."

"You may be excused," the judge told the jury.

He ordered that Maria come back to court for sentencing in sixty days.

Sixty days later, Maria returned to court for sentencing. She sat at the shiny, oak wood defense table. Maria conversed with her lawyer about what to expect on her sentence. She wore a pink dress with pink and white high heels. She had her hair in a French braid style going towards the back of her head that hung loosely past her shoulders.

Once the judge entered the courtroom, he got right down to business.

"Ms. Valentine I have read all the presentencing reports and the psychiatrist accounts of your mental state after your mother passed away. It seems in their reports that you were going through some temperamental problems. I also see where you never had been arrested a day in your life, but that still gives you no right to do what you did young lady," the judge scolded.

"Does the prosecution have anything to add before I impose sentencing?"

"Yes. Your Honor!" Jamie Lopez stood.

"I'd like to recommend that Ms. Valentine receive the maximum penalty that's allowed in this case. She's a very dangerous person who cared so little about life that she took it just to steal money from a bank. Even though she wasn't found guilty of the murders and attempted murders, she still played a major part in the ferocious shoot-out with authorities. The same authorities who uphold the laws of our great nation. Yes. Your Honor. She should receive the full consequences of this savage act she participated in. That'll be all Your Honor!"

"Mr. Rainey, do you have anything to say on the defendant's behalf?"

"I most certainly do Your Honor."

He stood up beside Maria and squeezed her hand.

"I would like to ask that Ms. Maria Valentine be given a sentence under the D.C. Youth Correctional Act because of the emotional trauma she experienced due to her mother's death.

Your Honor, you even said it yourself, she wasn't in trouble with the law up until that point in her life. She has already suffered tremendously with the loss of her friends and mother. Now she must face this fact for the rest of her life. That's sentence within itself. Giving her a lengthy sentence will only be punishment for this young lady, not rehabilitation," he sighed.

"This young woman needs psychological treatment, not harsh treatment. Under the Youth Correctional Act, I'm pretty sure she'll get all the help she needs. Your Honor, this young girl has been going through traumatizing anguish and pain. She didn't know how to ask for help. Furthermore, she didn't know where to receive help from. This is a young lady that lost her mother, the first and only love she ever knew. Then she was forced to care for her younger brother. She's not responsible for her actions. She wasn't conscious of what she was doing. You read the reports yourself from the mental health specialists. The law states that when someone is unmindful of the crime they commit, they should not be held accountable for that crime."

He paused before continuing.

"Your Honor, we don't want to destroy this young woman's life before it has even begun. That's what you'll do if you send her into a harsh penal institution. You can't fault her for our faults. Yes, we were at fault because we are the people of this great nation that weren't there to assist her during her time of need when her mother passed away."

"Please, Your Honor, I ask you to show some compassion on this poor young lady's soul and give her a chance. Just one chance. That'll be all Your Honor. Thanks," he said.

He remained standing while holding Maria's hand.

"Now what do you have to say young lady before I impose sentencing on you?"

"Your Honor," Maria took a deep breath and started speaking from the heart.

"I feel very saddened about what happened to my friends and the bank guard along with the rest of the people inside the bank. I do feel responsible for the guard's death and my friends. That will be on my conscience for the rest of my life. I'll never get over the fact that I could've prevented this some way somehow, but I didn't. I live with that. I live with being a part of this miserable tragedy," Maria choked up.

A few tears slid down her face.

"I, I always have to live with knowing that their blood will always be on my hands," she cried softly and wiped her nose.

"Your Honor, I know you may have heard that many times before from others, but if I could change their deaths for mines, I would without hesitating. That's impossible, I know, but that's what's in my heart. Your Honor, when my mother died, it took something out of me, something that I can't explain. All I know was that I wasn't the same anymore. Sometimes I would find myself wishing I was dead," she cried harder.

Her attorney consoled her.

"No, I deserve this pain. I did something wrong and I'll be the first to admit it. The pain was too hard for me to handle. I wanted to be with my mother. Your Honor, I do regret what happened. I have the utmost remorse for it. I don't know what else to say other than I'm very, very sorry. I'll always endure this agony for the rest of my life. I will forever mourn the loss of my friends and the loss of the people we affected that morning."

Maria continued crying and took a seat.

"I do take into consideration your unstable condition and I do understand the prosecution's arguments as well. Young lady, you committed a very terrible act. It lead to many people dying and their families and children suffering," the judge sighed.

He was looking directly at Maria.

"Given the account that your condition is by law viable and given the facts that you never been in trouble before, I do feel that you can benefit from the Federal Youth Correctional Act 50- 10-B. Get your life together young lady. That'll be all. Next case!"

Maria looked at her lawyer and said, "Wha-what did he just do?"

"He put you in good shape. He just gave you a six year Youth Act, meaning with good conduct and completing all the programming, you'll do about a year or eighteen months tops," he informed her.

In the back of the courtroom, Billy Boy turned on Cindy and asked, "What just happened?"

"The judge gave her six years. She can achieve her freedom within a year to eighteen months. That's not bad at all."

"That's what your mouth say!"

Billy Boy frowned.

"I have to be away from her all that time!" he fussed.

Sunny and Cindy tried to calm him down.

As the U.S. Marshall escorted Maria out of the courtroom, she turned around and looked at her brother with tears streaming down her face. She smiled knowing in her heart that she received a tremendous stroke of luck with the sentencing.

Billy Boy started crying as he watched his sister being lead off to prison.

"It's gon' be okay baby. It's gon be okay," Sunny said.

She was trying to be strong, but tears started falling down her face as well.

Sunny and Billy Boy were somewhat pleased with the sentence Maria had received. Cindy had to explain to them that she got off with a slap on the wrist.

"Shoo', for what she was charged with, she damn near jumped the moon! She could have got found guilty on murder and them other crimes and been up shit's creek for real!" Cindy told them.

Sunny and Billy Boy watched Maria's back and the door to her freedom close behind her.

Cindy stared at Maria's brother and best friend all the while thinking, "I guess the good Lord was really with her butt. He saw that she deserved another chance at life."

"How blessed a person can be at some critical times," Cindy mumbled.

"What chu' say Cindy?" Sunny asked.

They walked out of the courtroom.

In response, Cindy just smiled and nodded her head.

"Nothing girl, it's nothing," she stated.

Deep down, she was hoping that Maria's tomorrows would turn out far better than her yesterdays.

Coming Attraction

Synopsis for NO CUT CARDS ...

After being Left 4 Dead by the Criminal Justice System, Gunslinger and Wolftrap got their Life sentences overturned on a legal technicality... Hell bent on Revenge, they return to the gritty Streets of Washington, D.C. to settle some unfinished business ...

They have No Cut Cards when it comes to applying their trade of kidnapping, robbery and murder. When they eliminate a major figure in the Drug Underworld, all hell breaks loose. Their victim has some very powerful friends who want Gunslinger and Wolftrap dead, which put them in the crosshairs of a very crafty and ruthless killer.

As these two savage hunters become the hunted, the bullet riddled and bloody outcome with a strange and surprising twist will leave you spellbound, and gripping the edge of your seat...

No Cut Cards is a classic read that you do not want to miss...

By: Mr. Michael Lucas

Coming Attraction

Synopsis for THE BLUE EYE GANGSTER ...

Note from the Author

This Novel is a work of fiction, and certain instances, reflects on some of the most trying times of my life, but, it's characters are fictitious and are not intended to reflect the life or lives of no real individual. Any resemblance to an actual individual is strictly coincidental.

This Novel exposes the life of crime of young urban youth early in their lives of ' Drugs, Sex, Money, Robbery, Burglary, and Murder.

A young Kid growing up in a dysfunctional environment without his biological parents, being raised by his grandmother, but, taking life on alone. The Character is, "Macco Blue Eyes". Who gets caught up into the 'ghetto life' as he goes on his first burglary caper, being drawn into a spider's web of the "Systematic Plot of Society."

"The Blue Eye Gangster"

By: Mr. Michael Lucas

We Help You Self-Publish Your Book

Crystell Publications can help you self-publish your novel. Regardless of your status, our team will help you get to print. Our BLOW OUT prices are for serious authors only. **Don't have all your money? .... No Problem!** *Ask About our Payment Plans*

Crystal Perkins-Stell, MHR
Essence Magazine Bestseller
We Give You Books!
PO BOX 8044 / Edmond – OK 73083
www.crystalstell.com
(405) 414-3991

Our competitor's Cheapest Plans-
AuthorHouse Legacy Plan $1299.00- 8 books **Xilibris** Professional Plan $1249.00
iUniverse Premier Plan $1299.00-5 bks   10 bks

Hey! Stop Wishing, and get your book to print NOW!!!

–Recession Big Flex Options 100 Books–					
Option A	**Option B**	**Option C**	**Option D**	**E-Book**	**Option F**
$1399.00	$1299.00	$1199.00	$839.00	$695.00	$775.00
255-275	205-250	200 -80	75 - 60	255 pages	50 or less

Grind Plans 25 & E-Book	**Hustle Hard**	**Respect The Code**	**313 Deal**
Order Extra Books	$899.00	$869.00	$839.00
	255-275pg	250 -205	200 -80

Insanity Plans 2 Books & E-Book & POD	**Psycho**	**Spastic**	**Mental**
Extra Books Can Be Ordered	$759.00	$659.00	$559.00
	225-250pg	200-220	199- 100

All Manuscript Options except the E-Books include:
2 Proofs–Publisher & Printer, Mink Magazine Subscription, Free Advertisement, Book Cover, ISBN #, Conversion, Typeset, Correspondence, Masters, 8 hrs Consultation

$100.00 E-book upload only   **$75** Can't afford edits, Spell-check
$275.00-Book covers/Authors input   **$499** Flat Rate Edits Exceeds 210 add 1.50
$269.00-Book covers/ templates   **$200**-Typeset Book Format PDF File
$190.00 and up Websites   **$200 and up /** Type Manuscript Call for details
$375.00, book trailers on Youtube

We're Killing The Game.

No more paying Vanity Presses $8 to $10 per book! We Give You Books @ Cost. **We Offer Editing For An Extra Fee- If Waved, We Print What You Submit!** These titles are done by self-published authors. They are not published by nor signed to Crystell Publications.

Made in the USA
Middletown, DE
01 April 2023